PRAISE FOR GREGG OLSEN

THE HIVE

"Readers who relish the aftershocks of cult exploitation will turn every page with keen anticipation."

—*Kirkus Reviews*

"*The Hive* is Gregg Olsen at his finest. Exciting, anxiety provoking, and twisty . . . You will stay up all night reading . . . not wanting to put it down until the final and shocking conclusion. This book will take you right down a rabbit hole you never suspected."

—*Mystery & Suspense Magazine*

"Mesmerizing! Gregg Olsen tautly reveals layer after layer of lies, secrets, and betrayals in an increasingly horrifying exposé of one cult leader and her terrible sway over others. Forget the evil men do. These women will have you fearing for your life."

—Lisa Gardner, #1 *New York Times* bestselling author

"*The Hive* is a riveting thriller, a tsunami of a story that starts out strong and absolutely knocks you over at the end. The characters are fascinating, their world so real and absorbing—I was transfixed from the very start. Gregg Olsen is such a compelling writer."

—Luanne Rice, *New York Times* bestselling author

"In this gripping thriller, everything is not as it seems, and beauty is only skin deep. *The Hive* is a brilliantly engrossing read—exactly what we have come to expect from Gregg Olsen."

—Karin S̶l̶a̶u̶g̶h̶t̶e̶r̶, *New York Times and*

int̶

"A charismatic wellness guru, a dead young journalist, and a slew of secrets are the ingredients that make up this fiendishly fun thriller. *The Hive* will have readers buzzing."

—Greer Hendricks, #1 *New York Times* bestselling coauthor of *The Wife Between Us*

"Gregg Olsen's *The Hive* is a fast-paced, intriguing, intense, and suspenseful read that is as creepy as it is fantastic. Brilliant, thought-provoking, heartbreaking, and original, *The Hive* will keep you up at night and leave you reeling long after you've finished it. Every page carries weight in this novel. There are plenty of twists and turns to satisfy even the most seasoned crime fiction reader, and the characters feel authentic and alive in ways that only Olsen can achieve."

—Lisa Regan, #1 *Wall Street Journal* bestselling author of the Detective Josie Quinn series

"Die-hard Gregg Olsen fans will love *The Hive*; new readers will become fans. Olsen deftly guides the reader through the pages, cranking up the suspense as long-held secrets rise to the surface. The result is compulsively page turning as Olsen keeps the reader's mind buzzing in suspense. He hooks the reader as a dark crime from the past collides with a crime from the present."

—Kendra Elliot, *Wall Street Journal* bestselling author

"Gregg Olsen's *The Hive* begins with a fascinating premise and a spellbinding opening scene that held me in its grip as I flew through the pages. Olsen expertly weaves together a multilayered tale told by a complex array of unforgettable characters in his latest jaw-dropping thriller. In this dark and dangerously addictive read buzzing with secrets, betrayal, and murder, queen bees and wannabes take on a whole new meaning. Not to be missed."

—Heather Gudenkauf, *New York Times* bestselling author of *This Is How I Lied*

IF YOU TELL

"This riveting account will leave readers questioning every odd relative they've known."

—*Publishers Weekly* (starred review)

"Olsen presents the story chronologically and in a simple, straightforward style, which works well: it is chilling enough as is."

—*Booklist*

"An unsettling stunner about sibling love, courage, and resilience."

—*People* magazine (book of the week)

"*If You Tell* accomplishes what it sets out to do. The result is a compelling portrait of terror and a powerfully honest, yet still sensitive, look at survival."

—Bookreporter

"This disturbing book recounts the unimaginable abuse and torture three sisters Nikki, Sami, and Tori Knotek endured from their own mother, Shelly . . . the strong bond they form to survive and defy their mother's sadistic tendencies is inspiring."

—BuzzFeed

"A true-crime tour de force."

—Steve Jackson, *New York Times* bestselling author of *No Stone Unturned*

"A master of true crime returns with a vengeance. After a decade detour into novels, Gregg Olsen is back with a dark tale of nonfiction from the Pacific Northwest that will keep you awake long after the lights have gone out. The monster at the heart of *If You Tell* is not your typical boogeyman, not some wandering drifter or man in a van. No. In fact, they called her . . . mother. And yet this story is about hope and renewal in the face of evil and how three sisters can find the goodness in the world after surviving the worst it has to offer. Classic true crime in the tradition of *In Cold Blood* and *The Stranger Beside Me*."

—James Renner, author of *True Crime Addict*

"This nightmare walked on two legs and some of her victims called her mom. In *If You Tell*, Gregg Olsen documents the horrific mental and physical torture Shelly Knotek inflicted on everyone in her household. A powerful story of cruelty that will haunt you for a long time."

—Diane Fanning, author of *Treason in the Secret City*

"Bristling with tension, gripping from the first pages, Gregg Olsen's masterful portrait of children caught in the web of a coldly calculating killer fascinates. A read so compelling it kept me up late into the night, *If You Tell* exposes incredible evil that lived quietly in small-town America. That the book is fact, not fiction, terrifies."

—Kathryn Casey, bestselling author of *In Plain Sight*

THE LAST THING SHE EVER DID

"Gregg Olsen pens brilliant, creepy, page-turning, heart-pounding novels of suspense that always keep me up at night. In *The Last Thing She Ever Did*, he topped himself."

—Allison Brennan, *New York Times* bestselling author

"Beguiling, wicked, and taut with suspense and paranoia, *The Last Thing She Ever Did* delivers scenes as devastating as any I've ever read with a startling, pitch-perfect finale. A reminder that evil may reside in one's actions, but tragedy often spawns from one's inaction."

—Eric Rickstad, *New York Times* bestselling author of *The Silent Girls*

"Olsen's latest examines how a terrible, split-second decision has lingering effects, and the past echoes the present. Full of unexpected twists, *The Last Thing She Ever Did* will keep you guessing to the last line."

—J. T. Ellison, *New York Times* bestselling author of *Lie to Me*

"Master storyteller Gregg Olsen continues to take readers hostage with another spellbinding tale of relentless, pulse-pounding suspense."

—Rick Mofina, international bestselling author of *Last Seen*

"Tense. Well-crafted. Gripping."

—Mary Burton, *New York Times* bestselling author

"With *The Last Thing She Ever Did*, Gregg Olsen delivers an edgy, tension-filled, roller-coaster ride of a novel that will thrill and devastate in equal measure."

—Linda Castillo, *New York Times* bestselling author

LYING NEXT TO ME

"*Lying Next to Me* is a clever, chilling puzzle of a tale. A riveting, sharp-edged page-turner, it's Gregg Olsen's best book yet."

—A. J. Banner, *USA Today* bestselling author

"A dark, claustrophobic thriller filled with twists and turns. A brilliant book."

—Caroline Mitchell, #1 international bestselling author

"In *Lying Next to Me*, [Olsen] has given us a first-rate work of psychological complexity as well as a mystery that is full of twists and is quite a grabber."

—Popular Culture Association

I KNOW
WHERE
YOU LIVE

ALSO BY GREGG OLSEN

FICTION

NONFICTION

*If You Tell: A True Story of Murder, Family Secrets,
and the Unbreakable Bond of Sisterhood*

*A Killing in Amish Country: Sex, Betrayal,
and a Cold-Blooded Murder*

*A Twisted Faith: A Minister's Obsession and the Murder That
Destroyed a Church*

*The Deep Dark: Disaster and Redemption in America's Richest
Silver Mine*

*Starvation Heights: A True Story of Murder and Malice in the
Woods of the Pacific Northwest*

Cruel Deception: The True Story of a Mother, a Child, a Murder

*If Loving You Is Wrong: The Teacher and Student Sex Case that
Shocked the World*

*Abandoned Prayers: The Incredible True Story of Murder,
Obsession, and Amish Secrets*

American Mother: The True Story of the Seattle Cyanide Murders

*Confessions of an American Black Widow: The True Story of Black
Widow Killer Sharon Nelson*

*If I Can't Have You: Susan Powell, Her Mysterious Disappearance,
and the Murder of Her Children*

I KNOW
WHERE
YOU LIVE

GREGG
OLSEN

THOMAS & MERCER

Text copyright © 2022 by Gregg Olsen
All rights reserved.

Published by Thomas & Mercer, Seattle

www.apub.com

Amazon, the Amazon logo, and Thomas & Mercer are trademarks of Amazon.com, Inc., or its affiliates.

ISBN-13: 9781542016476 (paperback)
ISBN-13: 9781542016483 (digital)

Cover design by Rex Bonomelli

Cover image: © Nils Ericson / Gallery Stick; © Viorel Sima / Shutterstock

Printed in the United States of America

For Liz Pearsons and Dilly

AFTER EVERYTHING HAPPENED

Violet

My phone stares back at me while my husband drinks his favorite IPA, scrolling downward on his own device. Zach is handsome, with a skin tone that nods to an ethnicity recently sorted out by saliva in a tube. *Five percent Native American* says the bar chart printout. His hair flows jet black and thick. His caterpillar eyebrows will surely need hedge clippers when he's older. He works in what I call the Algo Tweaker offices at Facebook in Bellevue, east of Seattle, where we live.

My own DNA profile is exceedingly and, I admit, disappointingly bland. A northern European and Scandinavian ancestry accounts for my need to dip myself in a vat of sunscreen, not to mention a stylist's heavy hand with color to give my nondescript light-brown hair a fighting chance to be noticed. Now, she's moved the color toward red, which looks good with my unremarkable blue eyes. *Good*, not great.

I check the time on my phone again.

Rose is a clock. She's programmed to always be on time, as though the bell from the school where she taught first and second graders still rings in her head.

It was the day after my wedding to Zach that I stopped calling my mother "Mom," the day after she let her father slither into my supposed special day. She had assured me Papa, my grandfather, wasn't going to come, but she let him anyway. Because he said he'd behave.

Her name suits her. Probably always did. Roses are pretty and smell good, but those thorns . . . Sometimes you don't even see them when you bury your face in a bouquet of heaven, pulling yourself inside, deeper. Then you bleed.

I crack open a beer. Zach gives me a look when I sit down at the kitchen island. The beer is good when my mood is not. Until recently, calls from Rose have been dispatched into the send-to-voice mail category—the wasteland for those who bother to leave a message. Lately she's on a loop, grieving the dissolution of her marriage to my father and the emptiness that comes with figuring out what's next when you know that he's moved on to something better. Far better. And you are sitting there, alone, face planted against the glass of a window wondering why things had to be this way. Why you have nothing, and someone else— make that everyone else—has so much.

My phone buzzes. I gulp some beer.

"Hi, Rose," I say, forcing my tone to sound upbeat, though not overly so. She's had enough false cheer from an array of confidants. Fuck it. I *am* her lifeline. "You're right on time."

"Please don't call me Rose."

Her tone isn't cheerful, and I don't expect it to be, considering everything.

"You're a machine," I reply. I don't ask how she's doing. That's not a question that I would ever dare ask. Too loaded. Too much of a trigger.

"How's Lily?"

"Fine, Rose. She's fine."

"I know she's angry. I get it. There isn't anything I can do about it now, Violet. Can't she see that?"

"Apparently not," I say, before adding, "at this very minute. Later, Rose. She'll come around later."

"You think so?"

There's that sliver of hope in her voice that comes with every call. I don't know whether Lily will ever come around. I honestly don't see the need for the hard line they've both drawn in the middle of their relationship. Unproductive. Waste of time. Not my problem. I've put Mom—rather, *Rose*—in a box. A cage.

We talk a bit more. She asks about Zach, and I put her on speaker. He tells her that he's doing fine at work and that I'm being indecisive about a boat he insists we both want to buy.

She says she's thinking of taking art classes. We end the call as we always do. She says she loves me and Lily. Zach too. She asks if I've seen Dad lately, and I lie like I always do. I see him and Rose's replacement at least two times a month.

She leaves with a parting shot. "I hope the SOB knows what it's like to be abandoned someday. She's too young to stick around with a wadded-up old man to watch after."

"Bye, Rose," I say.

"I'm your mother," she snaps. "Don't call me that."

I end the call.

My eyes stay on the black mirror of my screen. I drink the last of the IPA. I wonder if this is how alcoholism starts. I feel a numbness take over. It isn't the single beer that's taking me to that place. It isn't my mother's rage over the divorce. It isn't that my sister won't talk to her. It's none of that. It's a numbness that comes from knowing that the truth is no panacea. Scraping away the dirt from a secret doesn't always set you free. Sometimes it's the very opposite.

I consider that as I sit there, phone back on, scrolling through my sister's Instagram. Lily is more beautiful than I am, and that never really bothered me. She has the kind of silky wheat-blond hair that can be made to do anything she wants. Nearly just by willing it to. Her eyes are coppery, not brown. Embers. Sparks. One time we saw a psychic at the fair who said she had a "fierce" aura. I see it in her gaze as I time travel through a year of posts on her feed. I note their absence in the last few months, only a handful of images from college life—no record of what she was doing because, frankly, there was nothing to brag about. The holidays are marked by a selfie with all of us—Rose, Dad, me, Nana, and, of course, Lily.

It was the last time we were all together, our nuclear family. Just a few months after the wedding, when everything collided in that messy, unsuspecting way disasters often do.

Just then, I think of the sweater Nana knitted for me when I was five. How I tugged at a loose yarn along the waistband. Absentmindedly, at first, then with compulsive purpose. It kept growing. Longer, longer, longer. I knew that I was ruining the sweater, but it became compulsive, obsessive. It was like that the day of my wedding to Zach.

Something started that night and there was no stopping it.

Rose

The world moves all around as the phone goes quiet.

My oldest daughter calls me by my first name to hurt me. My youngest has, as the kids say, ghosted me.

I make my way down to my cell. My eyes catch the flicker of a television in the common area—a talk show. Mouths move. The bald host shakes his head, squints his eyes, like he's outraged. A young woman buries her face in her hands, while another guest—her mother, I presume—points a daggerlike finger at her. They are talking, crying, but I hear nothing. I think back to the conversation with Violet. Has she put me on mute? If I screamed into the phone that I'm truly sorry, would she hear me?

Perching on the edge of my foam mattress, I catch my breath, steady my nerves to allow the realization to coalesce. It's overdue. It grabs me by the throat and squeezes. Hard. And in my heart, I accept the one truth that is indisputable now: not all crimes are equal.

When you are a mother, you can do much, much worse than kill.

THE FUSE

Violet

The fuse ignited a year ago during a tussle over a dress. I didn't know it at the time, though I probably should have heeded the tightening muscles on the back of my neck. Tension, as a rule, wasn't unfamiliar to me or Lily. But it was a polite, sneaky kind of tension. Our mother treated us as though we were students in one of her classes. She was sweet. She didn't yell. Her tone assumed that we were somehow in agreement with whatever she was saying. It worked for six-year-olds. Not so much for twenty-three-year-old me or my eighteen-year-old sister.

It started the night Zach and I told my parents that we were getting married.

"You'll be the loveliest bride ever," Mom said, loosening her embrace and staring into my eyes. "And I saved my dress for you!"

Lily rolled her eyes. An ice cube smacked Dad's front teeth as he swigged his scotch. Zach sat stock-still, the proverbial deer in the headlights.

Lily and I dutifully followed Mom to her bedroom closet, holding our breath. Her wedding dress was from the 1980s. It was an unqualified horror show with beach-ball-size balloon sleeves and a freakishly beaded Vegas headband that looked like something worn in a Jazzercise class. *Feel the burn. Work it, ladies! Now we're having fun!*

"It's fine if you don't want to wear it," she said, her words laying the trap as she released the dress from its hermetically sealed coffin, a white cardboard box with a cello lid to protect it during its nearly thirty years of justified confinement. Lily and I had seen the tomb of the unheralded atrocity over the years, tucked away in the back of a closet that held plastic tubs of our schoolwork, pictures, and things our mother saved because she couldn't bear to part with anything that even hinted at sentimentality. That dress, we thought, was just one of those things. It had never really dawned on us that she'd been saving it for another trip down the aisle.

My trip down the aisle.

"I even kept my shoes!" Mom cheerfully announced, holding up white kitten-heeled pumps, also wrapped in noisy cellophane.

"I couldn't, Mom," I told her, trying to find the right balance of affect. Kind. Surprised. Unworthy. "It's too special." I searched high and low for the right combination of words. "Sacred," I added.

Lily put her hand over her mouth, pretending to stifle a cough.

Mom unfurled the great white elephant—its satiny fabric and puffy sleeves finally unencumbered. The smell of mothballs that reminded me of Nana's sweaters wafted through the air.

But not a single moth.

Damn.

"It's too beautiful, Mom," I said. "I couldn't. Besides, you were so petite."

Don't make me make you cry, I thought.

Mom cried, of course. She was pretty adept at that. When she accepted that there was no way that the gown could be altered to fit my taller frame, she still rambled off a few solutions to make it "more your own."

Add lace.

Maybe remove some fabric from the sleeves.

Girls are wearing minidresses now, you know.

I pushed back and left no doubt that I was making my own decisions.

"Mom, I'm going to do what I want to do."

Surprisingly the tears didn't flow this time.

"Okay," she said. "Fine. It's your wedding. And, besides, I only want the best for you. I always have."

Lily started to laugh.

Mom glared at her.

In my family, one win is considered a streak. I went for another.

"I have one more demand, Mom. And there's no budging on it. Like you said. It's my day."

She knew what it was. Her lower lip trembled.

"Are you sure?"

I pressed the lid down on the dress coffin. "Absolutely."

CHAPTER ONE

June 17
Olalla, Washington
Violet

My mother perches on the edge of the white sofa in the bridal suite, one that I'm certain has been a refuge for crying brides and bitter MOBs from the day it was installed in the modern Victorian. When I said I wanted a beach wedding, I was thinking Maui. Maybe Cabo. Not ten miles from Gig Harbor. Mount Rainier bursts over the top of forest-smeared Vashon Island, a breathtaking view highlighted by the indigo salt water of the Colvos Passage. I doubt many brides notice it since the full-length mirror commands all attention. Then there's the drama. Backbiting. Tears.

Mom sniffs and I look in her direction. Her ombre hair is stiff and emanating the acrid smell of White Rain—the same drugstore hairspray Nana, my grandma, still uses. She's dabbing at wet eyes and making a whimpering sound that pretends to reflect her joy over the moment we're sharing. I know better.

She's really thinking about that relic of a dress from her wedding, and the crumbling state of her marriage to my father.

Taking their cue from the roll of my eyes, my bridesmaids depart the suite in a string of robin's-egg blue—a color concession to appease Mom after I deep-sixed her dress. I've known most of them since grade school. We went through everything together the way only a pack of teenage girls can, floating above the fray. Though it sounds ugly, an attitude of invincibility and entitlement topped off the sundae of our perceived perfection. Honestly, I never felt that I was one of them. Not really. They were flawless. I was the one who struggled to land a spot on the drill team, a coveted place in the cafeteria seating arrangement. A date with a football player—a nonstarter, even.

"Paris should have let her dress out a bit more," Mom snipes as the door shuts behind the girl I experimented with at a sleepover, the one my mom said had a vulgar figure. "She needs to slim down."

"Paris is a size eight," I shoot back. "And please don't be mean. She looks great. Everyone does."

She pinches her lips. "I'm not being mean. I'm worried. What if a seam splits?"

"If it does, Paris will laugh it off and become an Instagram star."

Mom dabs at her eyes again. Knuckles now white, she bunches up the tissue.

At the other end of the couch, Lily stares at her phone, her calloused fingertip scrolling evermore.

I look in the mirror.

"You are lovely, honey."

"Thanks, Mom."

She exhales. "I have something to tell you. I'm not sure about it. And I'm really sorry."

"I'm all right, Mom. I like the way I look."

"It isn't about the dress."

Her head is bowed. She shuffles her ancient white Liz Claiborne pumps—the same pair she wore at her own wedding. It's like watching Dorothy click her ruby slippers back and forth at the end of *The Wizard of Oz*. "I told him not to come."

I know immediately who she means. My only line in the sand. I didn't fight her over the table decorations. I didn't argue that robin's-egg blue was her favorite color, and I preferred more of a pale lavender. She insisted on a buffet, for God's sake. She ran the whole thing like a first-day-on-the-job prison guard. I let her. I did. But when it came to my lone request, I thought, this time, she'd put me first.

"If you told him not to come, then why is he here?" Panic fills me. "He's here, right? That's what you're saying, right?"

"What could I do? Nana wasn't about to miss this day."

I fight to hold it together. I could have guessed it. I should have known.

"You said Nana understood."

"Honey," she says, getting up and coming to me. *At me.* Her damp tissue falls to the floor, a sodden pom-pom. "I thought she did. We agreed."

I feel the sweat accumulating under my arms. Ironically, those balloon-puffed sleeves would be just the ticket about now. The last thing I want is to be the pitted-out bride in front of a group of people who purportedly love me. But everyone loves a messed-up wedding even more.

"What am I supposed to do?" she asks. "Hire a bouncer or an armed guard? Honestly, what do you expect of me? I've always done the best for you and your sister. You can never say I didn't."

My eyes catch Lily's across Mom's shoulder. "Really, Mom? You want to go there right now? Right here?"

"It was a long time ago."

The passage of time is a foolish and ultimately futile healer. She knows that, but I remind her anyway. "It plays in my mind all the time,

11

Mom. So don't tell me that it was a long time ago. Time doesn't erase what happened."

She shakes her head in that way that's meant to make me feel like a kid. "You sound like that god-awful school counselor."

I saw a counselor in junior high when my mother and I were going through an especially bad patch. "Mom," I say firmly, "I sound like me. I guess that my voice was like some fucking dog whistle that you and Dad simply couldn't hear."

"That's not fair."

"None of this is fair."

We stare at each other, reenacting an impasse forged when I told her how Papa had touched me. I had just turned seven, and the two of us were alone in the living room. Lily was napping. Dad was at work. Mom was reading a Jean M. Auel novel. I was playing with Barbies.

"Down here." I indicated the place on my body. "And he put his thing in my—"

"You're lying," she said, cutting me off.

"He did. I'm not."

She slammed down her book and paced the living room, grinding a path into the immaculately Hoovered green carpeting.

"You made this up," she accused me. "What an absolutely ugly thing to say."

I tried to protest, but I wasn't effective. And, really, I didn't know what to say after that, or how to make her see the truth. It wasn't that I didn't know what had happened to me. It was just that I thought my mother would put her arms around me. Tell me that it would be all right. That I'd be safe. That nothing like that would ever happen to me again.

Instead, she dropped the sweet first-grade teacher façade and held me by the shoulders.

"You are a devious girl." Her face red, her eyes black buttons. "If you ever say anything like that again . . . if you ever hurt Papa or Nana with such an ugly, ugly tale, you will find yourself in foster care. Don't doubt me."

"I'm not lying," I said, trying to extricate myself from her grip.

"Stop it. I mean it. Stop it!"

She scared me. Really scared me. So, I set the memory aside—like all the photos people my parents' age have stored in Rubbermaid bins for future scrapbooks. Fact was, I was never alone with Papa again. At least, not for more than a minute or two. One of those times, when I was a year or so older, he said something that I wanted to believe.

"I'm sorry about what happened."

"Really?"

"It was a mistake," he said. "An accident. Papa had too much to drink, honey."

I couldn't fathom how putting his penis in my mouth had been an accident. When it never happened again, I figured that he'd meant it. Even though I didn't trust him, he no longer scared me. I hated him.

More than that, I couldn't understand my mother's defense of her father. She had called me a liar. She threatened to wash my mouth out with soap. She told me that if I ever lied about that again, she'd put me in foster care.

I believed her.

Her absolute rebuke of what I'd confided that afternoon became the shaky foundation of our relationship.

And the cause of everything that would come.

Rose

My phone pings.

A text message from my mother.

A bomb is about to go off. And I can't stop it from happening.

I make the best of a tepid cup of Earl Grey in the bridal suite of You and Me by the Sea, the venue selected for Violet and Zach's wedding. I should have taken a shot of whiskey with the boys when I had a chance. I pick at the lemon cookies while my girls get ready. I'm sure other mothers do this too. They run through the highlight reel of their little girls' childhood. Their hopes for their children's future. A good job. A husband. Endless possibilities.

Violet stands in front of the mirror pretending to be self-absorbed. She is not that at all. Never has been. She studies her reflected image with a micro-gaze as she weighs the subtle flaws that make her even more beautiful than bland perfection could ever be. Her lower lip is fuller than her upper, giving her a perpetual pout. Her nose is a better version of her father's, while Lily's is a better version of mine. In the genetic lottery, Lily won the nose prize. Hair too. Violet, however, always manages to put everything together in a way that leaves no doubt she's beautiful.

I look at the text exchange between me and my mother.

Mom: We're here.

Me: Good mother of God! How could you? You were going to keep him home.

Mom: You never really believed that. Not really.

Me: I hoped it.

I steady myself as I stand and tell Violet that Papa is downstairs. The mood in the room turns like a flash flood.

"Mom," she tells me. Her voice is tight. Angry. "You fucking promised!"

I try to deflect with teary eyes and well-used tissues. I don't understand how Violet can summarily dismiss all I sacrificed to raise her and her sister with a husband who was always out of town. How I carted both of my girls from recitals to softball games to study sessions. Everything was for them. I tried. I did.

Their grandparents just wanted this one thing.

"I know," I say. "Of course." I stop myself from reminding her that my father has apologized, that she shouldn't hold what happened against him forever. I've tried that. My father had what my mother called "wandering" hands. I accepted her reasoning because she was my mother.

I've often wondered over the years why Violet never fell in line.

"Are you going to tell him to go?"

I shake my head. "Just leave it, Violet. Focus on the now. Not the past."

Lily peers up from her phone for a split second, then goes back to whatever she's feigning is more interesting than the explosion happening in front of her.

"What he did can't just be ignored, Mom. You can wish that all you want. You can say it to me over and over and over, but it doesn't take any of it away. Papa is a pervert."

That word!

My hand levitates from my body and I slap Violet. Hard. A loud slap. The kind of slap that leaves a handprint. My hand throbs. Pulses. Stings. For a second, I can't breathe. My daughter's face is red where I struck her. She doesn't say a word.

None of us do.

I've never hit her like that. I spanked her once or twice, half-heartedly, to be clear.

My girls stare at me with the kind of gaping reserved for a mass shooting. Disbelief and condemnation pour from their eyes.

And still no words.

I hit her because of what she called my father. It will be months before that truly sinks in. And I did it on her wedding day.

Violet turns away. She refuses to cry. She's held hurt deep inside before.

Lily goes to her sister and wraps her arms around her.

"I'm sorry," I finally say. I am. But I also lie. "I have no idea where that came from, Violet. Forgive me."

She gives me a hard, bitter look. "I don't know how you could have made this day any worse, but hitting me because you can't deal with the truth certainly qualifies."

"It was a slap," I say defensively. "I didn't hit you."

Violet reaches for her makeup bag. "In your fucked-up idea of family solidarity, you picked the wrong family. You should have picked ours. You should have picked me."

Her eyes drill into mine. "You don't know that a mother's number-one job is to protect her children."

Lily starts to speak, and I welcome the support.

"I guess the show's over," she says. "I'll go check on how things are going downstairs. Better than here, I hope. And, Mom, if I ever get married, which I hope I never do, I'm not wearing your ugly fucking dress either."

Lily

Shit show. Dumpster fire. Either will do. I go downstairs. The image of my sister's red-blotched face and my mother's shock at what her hand had done was a social media moment that I regrettably missed. Telling someone about your mom slapping your sister on her wedding day is good for a laugh or two. However, posting it on TikTok for strangers to see is worth a bazillion likes.

I'm not surprised by the slap. I'm not surprised by anything. Not anymore. In the run-up to the wedding, Violet told me what Papa had done to her when she was little. At first, I didn't know how to deal with it. I didn't know for sure if it was true. If it happened, why hadn't I figured it out—even at a much later date? Why had my mother aided and abetted her father? Besides, I had no real frame of reference for what Violet said he'd done. Papa never touched me.

Not even once.

I see the old man, Nana by his side. He's wearing his best suit, holding a drink and talking to relatives like he's an invited guest.

Not a pervert wedding crasher.

My stomach turns a little, and I take a deep breath and make a beeline to my father.

Dad doesn't know what Papa did to Violet. Mom insisted on silence. I'm not even sure Nana knows—or, in any case, would allow herself to truly know it. My family should have opened a mini-storage. Compartmentalizing things has always been our superpower.

"Dad?" I rescue him from a third cousin visiting from Spokane. "I need to talk to you."

He gives the cousin a smile and looks at me with relief. I catch a glimpse of the scene outside through the massive windows facing the water. With a thirsty assist from the geekiest of groomsmen, the bridesmaids are slurping Fireball shots on the beach.

I lead Dad toward the butler's pantry, but it's full of staff with tweezers fussing over a silver platter of stuffed mushrooms.

"What is it?" he asks once we're alone.

"Violet didn't want Papa here."

He gives me the exasperated look all girl dads master. "Jesus," he says. "I wish she'd get over it." His brow furrows. Deep lines. "Look, what am I supposed to do? He came. Am I supposed to tell him to go home? Can't you girls just let it go? Assume he'll get drunk, collapse, and that will be that."

Dad thinks it's about Papa's alcoholism, the source—so he believes—of every ruined family get-together.

I want to set him straight. I can't, though. I made a pact with my sister.

"It's better for everyone. Violet insisted."

I'm wiser now and I know it was only better for Papa.

"Can't you just tell him to leave?" I ask. "Do this for Violet?"

Unfortunately, Dad actually likes Papa. Drinking buddies, I guess. Fishing too. "I don't think I can do that, honey. I'll watch his booze. If he gets out of hand, we'll have someone take him home. He's old, Lily. He's happy to be here. Let him have this."

Except for cheating on Mom, Dad is mostly decent. He has dark-blue eyes and hair that went white at forty. He's reed thin, with long, sinewy arms. He believes in God but never proselytizes. Makes a good living and saved enough to fully fund our college expenses. He even coached our basketball teams—and made us earn starter status. All of that considered, he still lacks in the area that we needed him most. Richard Hilliard doesn't see anything beyond what's in front of him. Or rather, what his nonconfrontational nature allows him to see.

I know he'd kick Papa out the door—maybe even kill him—if he knew that he'd molested Violet. However, a deal's a deal. Mom, Violet, and I are wrapped tight in our secrecy.

He gives me a quick hug.

"Did you know Spokane is getting a new Applebee's?" he asks, defusing the moment with a side-eye aimed in the chatty cousin's direction.

I'm still pissed off, but I can't stop from breaking into a smile.

"Now you do," he says.

✄

A half hour later, we're all outside. Mom, Papa, and Nana sit in white folding chairs stuck in the sand. A harpist with waist-length hair plays Pachelbel's Canon in C, and my big sister, in a dress of her own choosing, walks along a path to the beach escorted by our father. Violet is not only about to marry a man she loves but also complete her escape.

As she and Dad approach me and the other members of the wedding party, I think about my role in the family. I'm the quiet one. The little sister. The last one to ask for anything.

I'm the one who just takes it all in and figures out how I can benefit from my mother and sister's disagreements. To add anything is to earn the wrath of the other. Even a nod can be fuel for an arrow in the back later. In this moment, I'm completely on Team Violet. After getting the huff-and-puff dress out of the way, she made only one request of our mother.

While my sister changes and the food is being prepped, my best friend, Maddy, and I sit on a driftwood log and get high.

"I didn't know Violet would be so emotional," Maddy says. "Looks like she's been crying."

I release the smoke from my lungs. "Mom smacked her."

"She what?"

I fill my lungs with smoke and hold it in, nodding. "Yeah, pretty messed up."

"Seriously, Lily?"

"Don't ask why, but I have a feeling we're in for more family fun tonight."

Maddy reaches for the roach. "Cool."

Chapter Two

Violet

Out on the patio, I let the familiar cadence of the waves soothe me. Despite my grandfather being present, my mother slapping me, and the lack of white sand beneath my feet, I'm married to the man I love. I can see my future clearly. Not just away from here but going somewhere. With someone who will never let me down.

Like members of my own family.

Mom, with an extended index finger, is directing the caterer to do something with the buffet table while Nana looks on. Dad is playfully lamenting the cost of the wedding while he jangles the car keys in his front pocket. And Lily, as always, is taking pictures with her phone.

It's a technique she's mastered. Being there but not being part of what's going on. I wish I'd thought of that for myself.

Zach leans in and gives me a kiss.

"This time tomorrow, piña coladas."

I start to say something about coconut prawns when a hacking scream erupts from the buffet table.

My Nana's COPD croak is unmistakable: tires on a gravel road. Her faded green eyes are terror struck, and she drops to her knobby knees next to Papa. In doing so, she tears the back of her dress, exposing her girdle (her "little helper"). Her purse opens and its contents skitter across the floor. Papa is on his back, eyes open, his breathing wheezy. The fall has jettisoned the clear tube from his oxygen tank.

I'm frozen. I could bend down and shield Nana's modesty. I don't, though. I just stand there with Zach like a cake topper and take an inventory of all the guests in their dressy-casual clothing and increasingly boozy breaths. Shock. Fear. Curiosity. When scenes of life and death are performed, people play to type. For some, I suspect it's a conditioned response, an affectation that exists solely to conform to the situation.

Empathy signaling.

Just then, I see it. Papa's EpiPen is among the contents of Nana's beaded clutch.

Right there.

He wheezes, trying to speak. His eyes are filled with terror.

One of the guests, a neighbor who is a physician's assistant, nudges a path to Papa while his husband frantically phones for an ambulance.

"Barely two bars of service," the husband says, rushing toward the sandy beach with his phone held high like a torch.

Nana moves aside, never taking her eyes from Papa.

"Dave!" she moans. "Dave!"

"Mr. Bradley, can you hear me?" the PA asks, his voice low and calm.

Papa doesn't say a word. His thin lips have thickened. His eyes flutter. I think he can see me, but I don't allow eye contact between us.

And poor Zach, my husband of less than an hour, must realize he's married into a veritable freak show. I'd promised we'd get out of there after the cake, but it's obvious that Insta-moment isn't happening.

Zach draws me in tight. "He'll be all right."

I think about what to say. Really, what *not* to say.

"Yeah," I mutter, "he's a tough old bird."

Among other things better left unsaid.

Zach helps as I stoop to collect what fell from Nana's purse.

Dad, who likes to make a show of his alpha-maleness, takes center stage.

"Where the hell is Dave's EpiPen?" he asks.

"He didn't eat any shellfish, Richard," Mom says.

"How would you know, Rose? You can't control everyone's movements."

Ouch.

Mom pushes back. "This isn't the time, Richard. Are you drunk?"

Dad puts his hands up in the famed "don't shoot" pose. "Not now. But you can sure as hell bet I will be. The EpiPen? Where the hell is it?"

"He's having a heart attack," she says. "Don't put this on Mom. There's no need for a pen!"

Like the slap, this is another wonderful moment to add to the day.

Nana looks over at my parents and shakes her head, then awkwardly crawls closer to Papa, who appears to be asking for something, and puts her finger on her lips.

"Shhh, sweetheart . . . I know. I know." Then she leans closer and says something into his ear, all the while patting his hand tenderly.

It strikes me. No one but Dad has mentioned the lifesaving medication that Nana made sure went everywhere with Papa.

The crowd loosens to give the old man some space, and at the same time, Dad hooks his hands under Nana's arms and lifts her to her feet. Her makeup is a crayon rubbing smeared from the highest ridges of her wrinkled face. Her knees are bruised from her fall.

It takes seventeen minutes before the sound of sirens filters down the road to the wedding venue. I watch as the ambulance noses into a spot under a huge old cedar and two paramedics hurry over to collect my grandfather. The pair are about my age, midtwenties. They move in tandem; they even look alike. Same fade haircut. Matching goatees.

"Heart problems?" asks the one with the better goatee.

"He's old! Of course he does!" Nana indicates the oxygen tank. "Emphysema too."

"All right. Any allergies?"

Dad answers. "Shellfish. He hasn't had any." He looks at Mom. "That we know about. Stupid old man didn't bring his EpiPen either."

Shellfish.

My gaze rises past the guests' shoulders to where the staff is keeping busy—collecting dirty china plates, setting out a fresh coffee urn, and refilling the ice beneath the giant platter of shrimp. The shrimp was a last-minute addition to the menu. *My* add-on. Something I'd wanted because I had been told that Papa wasn't going to show.

I look away like I've been caught doing something.

In less than a minute, Papa is packed onto a stretcher. He motions me over.

"Violet," he croaks, "I'm sorry for ruining your special day."

Nana looks in my direction. Her gaze is peculiar. Her eyes have always been the kindest. Not now. Despite the tears, she looks hard. It startles me into answering.

"It's all right, Papa," I say, breathing in that grotesque smell of his, the one that takes me back to childhood and sometimes makes me vomit. "Don't even think about it. You'll be fine. That's all that matters."

The last part is a big, fat lie.

Mom knows it.

Lily does too.

I wish Nana did.

More than anything, I hope Papa knows it.

With one quick move, I take the EpiPen hidden in the folds of my dress and shove it into the thick layer of moss encircling the base of a large ficus.

I look up and notice my sister looking at me.

CHAPTER THREE

Violet

St. Anthony Hospital feels like a combination of a library and a train station. People move about, but it's noticeably quiet. Especially at night. We see Papa in shifts. Lily and Dad are up in his room now with Nana. Mom and I sit in the waiting area across from a small gift shop with premade bouquets and plush teddy bears clutching satin hearts to their chests. The young men emerging from the shop are all smiles. The older women, not so much. Hospitals are the bookends of all of our lives.

Mom gets coffee from a vending machine while I play with my phone—liking, scrolling through posts of food, babies, and puppies. It's a mindless endeavor, for sure, but it occupies my time and my brain.

"I can't vouch for it," Mom says, setting a paper cup in front of me when she returns. "The machine seemed a little wonky."

I drink it. Brown water at best. Maybe a hint of coffee.

"It's not bad," I say.

She knows I'm lying, yet she smiles and nods anyway.

"All I can think about is how this happened." Her words are a passive-aggressive weapon aimed at me. She stirs her coffee with a wooden stick, watching the oily cream swirl into a beige cloud. "The shrimp was on the other side of the buffet. Not anywhere near his favorites."

"Right," I say, holding my tongue. Thinking of how to say what I want to say. The exact words don't crystallize, so I throw out a plausible theory. "The caterers must have mixed up the serving utensils. It's the only thing that makes any sense."

She seizes on the explanation. "I thought that too. I noticed a couple of other housekeeping issues as they were setting the buffet. I don't want to accuse them. It was an accident."

"Right," I say.

The elevator opens and Lily and Dad emerge. Lily looks like her usual self. Jeans, T-shirt, and pink flip-flops. Her wedding-day hair and the glamour makeup erased. She looks her age, maybe younger.

Mom stands. "How is he?"

"He's still out of it. Docs are optimistic," Dad says without much conviction.

"Nana needs to get out of here," Lily says. "She's tired and stressed."

"I'll get her," Mom says, going to the elevator.

"I'm sorry about your honeymoon," Dad says to me.

I shake my head. "It's all right. You know Zach. He has travel insurance."

Rose

The wedding. Dad's collapse. The hospital.

All of it exhausts me.

As my fading mother says on the way home, sleep won't make a ding-dong difference. She's right, of course. We put her into Violet's old room. She's beside herself with angst. I literally unknot her fingers as she clasps her hands white-knuckle tight.

"Dad's stable," I remind her. "Doctor says so." I cover her with a down-filled comforter. Violet's collection of vintage Keane prints stares at us with those enormous, strange eyes. Vi loves them. Zach thinks they're creepy, so in her childhood room they've stayed.

"He looked so scared," Mom says.

I sit on her bed. "He's going to be fine."

She's not convinced. "Oh, Rose, we can't really know that. I think I should have stayed at the hospital in case something happens."

"There isn't anything for you to do." My tone is firm, insistent. "We'll see him in the morning. Get some sleep."

She's drained. We all are. What was supposed to be a magical day was anything but. Part of me wants to slap my mother. I don't care how old she is. I want to shake her. She promised she would tell Dad she was ill and make them both stay home. She didn't like it, but she said she understood.

I can't resist one jab in her direction.

"You shouldn't have come."

Her eyes are closed.

"You heard me, Mom."

No response.

"How could you be so selfish?" I ask her.

Her eyes snap open. Suddenly she doesn't seem so tired. Or worried.

"Selfish is keeping me away from my granddaughter's wedding. Honestly, Rose, I never in my life thought you'd pull something like that on me. I didn't deserve it."

"It wasn't you, Mom. It was him."

"Your dad should have stayed home, complained about it, got drunk, and passed out like he does every other night of the week. He didn't. He insisted he'd come. Why should I have to be dragged into it?"

It's after one in the morning. Too late for an argument. I feel tears coming to my eyes, and I don't bother to stave them off. I don't speak. I can't. If I do, everything will spill out over the bed, the floor, and the hall.

My mother mistakes my silence, as always, for agreement.

"Oh, honey." She takes her tone down a notch. "I'm sorry. I know this was a grueling day. Doctor says Dad might even be released tomorrow."

I give her a small, sad nod, letting her think whatever she likes, then I switch off the light and head down the hallway. Almost comically enough to make me smile, a song comes to mind: "A Thin Line Between Love and Hate." No truer words were ever sung. I know so from experience, not just with my mother but with myself.

I dislodge a bottle of Finlandia from a blanket of frozen peas in the freezer. I take in the dark of the night and survey the scene outside the kitchen window. The neighbor kid with the wannabe drift car comes home, and the garage door shuts with a staccato slam. A racoon forages along the fence line. The vodka doesn't dull, rather it seems to sharpen my senses. I hear Richard snoring. Lily's white-noise machine purrs from her room. Mom shifts her tired bones in Violet's bed, and I can hear that too. In all that clarity, my mind spins thoughts, thoughts I want to cease and desist. That I want to banish. Unthink.

The second drink flows down my throat like a stream, a tonic to help me come to terms with the mistakes that I've made. Another gulp. Our family problems have always been dust and dirt to be swept under the orange shag carpet of the family room.

But forgetting things—truly forgetting things—is futile.

CHAPTER FOUR

June 18
Gig Harbor, Washington
Kirk Hoffman

Digging into a new case can be like a grave robber's folly. Old bones
can only reveal so much.

I'm handy with a shovel, though.

My phone goes off and my eyes reluctantly peel open. No one
likes a work call on a weekend. My wife pushes herself away from me,
rolling onto her side of the bed. Gone are the days when she'd wake up
to find out what was wrong. I don't blame her. After twenty years of
police work, first patrol and then detective, cases do run together. What
was once shocking now seems so, so normal. What once elicited the
curiosity of guests at a dinner party (and amused them when I swore
I *couldn't divulge anything, but . . .*) now sparks deep discussions about
social injustice and snark about how most of my ilk need retraining.

Not that we don't, but suddenly I've found myself doing a job that
many people see as more harmful than good. My oath to protect and

serve is no longer appreciated but seemingly at odds with the way the world now works.

I press the phone to my ear. Mark, my sometimes partner, blathers that he's at the hospital and needs me to assist. He says an elderly man with emphysema has died.

"I think that's what they do, Mark," I tell him. "A hospital is a good place for that kind of thing."

"Not trying to be funny," he says. "Doc says something hinky might have happened. I wouldn't bust you out of your weekend if I didn't need you."

"I'll be there in a few. You buy the coffee. And have it ready. I don't want to be fishing around for change."

I close the window and my wife stirs. I plant a kiss on her cheek. She nuzzles her face into her pillow, making grumbling sounds. As I dress, I think about the invisible wall between us, how we never talk about *it*. How we're both afraid that if we acknowledged the space between us, our marriage would succumb to our realization that it hasn't worked for a long time.

The cat rubs up against me and leaves a swathe of white fur on my pants as I pass through the kitchen. Glad for the company. Hate the fur. The house is empty since our daughter left on a church mission trip to Mexico.

Mark Danson is a good ten years younger than I am. He transferred in from the state patrol in Olympia. He was tired of the road, had good instincts, and, best of all, his age and lack of experience with homicide investigations made him the cheapest of the candidates. Captain hired him on the spot.

I find him in the lobby at the hospital. He's looking in my direction, holding up two cups of coffee. Kind of reminds me of an airport limo driver just then, waiting at the gate holding a card with my name on it.

"Black, two sugars." He hands me a cup.

I gulp it down and give him a look of approval.

"What have we got?"

"Old guy. Caller to dispatch thinks he might have been offed during the night."

"Fine. Let's find the attending physician. Tell me about the vic. Everything you know."

Mark leads me to the elevator. The rubber soles of his new shoes squeak with every step. It's annoying, but I need my coffee too much to stop drinking and remark on it.

"Vic was at his granddaughter's wedding in Olalla. Fell to the floor and flopped around like a fish before the paramedics arrived. Has one of those portable oxygen tanks for emphysema."

"Yes, you said that on the phone. So, a geezer falls, has a hard time breathing, gets to the hospital, and dies. Where's the crime?"

The elevator door opens.

"He'll tell you." Mark indicates a doctor with a cockscomb of black hair, and I now know for sure that my generation is crossing over to the land of AARP memberships and doctors the age of our kids.

Dr. Bob Amir takes us to a small conference room a few steps from the nurse's station. He removes his glasses and looks at us.

"So," he says, "I could lose my job for talking to you. I need you to understand that I can't have it coming back to me. I don't want to be labeled a troublemaker. At the same time, I just can't let it go."

"Understood," I tell him. "What is it you can't let go of?"

"First, I want you to know that I've told hospital administrators about similar incidents over the past month or so. Three times!"

His voice rises, and he checks himself, then scans the door.

"What happened three times?" I say.

"Amy Woods is what happened."

"What do you mean? Who is she?"

"A nurse," Mark answers for the doctor.

I nod. "A nurse did what? What?" I repeat when Dr. Amir hesitates.

"This is hard to say," he says haltingly. "Hard to know for sure. But in my heart, I feel it. I feel that she did something to that old man. Like I feel she has done to three others."

"Specifically?"

"I can only tell you that Nurse Woods is always there to call the code. And when she does, it's like she's called her family in for dinner. Like she revels in it."

"Revels in it?" I echo. "How's that?"

Dr. Amir gives me a deadpan expression. "You know," he says, "as though she's pretending to be concerned. She's smiling. Like she's enjoying it."

Mark glances between us. "Maybe she's a weirdo?"

I don't bust his chops over his grasp of technical terms.

"Did she actually do anything to arouse your suspicions?"

The doctor stiffens. "I never saw her do anything, if that's what you're asking. But Nurse Woods is always there, like that dog or cat in the news that visits nursing home patients the night they die." He reaches into the pocket of his white coat, then presses his card into my hand. "Need to get back to my work. I'll help in any way I can. Use my cell. In the meantime, talk to Bettina Gregory. She'll give you an earful."

"Who is she?" I ask.

Dr. Amir turns to leave. "A nurse. A good one."

CHAPTER FIVE

Seattle, Washington
Violet

My imagined remake of Nana's favorite oldie plays in my head.
It's my wedding and I'll cry if I want to.
I don't though.
Not my thing.
Zach and I spent our wedding night in a room at the Inn at the Market, a boutique hotel overlooking Seattle's Pike Place Market. It's more iconic and less tourist trappy than others might have selected for their wedding night. He and I have been together for two years and didn't need a rose-petal-strewn bed or engraved flutes of Moët to celebrate our first night of Mr. and Mrs.

Or to facilitate a wild night of sex.

We've had plenty of those. Zach once even talked me into an encounter in the service elevator at the offices of the Washington Apple Commission, where I work.

I guess he didn't really talk me into it. I willingly went along for the ride.

It isn't that I don't enjoy how our bodies lock together, the euphoria that comes now and then—mostly, but not always. Our lovemaking makes him so happy. He's like a weak little puppy after a clandestine session of sex. I much prefer how it makes him feel over how it feels to me. I've never told him—mostly because he's never asked—that he was only my second lover. By the time we matriculated to the University of Washington, Paris had a key chain with a bead for each guy she'd slept with. Seriously. She insisted that if guys could put notches in their belts, why couldn't she?

A true feminist. I respected her for that.

I slide under the covers next to Zach. He's muscular for a nerd but also funny. His concern for things comes from his brain and his heart. He's completely driven to create something revolutionary in the tech world, where he's staked a claim since high school. We're from the same town, but we didn't hang out as kids. I mostly remember his black-framed glasses forever sliding down his sharp nose. Zach had a kind of transformation the summer before senior year. Maybe just growing into his lanky body, I don't know, but he came back that fall the proverbial hot geek. I noticed, but I was too busy hustling for popularity then.

I never really got where I was heading, but he did.

He leans over and kisses me, a kind of semi-forceful smack that's akin to dipping a toe into a pool to test whether the temperature is conducive to swimming or not. I answer by murmuring and running my hands under the crisp hotel sheets, following his wispy treasure trail. I think of it as the road most traveled. By me. I play around down there a little, feeling him grow hard, then let him drift off into sleep.

We'll finish what I barely started later.

Promise.

I retrieve my phone from the nightstand charger and scroll through the wedding photos on Instagram using the hashtag #VioletZachWedding. Some images make me smile at the goofiness of my friends; some are cringeworthy and should have been relegated to

Snapchat. Paris and Michael are going to want to delete the photo of the two of them drinking from a mostly empty tequila bottle—if they ever need to look for new jobs outside of a distillery.

Thankfully, most guests practiced restraint when Papa slumped to the floor. There's only one shot of that and another showing the ambulance.

It's one of Lily's posts that sends my spine upright.

It's a short video of my mother standing next to her parents over by the serrano ham. Mom hands Nana a plate and turns away to help one of the older cousins. When Papa turns his back, Nana does something. Cleans the edges of the plate? Mom hands her a fork. Everything happens so quickly that I watch again.

I exhale and look over at Zach. He's asleep. My heart is beating so loudly, I'm sure it's the reason he stirs. I slide on top of him. I love him. I don't want to talk. I don't even want sex. I use it just then like someone changing the subject—even when the subject hasn't been broached.

"Babe," he says, "that feels good."

"Shhh," I whisper. "Let me take care of you."

Zach is at full attention. In every way.

I'm thinking about what I saw in the video.

Why did my sister post that?

※

While Zach showers, my mind remains stuck on Lily's video. I scroll through Instagram just to be sure. More uploads since I last looked. More congrats comments and enough emojis to fill the valentine section at a card shop.

I don't see the video post.

I search again.

Did I dream it?

I look at the time. Lily's sure to be up. She was always a disgustingly early riser, all smiles and unknotted hair.

"Did Mom call you?" she asks right away. She sounds anxious and my back stiffens. "She told me she was going to. She told me not to. I wanted to."

Lily rambling is not completely unusual.

"What's going on?"

"Mom didn't want me to tell you. She's going to call you later."

"Lily, get on with it."

I already know what she's going to say. It's just something I feel in my bones. Zach comes in from the bathroom and stops to look at me.

"Everything okay?" he mouths. His eyes are full of compassion. He knows me. Or, at least, he thinks he does. He knows what I let him know. Just like everyone else.

I put Lily on speaker. "Zach's here too,"

She exhales softly. Zach moves closer to me.

"You aren't going to believe this, Violet. Papa died overnight."

I hear what I think is applause, but it's only the inn's AC kicking on. Zach squeezes my free hand to let me know he's here for me.

"Oh wow. How's Nana? Mom? I'm coming home," I say.

"You can't, Violet. Mom doesn't want you to know. She wants you and Zach to go to Hawaii, and everything will get handled while you're away."

"Go to Hawaii and let Nana think I don't love her? Right. Like I could ever do that."

Zach squeezes harder and wraps his arm around me. "Hawaii can wait." There isn't the slightest trace of disappointment.

And so, apparently, can my reason for calling—the Instagram video. The one in which something puzzling was happening. Nana wasn't wiping off Papa's plate. Mom wasn't handing her a clean fork. They were putting something there.

Something to make Papa sick.

Or worse.

In any case, one of them succeeded.

CHAPTER SIX

Gig Harbor, Washington
Kirk Hoffman

Nurse Bettina Gregory corners me in the corridor while a writhing patient is pushed through the open jaws of a doorway to wherever they take the really loud ones. She speaks in a tone that suggests that she doesn't even hear the woman's yelps. I can't get it out of my head. Except for a butterfly tattoo and blue-dyed hair, Bettina's a ringer for every concerned young nurse on the floor. Her eyes are swallowed by hipster yellow frames, and her hospital lanyard is studded with pins that indicate support for various causes.

"I've seen Nurse Woods sound the alarm for two other patients," she says without hiding her disdain. "She just happens to be on shift when they die."

"I guess that means you were on shift too," I say. "I mean, you saw her?"

She bunches her lips and shakes her head. "I was on the floor. But she was in the room. She's always in the room when a patient codes. I've told every higher-up here at the hospital, and they do nothing!"

Her voice rises a touch, and she immediately tones it down. A second later, she leads us into a room with racks of folded white towels and other hospital linens. A dryer tumbles a load on the other side of the space. I tell her that I'm there to listen; it is my job to do so.

"Okay, fine," she says. "I have never seen her kill anyone. I have never witnessed her do anything other than act weird."

"How?"

She chooses her words with care. "Nursing is about helping other people. It is also a hard job and a demanding one. Some people come to it because they truly want to make a difference. Others come for the money."

"That's like a lot of jobs. Cops included."

"Okay, but there's also the third kind of person."

"All right, I'm listening."

"That kind of person gets off on the life-and-death drama. Most of us don't deny there's an aspect of excitement and the rush of adrenaline when there's a lot on the line."

I know of at least a half dozen cops and an equal number of firefighters who feel that way about their work.

"Nurse Woods likes the excitement," I say.

Bettina pushes her glasses up the bridge of her nose. "Loves it. She's an excitement junkie. Really. She thinks a cardiac arrest is a base jump with a bungee cord."

Her description makes me smile. Only inwardly. "Tell me about what happened overnight."

She goes on to detail the hours around Dave Bradley's death. Typical night. Pretty quiet. Hates the shift. Hates working with Amy. Hates this and that.

"Mr. Bradley was stable. There was no reason for him to die. Not on my watch. Amy goes into his room and all hell breaks loose. He's coded and flopping around. The man was practically a hundred years old. Every now and then, they need a jump start. She stands there like she always does. She has that stupid wide-eyed look like she's soaking in the moment. I don't get it. For someone who gets off on it, she sure is a passive player. It's like she lights a fuse and steps aside."

"What makes you think she caused the episode?"

"Because she's either a killer or the unluckiest nurse on the planet. Like I said, three times in a month. Must be a record of some kind."

"Or a coincidence?"

"That's what Dr. Amir said. At first. He thought a little differently when I told him what I'd found out about her."

This is the part where witnesses drop the bomb. It seems that Bettina likes drama as much as her rival.

I let her have the moment of anticipation she obviously wants. "And that was, exactly, what?"

"She was accused of the same thing in Oregon. Beat the charge. Changed her name. But lightning doesn't strike twice in the same place . . . and definitely not three times!"

She pushes a voided page from a prescription pad into my open hand. "Google this."

On the flip side are four words: Amy Atkinson, Eugene, Oregon.

While Mark interviews other staff, I lead Amy Woods into the vacant nondenominational chapel. Nurse Woods is tall, with closely cropped gray hair and a no-nonsense demeanor. The seriousness of the situation is clear on her face. There is no chitchat. Her words come at me clipped. Not as though she's being evasive, but she's brief in a way that suggests she's either a poor observer or a non-embellisher.

We sit side by side on an upholstered pew facing a stained-glass window, illuminated from behind by incandescent lights. In this room, it is always day.

"You were the last one to see Mr. Bradley alive?"

"As far as I know."

"What do you mean as far as you know?"

"Well, a hospital is a busy place, Detective."

"You also were the first one in the room after he coded."

"Yes. That's correct."

"Tell me about it."

"What is there to say? I answered the alarm. I called out for assistance, and we worked on the patient. It's what we do."

"Right," I say, not wanting to back her into a corner. I have nothing but the suspicion of another nurse and the backing of a doctor. "He didn't make it, though."

She doesn't answer immediately. I opened the door to a smart-ass reply, but Nurse Woods isn't the type to take the bait.

"No," she tells me succinctly, "I'm afraid not."

"You've been through similar scenarios before, right?"

The wheels are turning. I can see them move. Amy rotates her watch around her wrist while keeping her eyes on me. On the face of it, my question is not accusatory. But in the case of a woman who, at least according to other hospital staff, has had more than her share of recent deaths on her watch, it might seem so.

"Every nurse or doctor has."

"Of course," I say. "You've had a run of them lately."

She stops toying with her watch. "Detective, it's been a long shift. Please be direct. What are you getting at?"

"Just trying to put things in order so we can all go home and get some rest."

It's a lie. I feel like I've guzzled a case of Red Bulls. It's not from the caffeine in the crappy coffee. It's that needle poke in my gut that tells me there just might be something here. It's early in the inquiry, of course. I know nothing but what's been said to me. Old man comes in with food poisoning or anaphylactic shock. Stabilizes. Put on oxygen because of his medical history. Tragedy averted. A couple hours later, old fella codes and dies. None of that would bring me to the hospital, except for the caller who used the phrase "Angel of Death."

And she's sitting next to me.

Chapter Seven

June 27
Violet

Zach drives his geek starter car, a Prius, as we head south from Seattle on the interstate to Gig Harbor for Papa's memorial service. A Doja Cat remix rolls out from the speakers. Zach keeps one hand on the wheel and the other on my knee, drumming softly to the beat. My eyes stay fixed on the view outside the window. Circus and army surplus tents under the freeway, green fuselages of new Boeing planes, then the bottleneck of Southcenter Mall and farther south to Tacoma and the Narrows Bridge to the peninsula—the commuter's slideshow flashing by.

Rain pecks at the windshield.

"Hey," Zach says, turning on the wipers, "let's not make the day any worse."

"Right," I say.

I keep up the pretense that I'm upset, but not overly so. Like, it hasn't fully sunk in. It's the best I can manage.

What would my husband think of me if he grasped how I felt about Papa's sudden death?

When Lily told me Papa died, something strange and wonderful happened. It was as though I'd shed a lead chrysalis. The air that filled my lungs suddenly came to me easily, smoothly. No more gulps of oxygen in the middle of the night or at my desk at work. From the time I'd fully processed what happened to me, I'd been all over the incest survivors' websites. I'd even joined a support group for sexually abused children. I went a half dozen times, and while it was probably helpful to some degree, I wasn't sure what I was hoping for as far as an outcome. Maybe just to listen, nod in agreement, and comfort others.

To be fair, none of the other women seemed to be vying for "my abuse was worse than yours." Still, it felt that way to me. I hated Papa for what he did to me. I had neither forgiven nor forgotten. I couldn't grasp the purpose of the group.

I needed an end to thinking about what happened when I was a girl. I wanted the burden lifted away like a bandage being ripped off. Quick. A flash of pain, then over. I just didn't know how that would ever happen.

After one of the meetings, a woman in her late thirties who'd been abused by a neighbor asked if I wanted to get coffee. Her name was Ellie Greene. She had large expressive eyes and the kind of refined nose I thought I'd wanted as a girl. Like Lily's. Ellie wore a stack of bangles on her left arm to hide the telltale striations from a razor or box cutter.

She noticed my eyes landing there.

"That was, my doctor insisted, a coping mechanism. I considered it a distraction at best. Nothing helped me cope. Keeping a journal. Medication. Counseling. None of it, well intentioned as it was, did a fucking thing to make it go away. Only one thing worked."

The memory of that meeting remains vivid.

We sat across from each other at Starbucks in Tacoma. She waved to another patron, an older woman carrying a cardboard tray of lattes.

She leaned toward me. "Brother was abducted by a pedo."

Her words jolted me. "I'm sorry."

"Don't be. His abuser is dead. Cops filled him full of bullets. Rescued two boys from a basement dungeon. Genuine *SVU* moment."

Ellie seemed strong. She looked me in the eye. She dressed nicely. She had a husband and two small children. I thought she was a researcher at the university, though she'd never said so specifically. She appeared so together, yet she came to the meetings.

I set down my latte. "You said none of the talk therapy stuff helped you. To look at you, I just think, wow, she looks okay."

Ellie smiled. "Actually, I am. If you had met me five years ago, you would have said the same thing. I've always been good at hiding everything. We're probably a lot alike in that way."

Something told me I'm nothing like her. She really did seem fine. Strong. In group, she never cried. She held the hands of the newbies. She unreservedly gave out her phone number.

"You said only one thing freed you."

Ellie rested both elbows on the table, and the bangles on her wrist fell downward. Like a slinky, I thought.

"That's right," she said. "When I knew that my molester would never hurt me—or anyone ever again."

"They caught him. Sent him to prison?"

She shook her head. "No. Not prison. That's not a permanent cure for my problem. Or the next little girl that crosses his trail of slime. My molester went to prison for eight years. At the time, my parents and I stupidly considered that justice. Thought it meant I'd get better too—you know, not thinking about him popping up around the corner. Well, I didn't get better."

Her voice carried a harder edge. She rattled her bangles. "That's when I started this art project on my arm."

She gave me an ironic smile.

"Honestly," she continued, "prison for these guys is a joke. Drugs. Sex. Free food. And they know that they'll be released. All in good time. Just the way it is."

"And the victims," I added in the space she left open. "We don't realize that until they're free again."

"Correct. We buy into the justice theory."

"Then what?"

"He died in a house fire. An accident." She paused to sip her coffee before putting a finer point on things. "A happy accident."

Her eyes flashed so brightly, I found myself glancing away.

I knew there was more to the story, but I didn't ask for it.

It turned out I didn't have to.

"After the motherfucker burned up, my dad called me. He'd heard it on the news. His exact words were 'A gift from the Almighty came tonight, Ellie. That bastard is dead.' And you know what I did?"

"What?" I asked.

She shook her head and shrugged. "I cried. Funny, right? I bawled like I hadn't since I first told my parents what he'd done to me in his basement. This time, however, the tears came from joy. Really. Just a damn flood of joy came over me. I never thought I'd be happy about someone's demise. I was. I was freaking overjoyed. I still am."

I took in every word Ellie gave me. I squinted in the direction of a nosy girl eavesdropping on our conversation, and she went back to her phone.

"You probably didn't want to hear all of that," Ellie said as she slid on her jacket and reached for her purse.

"Of course I did."

"Well, it goes against what experts say. They tell people like us that we must overcome. Must be strong. Yada yada yada. Have to get past the abuse to get on with our lives. Like it's all incumbent on us and what we do to actually get better. It's not. To be a survivor is a made-up convention designed to make us live within the confines of the law. The truth is surviving childhood trauma isn't the same thing as living."

"I don't understand," I finally admitted.

"You will." She pushed her chair under the table as she got up to leave. "You'll see."

I didn't then.

I do now.

By the time Zach and I pull up to my parents' house so we can all drive together to the memorial service, I'm working my way through the internet using the key words "sexual abuse homicide."

Zach asks if I need a minute.

I don't. I turn off my phone and give him a kiss on the cheek. He's kind. He's thoughtful. He loves me. I still can't be sure, though, of one thing.

Would he love me if he knew what happened to me?

Would he love me if he knew what I was thinking just then?

"Thanks," I tell him. "Gonna be a rough day."

CHAPTER EIGHT

Rose

A lovely PowerPoint plays on mute in front of us in the chapel at Haven of Rest. It's a greatest-hits collection from my dad's life. I have a hard time watching it, and I wonder why I agreed to dig up photos for the damn thing. Some images are reminders of things that I haven't thought about in years. A few bring faint smiles of recognition. Dad playing Santa with the neighbor kids. Mom sulking in the background while my father's little fan club crawls all over him for attention. My eyes land on the face of my best friend, Jenny Little.

Mom is wearing the same dress she wore at Violet's wedding, somehow repaired in the interval. She sits in the middle of the front row, bolstered by Richard and our girls. Wearing that dress is Mom at her finest—thrifty and practical. She made such a fuss over the cost of it, I knew I'd see it at every special occasion until her own ride in a hearse.

I hadn't expected to see it so soon, though.

I let go of her arthritic hand, and she moves it away to sob into tissue pulled from a box proffered by the pastor, a young man with the incongruent frame of a linebacker and the gracious manner of a concierge at a high-end hotel. Mom likes him. Her drippy eyes signal a message, and he immediately tilts the large portrait of my father in her direction. Familiar to all of us in the front row, the photograph is black-and-white, taken when Dad was a young man. His hair was lustrous and his eyes flinty. He was smart, successful. On the surface, I'm sure it seemed to others that we had the perfect family. I was Daddy's Girl and, at the same time, my mother's Mini-Me.

Now Dad's gone. Mom's alone. My oldest is married. I am feeling as though things have spun out of control. I like control. Control, I'm sure, likes me. Loves me.

Mom smells of witch hazel, the tentpole of a personal skin-care regimen that also includes mayonnaise and cucumber slices done on a mandolin. Always English cucumber. She's kept all three items in the pink Norge fridge ever since I can remember. One time when I was a brat, I called her Salad Face.

She slapped me hard for that. When my own girls, especially Violet, attacked me as they grew to teen hood, it was with the "bitch" epithet.

Or worse.

Until the run-up to Violet's wedding, I'd never slapped either of my girls. My generation used reason, car pools to ballet practice, and trips through the Dairy Queen drive-through to shift behavior from atrocious and annoying to halfway acceptable.

My tactics were weak. Passive, even. I knew it was more than the times we were living in. I knew that it was also because I was gutless. I had no real spine.

I can forgive her for not being the perfect mother. When bad things happened, she had a way of pushing them aside with a distraction meant to make things better. *Don't look here. Look* here. *When you think happy thoughts, you become happy. The Power of Positive Thinking* is her second bible. Norman Vincent Peale is her Pope.

What a sack of bullshit.

Lily

I've only been to one other memorial service in my life. It was in the summer before fourth grade, and a neighbor boy three doors down died from cancer. I didn't even know he was sick. Mom sent me down the street with some cookies she'd packaged in an old Christmas shortbread tin. The fact that the tin had a snowman on it mortified me. It was July! When I tried to give the cookies to the boy's mother, she started to cry. Stood there just crying in the doorway. I froze, like the snowman. Mute too. I don't think I'd ever seen such anguish before, probably since. Finally, after an awkward minute or two, I hurried back home.

I never gave her the cookies.

Mom served them that night after dinner.

Now Papa is gone. Once again, I don't feel a thing that I should. I try to put on a show of sorrow for my grandmother's sake, though she's probably the toughest person here. She came from a family of German-born farmers on the western side of Nebraska. She was one of fourteen kids. "Poor" wasn't the word for her situation. She and her siblings didn't know any different. They played farmer until they had to work the beet fields.

"Chicken bones were our horses, and we pretended walnut shells were turkeys," she told us.

"Chicken bones," I repeated. "Gross."

I remember the prickly look she gave me. It was an expression I'd see often over the years. A way to keep us in line without the bother of words.

"Having nothing can be a source of imagination or the rope around your neck. You get to choose. And frankly, girls, you have a lot more choices than I ever had."

Nana earned her way through nursing school in Omaha during the war. She offered up endless, and repeated, stories about how she lived on ketchup soup and reused tea bags until the hot water stayed colorless. She didn't need or want a man—but then Nana did what she told us girls never to do: she picked poorly. She succumbed to Dave Bradley's charms; they married and moved west after he was hired by Boeing.

Marrying Papa wasn't the first mistake she made. It was, however, by far the biggest.

The living room of my grandparents' redbrick rambler smells of old people and smoked ham. I know all these faces, and I see how much they loved the man who we buried today. They look at my mother, my sister, and me with compassionate eyes, and I realize they knew Papa in a way that I never could.

The weather seemed to be his opening salvo to any conversation. Until I heard Violet's story, I thought he was just boring in the way old people can be. But maybe it was a subject of little or no controversy? No room for error in saying something that would awaken dormant memories. No questionable: *Remember the time we went to the beach . . .* Or suggestive: *You look pretty in that dress . . .*

Nana has powdered coffee creamer on the front of her dress that I ignore when she leans down to kiss the top of my head. I could easily tell her it's there. I could wipe it off. I don't. I just ignore it.

Like my family ignores everything.

My father is over in the corner next to a gigantic Christmas cactus talking to a neighbor. His palm is pressed in the small of her back as though his touch is needed to steady her as she teeters on spike heels that lift her legs up the high hemline of her pencil skirt. I've seen her around. Her name is Shondra. She's about forty, slim but curvy at the same time. My dad likes her. He likes every woman in the room. She, however, seems to be a favorite.

I walk over to join them.

"Mom needs you, Dad."

"All right, Lily," he says, knowing Mom gave up on needing him long ago. My parents think that whispering when they fight is a winning technique for keeping a lid on their troubles. The walls in our house are thin. Very little goes unheard.

Like the existence of Shondra.

Dad touches her back again and leaves the two of us standing there. Shondra is holding a cup of tea now.

"Looking forward to going to college?" she asks after a sip.

"Looking forward to getting out of Gig Harbor, if that's what you mean."

She gives me a smile. "I know the feeling. At least, I know the feeling of wanting to get away and start your adult life. Funny thing is—if you are anything like me—you will miss it here. Not right away. But later."

I could say something about how summer can't speed by fast enough and that I will only return home for major holidays. Instead, I pivot from the subject.

"Thank you for coming, Shondra. My grandmother will be lonely. Please stop by and see her from time to time. Old friends like you mean everything."

With that, I go look for Violet.

Growing up, she had mood swings I didn't understand. I never knew what big sister I'd get. I'd come into her room, see her crying, and try to comfort her. Once in a while, she'd let me. Mostly, she'd snap. Tell me to get out of her face. One time I emerged from the bathroom after playing with our mother's makeup, and Violet told me I looked like a slut and practically rubbed my skin raw with a washcloth. I don't know where that came from. I was only ten.

Of course, I always loved Violet. Wanted to be her, even. And now our relationship has finally found firm footing.

Violet

I fill the teakettle and rearrange cookies someone brought on a ceramic platter. Store-bought oatmeal raisin, masquerading as home baked. It's a perfect metaphor for the entire day. Sham memorial. Fake tears. Stupid PowerPoint.

Zach has no idea. It feels a lot like betrayal to keep him from the truth of what he's married into. I see him from the doorway to the living room talking to one of Nana's friends. I can't face the people out there. They ask me how I'm holding up and say how sorry they are for my loss. I'm tired of pretending Papa's death was anything other than a great relief. I haven't felt better in my life. It's like Papa's death was one of those Hawaiian waterfalls not far from the hotel where Zach and I will be staying starting tonight—washing over me, cleaning off the dirt and filth of the things he did to me.

"Dad has his hands all over Shondra," Lily says with the subtlety of an Amber Alert as she enters the kitchen.

"What else is new?" I ask. Rhetorically, of course.

She answers anyway. "Papa's dead."

"Right, and the last thing the creeper did was ruin my wedding."

Lily plunks plates into the sink and runs the water. "Last thing he did. Doesn't that alone do anything for you?"

"Yes. But it was my wedding."

"Well, at least up to that point, it was perfect. Everything was perfect. Just like you dreamed it."

She's trying to lift my spirits, and I love her for that.

Just then, Rose comes in with a picked-over tray of cheese and fruit. She looks tired. Not sad. Only tired. I wonder how she really feels about her father's death.

"Rose—"

Zach pokes his head in and holds up his phone like he's a road flagger or something and we're supposed to halt.

"Vi, we need to get going. Security lines at SeaTac are long."

"I'm ready."

I give Lily a hug and lean in to do the same to my mother. Rose always felt a little brittle to me. This time, more so. I breathe in her perfume, a light hibiscus that she made at a perfumery on Sixth Avenue— the hipster part of Tacoma. She hugs me back, hard. Not boa constrictor tight, but with more force than usual. Longer than she ever has.

"I am so sorry," she says.

"It's okay."

We don't say any other words to each other. Just the same ones we've always said since she finally seemed to believe me. Was she really sorry? Was I really okay? Our exchange feels a little different this time. It passes through my mind just then as I pull back and look at her face. Her eyes are flooded with tears. For me? For her? For her mother?

In the car on the way to the airport, Zach gives me his usual succinct take on the day, the gathering at my grandparents' house, and the suddenly infamous Shondra Jones.

"A total shit show," he says.

I grin. "Agree."

He looks over at me. "Do you think your dad is fucking the neighbor?"

"I need a dozen mai tais," I answer, "before we get into any of that."

CHAPTER NINE

June 28
Rose

Richard is watching ESPN. Mom is asleep in Violet's room. Lily is out somewhere with Maddy. Violet and Zach are on their honeymoon trip.

And Dad is under a layer of dirt at Haven of Rest.

I am alone.

I visit the freezer and pour myself some cold syrupy vodka. I get on my school laptop and sign in to Facebook. Jenny Little has been on my mind since I saw her photo in the memorial's PowerPoint. She and I were inseparable through second grade. Her father was transferred to Wichita, and they moved away. We exchanged friendship bracelets and promised to stay in touch, but promises like that are hard to keep when you're seven.

I'm doing what my daughters think is hugely embarrassing— Facebook stalking, they call it. I don't make a habit of it, but every now and then, I like to see where my generation landed in life. Facebook has made that easy.

I find four variations of Jenny Little, but the profile picture of Jenny Little Hopper looks vaguely right. The location in Overland Park looks good too. I send her a friend request. I drink some more and find myself lost in a feed of other people's lives.

Not more than fifteen minutes later, Jenny accepts my request. A chat window opens, and I watch an animated bubble expand and contract while she types a message.

Jenny: Surprised to hear from you.

Me: Just thinking of you today.

Jenny: I think of your screwy family every day.

Me: I don't understand.

Jenny: Bullshit, Rose.

Me: What are you getting at?

Jenny: Ask your pig of a dad.

Me: You're mean. He's dead.

Jenny: Best news I've heard in years.

Me: Harsh. What are you getting at?

Jenny: Ask your mom. The fucking biggest bitch denier. It took me ten years of therapy to make it so whenever I went past a flower shop, I didn't puke on the street because I saw your stupid name on a sign.

Jenny: Ask your mom. Maybe she'll stonewall you like she did me and Lynette.

Me: Lynette?

Jenny: Lynette Riggs. He diddled her too. Ask your mom. When I talked to her, she acted like I was some stupid kid with false memory syndrome. I know what happened. That your mom covered for your dad is fucked up to the moon and back. All I can say is I'm glad that SOB was like a dog that didn't shit in his own crate. Wouldn't want anyone, not even you, to go through what I did. Glad the motherfucker is dead.

Me: Got it all wrong, Jenny.

Jenny: You know only what you want to believe, Rose. I get it. I do. I wouldn't want to believe it of my own father. The difference between you and me is that I wouldn't hide it. I wouldn't pretend things were hunky-dory.

Me: Sorry you feel that way.

Jenny: Bullshit. What I feel is based on what happened to me and Lynette.

Lynette, another name I hadn't thought of in eons. I stare at the screen and feel my hands tremble. I have no idea why. I suck in some oxygen and steady myself before typing.

Me: Lynette never said anything.

Jenny: Ever wonder why she smashed into that guardrail?

Me: She had too much to drink.

Jenny: She wanted to die. It was a suicide.

Me: It was an accident.

And just like that, Jenny leaves the conversation. I try to message her, but she's already blocked me.

Finlandia calls my name. Actually, screams it. I fill an empty glass, trying to forget Jenny's words at the same time I'm struggling to remember. To understand. She and Lynette were frequent visitors to our home until, suddenly, they weren't. Jenny moved away. Lynette didn't come over much after that, but we remained friends through high school. How was it possible that we could be friends and not share such a secret?

I drink more and somehow find my way to Violet's room, where Mom is sleeping.

I flip on the light with unexpected force.

Mom opens her eyes and looks at me, startled.

"What is it?" she asks, lifting her head from her traveling satin pillowcase. "Is it one of the girls?"

She twists in her fortress of comforters and sits up.

"I talked to Jenny Little, Mom."

I stand over her frail body. I could snap her bones just by sitting down. She reads me like a menu. She's always had that ability. Her expression—irritation, I think—tells me how she feels about Jenny.

"That little liar?" she asks. "What did she say this time?"

Shock penetrates even the numbness of the vodka.

"'What did she say *this* time?' Did you talk to her? What did Dad do to her, Mom?"

She slides deeper into the covers. Ending the conversation.

"Go to bed," she barks at me. "That girl was fixated on your father. On this family. She made up a pack of lies and caused us nothing but heartache. I don't want to discuss it. Good Lord, Rose, your father just died. You're being needlessly cruel. Doctor says I could have a stroke with all this stress. Can't you let things rest? You smell like a distillery."

I'm shaking when I leave the room and climb into bed next to Richard. He's sawing logs, oblivious. I close my eyes and catch an elusive memory of our baby rabbits. It was a few days after my seventh birthday when Jenny came over. Dad asked if she wanted to see the litter of mini lops we kept in a hutch in the garage.

"Maybe you can pick one out when they're old enough."

"Could I, Mr. Bradley?"

My mother piped up. "Only if your mother and father say it's okay."

Dad and Jenny disappeared. I was helping Mom slice fresh strawberries for the last two servings of angel food cake. About fifteen minutes later, maybe longer, they came back inside.

"We had a little accident," Dad said.

Mom hurried over and jerked Jenny away from him. He said something about one of the bunnies biting her while it sat in her lap. Dad took a bottle of scotch from the liquor cabinet and returned to the garage. Mom took Jenny to the bathroom and dressed her injury with a Band-Aid.

Over Jenny's sobbing, I heard my mother's voice.

"You're a good girl, Jenny, and I'm sure you didn't mean to scare the bunny. They bite when they get frightened."

"It wasn't the bunny," she said.

"Of course it was. Don't you worry. I won't tell your mom. You shouldn't either. If you're a good girl, you can still have a bunny."

Mom later told me that Jenny had learned a valuable lesson that afternoon.

"Sometimes things are better left unsaid."

I play back the foggiest part of the memory. I was in bed but I could hear my parents arguing. The words were garbled. I could only make out one thing. It came from Mom.

"In our own home. What were you thinking?"

In the morning, I find Mom dressed—coat fully buttoned—and sitting with perfect posture on the living room sofa, all packed and ready to go home. Lily is asleep and Richard has gone to work, an early meeting in Olympia.

"Rita is picking me up," she announces.

"Mom, is it about last night?"

She hardly looks in my direction, a silent rejoinder more devastating than her penetrating laser gaze. "You've really hurt me this time, Rose. The things you said. Honestly, I think I'm in shock. I can't believe I raised a girl who would spout such unfounded and hateful ugliness."

I seldom press a point with her. She always wins.

"It was the truth, wasn't it?" I ask anyway.

"What does it matter now? In our lives today? I've been through a lot of hardships and agonies, Rose, but, really, your midnight tirade truly takes the cake."

I attempt to sit next to her, but she puts her hand on the cushion to keep me at bay.

"I said I'm sorry."

"Sorry and two cents won't buy you a cup of coffee."

She looks defeated sitting there. Small. Somehow even older than she was only days ago. I hold back the memory that seeped into my consciousness before I fell asleep. Papa. Jenny. The rabbits.

I want to find out more.

CHAPTER TEN

June 29
Honolulu, Hawaii
Violet

The Royal Hawaiian is a Mary Kay cosmetics sales rep's vision of heaven. The color pink is everywhere. It's like someone picked up the venerable hotel on Waikiki Beach and dipped it in a vat of pink royal icing. Our lounge chairs have pink pillows, and the sun has turned me slightly carnation. The ocean breeze brushes my face as the sun sinks lower on the horizon. Zach is on his fourth mai tai. Maybe fifth? I decide I've had enough sun, and the book club pick from the girls at the office is such a downer, reading any more of its turgid prose will make me want to jump off a sea cliff.

I get up from my chaise. "Heading back to the room."

Zach gives me a boozy smile. "Really? Feels like we just got here."

I toss him a tube of sunblock.

"Just put some more of this on, babe. Yes, you tan. That doesn't mean you can't get skin cancer."

He motions to the server from the Royal Hawaiian's aptly named Mai Tai Bar that he wants another.

I don't say what I'm thinking. He looks happy. He's enjoying himself. He'll deal with the hangover tomorrow all on his own. Not a complainer, this one. In fact, Zach is nothing but positive about all things in life. He sees the world as a place of opportunity, possibilities. Whatever was done to you—and these days, it can be anything from what happened to me or the fact that you didn't get an Xbox for Christmas—should not impede you from reaching for whatever you consider the brass ring.

I weave my way past tables scattered under an unruly and beautiful banyan tree that forms a natural leafy canopy over the courtyard. It's an octopus, arms reaching over the space, tentacles dropping to roots like splashing rain. Inside the hotel, I retrieve a copy of the *Honolulu Star-Advertiser* from the concierge's desk. A woman my age sits there, leis ringing her neck. She gives me a nod as she smiles at a couple posing in wedding attire in a corner of the lobby that offers nothing special in the way of a backdrop.

"Saw them this morning by the tree," I tell her. "Covering a lot of ground here."

She grins. "Inch by inch. Wedding isn't for two days."

"Our photo session was an hour at best," I say.

"Mine too. Sunset cruise tomorrow?"

"Not sure. I'll check back."

She nods, and we watch the photographer position the couple by the entrance to the hotel gift shop.

I shake my head.

I can't even think of the last time I touched newsprint. Probably on my last trip—the organic food convention in Anaheim, almost a year ago. Immediately, a story on the bottom of the front page catches my eye. Like a barbed fishing hook.

Suicide Result of Coach Predator's Release?

I stand outside the door to our suite reading. When a maid pushes her rolling cart by, I swipe the key card and go in. My heart rate quickens, and I find myself slumping onto the bed, trying to catch my breath, taking in the story of Donita Lee, who was eleven when Lewis Faraday, her soccer coach, started grooming and molesting her over a two-year period.

> "Nothing is right about this," her mother, Kara Lee, said. "He served only ten years and she's served a lifetime sentence, then a death sentence. Her life was a mess. And his? Well, he's started over. We tried a hundred times to start over. Nothing worked."

Ms. Lee goes on to tell the reporter that her daughter had been in counseling, rehab, and was even arrested a couple of times for petty crimes.

> "She would not have been this kind of person if he hadn't done those things to her. She trusted no one. Not even us. She killed herself because it was the only way to find peace."

I know what it is like to be without the ability to truly believe or trust another person. I have been without it almost all my life. Until Zach, of course. The first time I had sex, I had to tell the boy to stop. When he was inside of me, I pictured a knife. Papa never did that to me. Yet in my mind, that's where I went with the idea of sex.

A penis was a knife. A hammer. Crowbar. Whatever hard and menacing foreign object that was meant to terrorize, it was.

I no longer feel that way, but the mere fact that it comes to my mind as I read Donita Lee's sad story tells me that something is still there, lurking in my subconscious.

I put the paper down and search on my phone for more information about Lewis Faraday. There are five articles in the *Advertiser's* database. The arrest, the conviction, a story about other victims coming forward after the trial, his early release, and finally, the article I just read about Donita's suicide at barely twenty-four.

The article detailing his release urges me to do another search on the sex offender registry.

I click on Faraday's name.

And there he is, a pipsqueak of a man at five foot five, a thin build. He's over fifty now but has a full head of dark hair and a wispy mustache. I want to read something in his eyes, his expression. An attribute that aligns with evil, cruel, predatory behavior. Knowing what someone had done changes how you see them. Yet, there's nothing there. He's bland. He looks harmless. If I was lost on the street, he'd be the one that I'd seek out for help.

If I were an eleven-year-old, I'd see nothing to be wary of.

It isn't Prada that the devil wears but a smile that belies the truth of his intent.

Faraday was only convicted on one charge of rape. But it's heavily implied that the police were investigating other accusations of molestation against him.

When I do it, I don't know exactly why. I take a screenshot of Faraday's address.

The door opens, and Zach, looking like he dived into a pool of Bloody Mary's mix, enters. He's a shade of red that reminds me of the peonies Mom planted in the backyard of our house in Gig Harbor the first year we lived there.

"You're going to hurt tomorrow," I say right away.

"I hurt now. Fuck, I'm stupid."

"Not stupid. From Seattle."

Chapter Eleven

Violet

There are things that have happened to me and things that I will do that my husband will never know. And yet, I'll tell a stranger.

Since Papa died, it's as if God gave me wings. The stones upon my back had dug in so deep, my skin had become mortar, but then, bit by bit, they began to fall away. My breathing has been softer than it's ever been. My steps, lighter. Sex with Zach has been better too. It was never bad, but there were always flashes of my first sexual experiences, ones that I couldn't talk about because whenever I wanted to tell someone, my throat became lined with cotton.

Or razors.

Maybe nails.

Things that should never be forced inside your throat.

Like what Papa did to me.

It isn't difficult to find where Donita resided, where her mother still does. Google has a lock on where everyone lives—real estate transactions, civil and criminal cases, social media posts. Bread crumbs are digital and everyone is there for the finding. In this case, however, the address appears in one of the photographs from the trial coverage in the Honolulu paper.

I park the ridiculous canary-yellow Camaro rental car in front of the Lees' home, a white single story with a wide porch. In front of the house is a heap of flowers, a sad splash of color, and cellophane rattling in the gardenia breeze.

I consider turning back, but the compulsion to knock on the door pulls me forward.

A woman cradling a mini dachshund that looks limp in her arms answers almost immediately. She appears as she did ten years ago in one of the articles: full-on anguish. She acknowledges me with a tentative smile and asks if she can help me.

I want to help her.

I give her my name. She listens, adjusting the dog in her arms.

"I'm sorry about your daughter."

We stand there in silence. It's awkward. I want to speak, but I can't.

"You're a survivor, aren't you?" Kara Lee finally asks.

I let the air out of my lungs. "How do you know?"

"You're not the first one to stop by. Come inside."

She leads me past what amounts to a shrine to Donita. It includes photos, memorabilia, things that I'm sure were displayed at Donita's funeral. More personal than a PowerPoint, I think. Everything is carefully arranged on a console table. Scuff marks on the tile floor indicate that the table was moved to a more central location, possibly for a gathering after her daughter's memorial.

"I'll be just a minute," she says as I take in the highlights of Donita's life.

I hear her pouring iced tea, and when she returns, we sit outside in a stunning tropical garden that Kara must give much of her time.

A way of coping with loss. One of the women in the Tacoma group said she turned her backyard into a replica of one of Wordsworth's gardens in England.

Kara hands me a glass. "You're here with a new husband on your honeymoon, but you wanted to see me?"

It sounds ridiculous, but it's true.

"I read the article. I felt the connection with your daughter."

She wipes the condensation from her glass. "There are a lot of you out there. All ages. All types of abuse done to the innocent, like my Donita."

"It was my grandfather," I blurt out. "He did it to me."

She closes her eyes and shakes her head. "I'm sorry." The ice cubes tinkle as she sets her tea on the table next to her. She wipes the moisture on her pant leg. "Monsters take all forms."

I don't respond right away. I don't want this to be about Papa.

"Lewis Faraday killed your daughter," I finally say.

Kara doesn't disagree. "That was a long time ago. What Donita did was a delayed response to what happened when she was a girl. It was playing in her head all those years. I didn't see it. I don't think anyone could. It was just something no one could stop."

"What happened to her never left her," I concur.

She fiddled with the rim of her glass. "Just like what happened to you. What your grandfather did to you still holds you tight, right?"

"It did for a long time." I fasten her gaze to mine.

"But not anymore?"

I shake my head. "Not since he died."

"Interesting."

"What happened is always going to be part of my story. It was only after he died that I didn't have to worry about it catching up with me, tearing at me. It was like what he did, the shame he brought to me, had become permanently dormant. There, but not threatening to rear up."

"I heard that from another girl. Her abuser had been murdered in prison, and she told me that his death gave her peace. Lasting peace."

The question I want to ask is a hard one, but I find the courage.

"You don't have peace, do you?"

"No. Not ever. My daughter is gone, and the predator that sent her to the grave is out there. Lives up on the North Shore. Works at a grocery store. Has a wife, even. People probably think he's wonderful, and if they know about his past—which I doubt—they probably think that my daughter made up the whole thing. She killed herself, didn't she?"

"Lives his life like nothing happened."

"Right. Like Donita was nothing. Just another girl foolish enough to let a grown man manipulate her. He never owned up to it. Never admitted it. Never said he was sorry. Nothing."

"He served his sentence."

"Part of it. They call that justice around here. He's free. She's dead. And I'm still serving mine."

She gets up and brings me her phone. I notice her hand is shaking a little now.

"Donita recorded this the day she died."

Kara doesn't like the word "suicide."

She pushes Play on a video clip, and as I watch, tears run from my eyes. Kara hands me the phone and looks away at the beautiful garden she's lovingly planted with her own hands. She's crying too. While she's fishing for a tissue, I air-drop the video to my phone.

Before I leave, I text Zach that the Dole marketing people are working on island time, which means that the meeting he thinks I'm at has barely started.

Me: Put on gobs of sunscreen and have a drink or two (or more) for me.

Him: One or two steps ahead of you. Hurry back. Love you. Honeymooning alone is kind of weird.

Me: I'll make it up to you.

The moment I'm back in my car, I call Ellie.

She picks up right away. "Aren't you supposed to be fucking your brains out or something?"

66

I let out a nervous laugh. She's crass sometimes, but I don't mind. She's earned every swear word that pops out of her mouth. She's been on the front lines and takes no prisoners. She understands the good fight. I'm beginning to.

I tell her about Kara Lee and Donita. "You should have seen her, Ellie. She's not even the victim here, but she's as broken as any one of us."

"Dominos," Ellie says. "In some families, the scumbags destroy everyone."

I think of Lily just then. Papa never touched her, but what he did to me changed her life too. She lived with my unpredictable moods, my bitterness, my walled-up rage. She didn't know why I wasn't everything a big sister should be.

"My sister," I say.

"Yeah. The tentacles have a long, insidious reach."

"Kara says that her daughter's abuser lives a new life on the North Shore as though nothing ever happened. Already has a wife."

"We live in a world where justice is a joke. After a sentence is served, these guys go on their merry way. Sure, they're on parole. Some have to take peter meter counseling. Some just fade away."

The light changes, and I drive by a homeless encampment, a man with a hand-lettered sign that reads, "Paradise Ain't Free."

"They don't fade away completely," I say. "They might be off the social grid, but they're on the registry."

Ellie doesn't respond right away.

"You there?"

"Yeah. Just thinking. Some hide in plain sight. Only if someone knows enough to go onto the offender's database will someone find them. Smart ones alter a letter or two in their names after they get out so they can't be googled easily."

"What about neighborhood notifications?"

"Right? Not happening. Not after a molester in Minneapolis got a huge judgment against a neighbor for harassment."

I know the case. "Well, they did burn down his house."

Ellie lets out a laugh. "You've been reading up. Good. Then you know where we stand."

I turn into the entrance to the hotel and park in front of the valet stand. A boy wearing a lei of koloa nuts opens my car door.

"At the hotel now, Ellie. I know where we stand. And I know what to do."

"Intrigued," she tells me. "Talk soon."

That night, Zach and I make sticky, sweet love in our suite. The air conditioner is on low, a hum punctuated with the intermittent sounds of the outside world. Waves breaking, the laughter of people having a good time, a cover band playing at the hotel next door—all merely a background to the thoughts that have consumed me since I returned to the hotel.

"I thought we'd be doing more of this," he says, sliding over on his side. He brushes my hair gently with his fingertips and leans in for a tropical-drink-infused kiss.

Coconut, I think.

"Sorry about today," I say.

Zach shrugs. "It's hard to leave your work behind when you're so passionate about it. I have a confession myself."

"I've seen you work your phone."

He grins. "God, are we both that bad?"

"Yeah. I think so."

"Our generation is so messed up."

"We're wired differently than our parents. It's hard to let go of the things that make us feel successful."

"We should be screwing instead of texting."

"Probably," I tell him. "What can we do about it?"

"Throw our phones in the ocean?"

I laugh. "That would last about a minute. You'd go after your phone faster than you would a drowning kid."

Zach makes a serious face. "I guess so. God, we're selfish."

"Just screwed up by technology. And that reminds me. I hate to do this, but one of the people from Dole that I was supposed to see couldn't make it. I have to go back tomorrow. Promise it won't be all day, though."

I close my eyes, but I can't fall asleep. I lied to Zach. It isn't the first time. My lies—by omission or outright—trace back to what happened to me when I was a girl. It's a shadow that hangs over all my relationships. If someone says something about child abuse, I choose silence over adding what I know. When Zach tells me about the traumas of his childhood—he had to wear braces for four years—I don't tell him to get a grip. I couldn't tell anyone.

Until I met Ellie Greene.

"As victims, we feel powerless," she said at that first meeting.

I raised my hand.

"I was a child," I said, pushing back. "I *was* powerless."

Her eyes scraped over the rest of the women in the crescent-shaped cluster we'd formed, with Ellie in the center.

"You're not a child now." Her tone was firm. Not cold but matter-of-fact. "You choose to be powerless now, Violet. It's really that simple."

Nothing about any of this seemed simple.

One of the other women, gray-haired and spectacled like Mrs. Claus, spoke up.

"I agree with Ellie. You are a grown woman, Violet. That you are here speaks to your courage and your desire to find a way forward after what happened to you. You know, how not to make it define every moment that passes. Consider yourself lucky. I didn't understand that until I was fifty-three."

Her words touched me. "What did you do?"

Her eyes bored into mine. "Confronted the asshole. That's what I did. I don't recommend you do what I did. I confronted my uncle at our Thanksgiving table. He was in his late seventies and half deaf. I know he heard every word and so did the rest of my family. My kids too."

"That's it? Confronted him?"

She gave me a nod. "Simple, right? I was shaking like a leaf, and my family acted like I'd shot the Pope or something, but it worked. Wish I'd done it sooner."

Another member of the group spoke up.

"I put up posters with the motherfucker's picture in the neighborhood where he lived."

Then another.

"I kicked my attacker in the balls at Fred Meyer. So hard, my shoe fell off. Right in line at the checkout counter. Called the pig a pervert. He yelped and doubled over onto the floor and squirmed in agony. I paid for my groceries and went home. Drank half a bottle of vodka that night, and the next morning, I woke up feeling better than I had in a very long time."

"I don't know if I could be strong enough to do anything like that," I finally said.

The room fell quiet.

"Really," I repeated, "I don't."

Mrs. Claus held my gaze. "Like Ellie says, you get to choose now. Who you are. What's important to you. And what silence does."

"Makes you sick," I said. "Takes over your life?"

Ellie came to me and put her hand on my shoulder.

"Those things are very true, Violet. Much more is at stake. Stepping up and avenging what has been done to you can put an end to the abuser's ongoing crimes. Some have gone to extremes to stop a victimizer."

"I don't know what you mean by 'extremes.'"

"Google 'Alaska pedophile vigilante,'" Ellie said.

Later that night, I searched for the case Ellie mentioned and found it right away. It involved a forty-two-year-old man, a victim of childhood sexual abuse himself, who'd attacked three registered sex offenders. The media dubbed him an avenging angel and noted how he'd used the sex offender registry to locate his victims.

He beat the men bloody with a hammer.

It was brutal but effective.

A trio of sex offenders lost their jobs and good standing in the community.

The vigilante tried to make things right. Tried to save others. For that, he was sentenced to serve twenty-five years for his attacks.

As I roll over on my side to feel the warmth of Zach's body, a relief from the chill of the hotel's air conditioner, it gels for the first time that the only thing the avenging angel did *wrong* was getting caught.

CHAPTER TWELVE

June 30
North Shore, Oahu
Violet

The Faraday home is a rental, five blocks from the beach. I know it's a rental because I checked the address on Zillow. It's a two-bedroom with a shiny tin roof and stucco siding. I park across the street, roll down the window, and turn off the car. I don't know what I'm doing. Not for sure. I notice some bikes leaning against the inside of the cyclone fence. Kids. My heart sinks to my lap. How is it that vermin like Lewis Faraday manage to crawl their way into the lives of women with children? As I marinate in an unsettling mix of fear and empowerment, the front door opens and a woman emerges.

The pervert's wife.

Tina Faraday looks to be in her thirties. Her skin is tanned, her lip color is coral. Silver hoops dangle from her ears. When she closes the door and starts for her car, I take a breath, get out, and walk in her direction.

"Ms. Faraday?"

She looks up from her open purse, her keys dangling from her manicured hand. Her eyes are alert, though wary. She has a pleasant smile, one I find off-putting, which I know has more to do with what I'm thinking than seeing.

"I'm here about your husband."

She studies me, assessing the situation. I wonder if she's trying to determine if I'm with the county, law enforcement, or if I'm a friend from Foodland.

"He's not here."

She's being careful. I wonder if she's had any other such encounters at her door. If any girls ever showed up unannounced. Did she conceal her worry and rising blood pressure with a smile like she's doing right now?

Tina doesn't ask why I'm looking for him.

"He gets home after six," she says.

"I came to talk to you."

"About?"

"You know."

The look on her face tells me I'm right.

Before she answers, a woman from the house next door calls over the running sprinklers, "See you and Lew tonight, Tina."

Tina waves and puts on a bright smile. "On the calendar!"

The neighbor disappears, and Tina's eyes immediately drop low, her gaze scraping the wide-bladed grass under her feet.

"Can we go inside?" I ask.

"I'll be late for an appointment."

"You can reschedule."

"Fine. But whatever you are doing here is bullshit. You people just can't leave him alone."

The house is smaller than it appears from the street. Our place in Seattle is tiny, but this is minuscule. A palm-leaf fan twirls in slow motion overhead.

She closes the door and turns to me.

"What do you want?"

I'm still not entirely sure.

"And who are you?"

I ignore that second question too. Instead, I make a statement that's meant to convey why I'm there but not my purpose.

"Your husband is a monster."

Her smile stays put. A protective tic, I think. She doesn't blink and she doesn't back off. "He's changed," she says. "That was a mistake. A terrible one. He didn't mean for any of that to happen with that girl. It just did."

"'Just did'? Like he had no part in it?"

"She was obsessed with him."

His story. His lie. She believes it all.

"He groomed her," I say. "He manipulated her. He ruined her life."

"What do you want? An argument? I can't win that, and I know it. My husband is a good man. A changed man."

"A good man doesn't molest little girls, and men like your husband are incapable of changing."

The tension between us escalates a notch. Maybe two. Tina is nuts for loving a monster, and I am crazy for chasing after one. One who didn't harm me or anyone I personally know.

Tina tries another tack.

"Do you want me to call the police?"

"Fine," I tell her. "Do you want me to tell your neighbors? His boss at Foodland? Go ahead and call the police." I indicate a photo on a side table—a boy and a girl, about ten and twelve. "They'll be glad to know about your children living under the same roof as a convicted sex offender."

Tina slumps her suddenly crumpled frame into a chair. I stay standing.

"My children don't live here. They live with their father. When they're here, I am here."

"Really," I say, not sure if I believe it.

"Yes. Really. What do you want from me?"

"If you're telling the truth, that your husband is repentant, that he has not touched a child since his release from prison, then maybe we can come to an agreement. I need you to watch this video, Tina. I want you to understand something that your devotion to your husband couldn't have taken into consideration. Not if you are human. And I know by the care that you're giving your children that you are."

I play the video. It's Donita Lee. She's recording from a darkened room. The background imagery is a bit strange. The décor looks like the bedroom of a preteen girl—lots of pink, wicker headboard, and a bedspread of French poodles edged with ball fringe.

"I am tired of being the girl who was raped. When people, even my own mother, look at me, it's with pity. I see it in their eyes. Lewis Faraday turned me into something other than what I was. What I am. What I will be. How would you feel if you only saw sad eyes? Or even worse, eyes that turn away? I should have stopped it. I should have told my mom, but I thought she would be mad at me. I wish that instead of always asking me if I'm okay, if I needed to talk, or whatever, that she had gotten mad at me. Grabbed me by the shoulders and shook. Made me feel like an idiot for letting Lewis touch me. Anger is something I could channel into something concrete, instead of wallowing in misery."

I look over at Tina. Her eyes are damp. Good. She knows the ending of Donita's story. She's got to know that her husband put a young woman on a path to suicide.

"Do you want to see any more Donitas?"

"I don't know what you mean. What are you asking me to do?"

"Leave him. Pack up your things. Take your kids far away. Go online. Expose him. Tell the world what he did. Where he goes. Who his friends are. Post his photos on every site you can think of. You know him, Tina. You can expose him. You can ruin him. Only you."

"He's my husband. I love him."

I hold up the phone with the frozen image of Donita Lee.

"He killed her. Just as sure as a man with a gun. Hers was just a slow death."

"You're crazy. Get the hell out of here."

Chapter Thirteen

Violet

Maybe Tina Faraday is as wrong as she's right.

Right that I might be crazy.

Wrong to love a monster.

I thought the video would snap her out of whatever delusion she'd bought into when it came to her husband. Nana, never short on clichés, would say a leopard never changes its spots. Monsters like my grandfather and Lewis Faraday simply hibernate with one eye open. They can't stop. There is no treatment, no cure.

It makes me wonder how many other girls Papa might have molested. Was he an outlier with only a single victim? Was I really the only one?

As I pull away from the Faradays' place for the drive to Foodland, rain rolls off my windshield like the rinse of a car wash. I park in the only spot available, a slightly sunken area that reads like a wading pool. I check myself in the mirror. I don't have any idea why. This isn't a job interview. This isn't an appointment with someone who might benefit my life.

This is a confrontation.

A declaration of war.

I throw my purse into the front of a shopping cart. An old song by the Cars plays on the store's scratchy PA system. Moms in muu-muus and men in sloppy long board shorts roam the aisles. The moms have actual food in their carts. Tourists are cutting expenses by loading booze-in-the-blender fodder and bags of Doritos and Maui-style potato chips.

I see Faraday by the deli counter stacking logs of salami into a bin.

I say his name.

His eyes dart in my direction. "You must be my wife's visitor."

Visitor? That seems so innocuous. I am more than that. I'm like the bill collector who never goes away—the one who calls every night. Or pounds on your door. Or visits you at your place of work.

"She said you had kind eyes."

Bullshit.

"We need to talk," I say as he puts the last log of salami on the top of the pyramid.

"Outside," he says. "We have a smoking area."

He looks over at the woman behind the counter. She's writing out a price change on the poke, a manager's special.

"Minnie," he tells her, "taking a break here with my cousin from the mainland."

Minnie tightens her jaw. "Okay, Lew. Don't be long. More cheese needs to be re-merched."

I follow him to the back door, past the customer bathrooms and staff lockers. He's wearing khaki shorts and a bird-of-paradise Aloha shirt, the Foodland uniform. His team lanyard swings like a pendulum in the darkened passageway. When he flings the door open, sunlight zaps my eyes, and he spins around, facing me.

"What in the hell do you want?"

My heart is pounding, but I hold my fear inside as I offer the single word that serves my purpose.

"Justice," I answer.

He slides onto the bench seat of a picnic table. He doesn't look me in the eye.

"I served my time."

"This isn't about you. It's about Donita."

"That's not my fault."

"You don't see any correlation between what you did to her and what happened to her?"

"I am sorry about what happened, but I didn't hurt her."

"You raped her when she was a child."

"She was a teenager, and we were in love."

"She was eleven when you started."

"Well, almost twelve."

I ignore his self-serving math.

"You were her soccer coach, a grown man. You messed with her head and her body. You know it. I know it."

His face turns red. Good. Shame is good. It is also rare when it comes to these guys.

"Look, I'm doing the best I can," he insists. "I meet with my counselor. I don't drink anymore. I've started a new life. I hate perverts as much as you do; I'm not one of them."

Ellie told the sexual abuse survivors' group that offenders justify what they do. *In love. Girl wanted it. Teaching the boy the ropes. She came on to me. I was drunk when it happened.* A litany of excuses to put the blame on the victim. The manipulation can be so convincing that some kids come to accept that it was their fault.

"What more could I do to make things right?"

I wait in silence for a long time. I imagine him hanging from a short rope, twisting in the wind as he takes his final breath.

"You seem to have a nice life," I say.

His expression changes as he weighs the intent of my words as a threat or a reiteration of his own.

"I have no idea who sent you or what you want from me, but you need to know that I am sorry for what I did to Donita, and, yes, I'm sorry for what happened to her. I made a terrible mistake. I regret it. Why can't people just let me start over?"

"It looks as though they have."

The veins on this temple pulse. "What is it you want from me?"

"I want you to prove that your life, your new life, is something that you would fight for. That given the choice, you would do the right thing to keep it."

He doesn't say a word, but the sweat on his brow is glistening now. His eyes narrow as he tries to imagine just what it is that I'm after.

I slide my phone over to him. "Go on," I say. "Look at it."

I play Donita's video.

He sits there, eyes on the girl. When the video ends, he pleads with me.

"I'm really sorry."

"Are you, Lewis? Really?"

"I'm never going to do it again."

"So you say."

"It's the truth. What do you want me to do about it?"

A beat of silence passes between us as we assess each other.

"Tell Kara Lee you're sorry," I say. "That you knew what you did was wrong. You weren't a fool in love."

He looks down at the table.

"I can't face her."

I could play it two ways. I pretend to be empathetic to the difficulty of my demand and get him to see that he could make amends.

Which he never really could.

Or I could play hardball.

Hardball it is.

"I will make sure that everyone knows what you did and who you are. You won't be able to hide under a rock anywhere in Hawaii. You can't leave here because you can't leave the state. You'll feel how small this place can be. I'll push you right toward the edge. The same way your crimes pushed Donita."

He fumbles for a cigarette while the color on his face darkens beneath his tan.

"I said I was sorry."

"Now is your chance to make amends," I tell him. "This is your one shot. Are you going to take it?"

His wispy mustache droops at the edges. He wipes his brow, then his upper lip. He's sweating through the shiny rayon of his store uniform. He's feeling pressure, not outrage.

A stream of smoke whooshes from his nostrils, and his façade mutates from remorse to anger.

"Who in the hell are you? This amounts to blackmail."

"Maybe so," I say. "And maybe it's the only thing you can do for Donita's mom. She might hug you and say she forgives you. She might shoot you. But you owe her."

"I can't do it. I won't."

"You can't turn back the clock, Lew. You can't undo it. It doesn't matter what you do for the rest of your life. You will always be known as a pervert. That is, if there's a way to remind everyone. With one click, I can make that happen. With one phone call. With a flyer pasted on your neighbors' doors. They don't know. Am I right?"

I ask for his cell number, and he surprises me by providing it.

"Do it tomorrow." I walk away without looking back.

⚓

Back in the all-encompassing pink of the Royal Hawaiian, Zach suggests room service. "You know, lobster or something ironic like that."

"Oh, babe," I say. "I feel like going out. Let's find a club and party."

He arches one of his magnificent brows. "Really? I thought you'd be wiped out from the Dull Pineapple people."

His pun brings a smile to my lips.

"On the contrary," I say. "I feel energized. Let's make a night of it."

CHAPTER FOURTEEN

July 1
Honolulu, Hawaii
Violet

Last night was a long one. A fun one, though. Zach and I hit a few Honolulu hot spots with live music. No karaoke, please. I even got him to bust out his charmingly awful dance moves. No small feat. The lights were flashing and the music throbbing all night long. I had my mind on two men. Zach, of course. And the freak on the North Shore. The freak that had only one job to do. Eat a bucket of dirt and tell Donita's mother that he was sorry. That he was wrong. That he'd trade places with Donita if he could.

I text Faraday before my morning run on the beach.

Me: When are you going to see her?

Him: I'm not. I won't.

Me: Do it. You owe her.

Him: Fuck you. Crazy bitch.

Me: Crazy is fucking a schoolgirl.

I assess the situation. A bold move works in advertising and promotion, but apparently that's not the case with sex offenders. I think of another way. More of a guerilla marketing approach, maybe.

I spend the day with my husband. It is, by every measure, a perfect day. Trade winds. Surfing for him. Swimming for me. Pineapple. Coconut. Rum. Mahi-mahi encrusted with macadamia nuts. Hot sex in our room.

I love every minute.

I can compartmentalize things like my dad's tackle box.

When Zach slips into his deep, purring snore, I dress and go to the copy center. The coupon seekers searching for discount luaus have gone. Good. I check the paper tray. Enough for what I need. I connect my phone to the printer over Wi-Fi and study the first copy as it whirs and clanks its way into the tray.

Lewis Faraday's picture, culled from the registry, is at the top of the page.

Under that:

Your neighbor Lewis Faraday (221 Plumeria Drive) is a child molester on the sexual assault offender registry. Look it up. He was a soccer coach in Ko Olina when he repeatedly raped an eleven-year-old girl named Donita Lee. Donita committed suicide upon learning about his early release for good behavior. Don't be fooled by his pleasant manner. He is a monster and will offend again—if he hasn't already. Your children are at great risk.

I print out twenty-five copies, more than enough for his street and the bulletin board at Foodland.

It's still dark as I drive, and I take in the lonesome stillness over the Pacific. I don't feel lonely. I feel strong. White undulates along the shore, a lacey edge of foam. The music from the radio is classical, and it both calms and emboldens me. I'm doing something. I'm not standing around waiting for something to happen to bring a sense of closure. What in the world does closure really mean? I know it's meant to bring someone solace or comfort after a tragedy, but it's a milestone that eludes me and many other survivors of sexual abuse.

When I return to Faraday's tidy neighborhood, a man with a short military haircut is backing his blue pickup out of the driveway and onto the quiet street. An army base parking sticker indicates where he's headed. I park on the other side of the street and pretend to be looking at my phone. He's the only sign of life up and down the block. I profile the man. Truck. Hair. Job. He would be an ally if he only knew about what the nice grocery employee did before he moved in among the others. Maybe he'll be the one to take matters into his own hands. He'll be the one to make sure that Faraday pays not only for what he's already done but prepays for what he will undoubtedly do in the future.

When the pickup disappears, I quietly plant my feet on the street. I can do this.

Someone must do it.

For Kara's daughter, Donita.

For Kara.

I zigzag across the street from house to house, over wide-blade grasses that lay tight to the earth, and I tuck one of my flyers under welcome mats or inside screen doors. A baby cries in one house. I tell myself that I'm saving that one by alerting his or her parents. When a dog barks as I approach another house, I stand still for a second.

I don't speak.

But inside, I tell the noisy terrier not to bark.

I know a thing or two about solo conversations. I had a running silent monologue after Rose refused to believe that Papa had molested me. I wanted to kill her. I wished it. I dreamed it. One time when she was late from a school function, I wished so much that she would be dead. I knew she had to be. That God had finally listened and struck her down. I was so sure that when I set the table that night, I didn't put out a plate for her.

When she came home, I ran to my room. I told everyone I was sick.

Back and forth I go, working my way down the street. When I reach the house next to Faraday's, I notice a cardboard box by the front door. Inside is a table lamp that someone is DIY-ing to a ruby shade. Without even thinking, I seize the can of spray paint.

Faraday's car is an old gold-colored Subaru. I recognize it from the lot at Foodland because of the stickers on the rear windshield—stick figures of a dad, a mom, a boy, a girl. It's like an advertisement of normality. In this case, it's a smoke screen and a lie. There is no normality when daddy is a child molester. No matter how hard he may try, he can never stop being what and who he is at his rotten core. I tuck a flyer under the wiper on the driver's side and get to work on the side facing the street. I'm going for maximum impact, maximum exposure.

My hand moves quickly, and the overspray lands on my bare toes, forcing me to step back and really take in what it is that I'm doing. I'm no Banksy. I'm clearly no sign painter either. Hell, I'm not even sure what I'm painting. It's a compulsion, and it feels scary and exciting at the same time.

I finish just as he comes out the door.

"Hey, what are you doing?"

I'm standing there literally red-handed.

"Stay away from me," I say, brandishing the can like a weapon.

He yells for his wife to call the police.

"I wouldn't do that if I were you." I'm thinking more of myself than him as I imagine that the tables would turn and I'd be the one arrested for defacing his property.

Faraday comes around the car and sees what I've done. I stand my ground, the nozzle of the can pointed right at his suddenly red face. I could blind him, then run away. I could also scream for help. His eyes shift from alarm to rage as he reads what I wrote on his precious gold Subaru.

I Rape Little Girls

"Give me that goddam paint!"

His wife comes out of the house, a little slowly. Tina Faraday stands there awkwardly while her pig of a husband tries to pull the can from my hand. I refuse to let go. Instead, I send a shot of paint at his face, and he screams.

"He was attacking me!" I yell as loudly as I can. "I thought he was going to kill me."

My words are dramatic, but this situation calls for a drama that I'm making up as I go along.

"God! I can't see," he says, hunching over, tears raining down. It looks like he's bleeding from his eyes, but it's only the paint. His eyes are puffy and circled in red, a rapid and painful result of what I've done.

Hurting a monster like Lewis Faraday feels good.

Tina approaches and surveys my handiwork on the car.

"Get me an ambulance," Faraday cries out as he scrunches his burning eyes closed, then open. "Don't just stand there!"

"I had a touchy-feely uncle," Tina says to me. "And I think about what he might have done to me if my mom didn't kick him out of the house."

"Are you going to call an ambulance?"

She looks at him. "No."

I take a breath. *She* believed me. *Her* mother believed her. I remain motionless and hold that deep inside. A surge of power comes over me. I didn't have any idea what I truly hoped to accomplish with the flyer. If I'd just put up a post online that child molesters are bad people, I'd have gotten thousands of Likes. I would have felt pumped up a little, but the next day, interest would move on. Instead, I took matters into my own hands. Not with a keyboard. Not relying on the vapor of the internet. Me. Paper. Paint. I made Faraday beg for help. Hurt. I'd given him a tiny bit of payback for what he'd done to Donita and Kara Lee.

"You are such a bitch, Tina," he says. "You always have been. I should never have married you in the first place."

"I wish you hadn't. I wish I weren't such an idiot. I fell for your story, Lewis. I admit it. So, it's on me. I also looked the other way until a stronger woman"—she stops and rivets her eyes on me—"set me straight. There's no fixing the likes of you. I see how you look at them. I'm stupid and weak. Not blind."

"Them? What in the fuck are you talking about?"

"The girls."

"What girls?" he asks, playing dumb, all red-eyed, and still defiant.

Tina's shaking now, though I know she's trying not to. She's going to let out something, and it will be ugly. Good. The look on her face reminds me of watching someone as they wrestle with the idea of throwing up or maintaining control until a quiet place can be found and they can vomit without an embarrassing scene.

"All little girls," she says, sweeping her gaze first to him, then to me. She wants both of us to know that every word carries enormous weight. "You watch the Disney Channel with the kids—not to be with them but to look at the girls on the TV as they dance and sing and pose. I don't know how that channel hasn't been shut down. It's a feeding station for men like you, Lewis."

Faraday tries to go to her, but she holds up her hand, and he immediately switches his affect.

Not sorry.

Not a bit repentant.

Just the man he always was.

"You're delusional, Tina," he says.

She holds her ground, something I suspect she has never done with her damaged-goods husband. Women married to pedophiles always say that they didn't know—because they didn't *want* to know.

Tears come, but she's full of resolve. "I was delusional. I was. I know it. When I found those panties in your car, I believed your story that they'd gotten mixed up at the laundry. Idiot me. When I offered to take them back, you pitched a fit and said you'd do it. That it was part of something you needed to be a better man. Like a test. Although, it wasn't really a test. Was it?"

He doesn't answer as we both watch Tina reach into the front pocket of her white denim capris and retrieve a tissue.

It isn't a tissue, though.

Instead, she holds out a pair of child-size mint-green panties. Carter's, I think.

"I found this in the bottom drawer of your night table."

He swivels in my direction. His eyes now swollen and bulging. I don't take a step back. I won't give up any ground either.

She and I will never see each other again, but we've bonded now.

"You goddamn bitch!" he yells at me. "You put them there."

I make a note of that. Not a bad idea, though I didn't.

"Lew," Tina says, "I'll put your things outside tonight. I'm going to call Foodland too. You'll need to find another rock to crawl under."

CHAPTER FIFTEEN

Gig Harbor, Washington
Lily

It's midafternoon, and I confirm the time difference between here and Hawaii. Five hours behind. I'm home alone, but I shut my bedroom door anyway. I don't want to bother Violet on her honeymoon, but she hasn't returned any of my texts from earlier in the day, which is unusual.

Me: Call me.

Me: It could be big.

Me: This is worth a call. Not a text. I'm waiting.

I wonder for a moment if she's lost her phone. Her unresponsiveness is that out of character.

Violet sounds out of breath when she answers my call.

"I thought you were dead. I didn't interrupt you and Zach, did I?" I ask.

"Uh, no," Violet says. "Just running some errands and am hurrying back to Zach in case he needs more sex from me."

"You're disgusting."

"You brought it up."

"I know you're coming home tomorrow. Mom told me not to call. I don't think this should wait."

"Are you all right?"

"It's not about me. It's about Papa. You know Mom's been talking with the detectives, the hospital, about his death?"

"Right."

"Well, something's happening, Violet. There's an article online."

"Send me the link."

"I just wanted to warn you, that's all. Just a heads-up. The police are investigating what happened as a homicide."

"The link, Lily."

I send her the link.

"That nurse that was on duty was involved in a murder case in Oregon. Social media trolls are calling her the Angel of Death."

The phone goes silent.

"You still there, Violet?"

No answer.

"Violet?" I ask again.

This time she answers. "Reading now," she says. "I didn't know that the medical examiner said Papa died from asphyxiation. I thought he had a heart attack after the allergic reaction."

"Me too," I say. "The nurse suffocated him, I guess."

"I don't give a flying fuck, or as Nana would say, a flying fig. I'm glad the old bastard is dead, and if some people want to call the nurse an Angel of Death, I'm fine with that. I'd call her an avenging angel."

Avenging angel? *That's a new one.*

Ever since Violet started going to a support group, I've seen this change in her. She's become stronger. More inclined to tell people what she really thinks. The group prompted her to finally confide what Papa had done.

"You're sure not holding back anymore," I say, trying to lighten the moment.

"It's how I fucking feel."

"Okay, but what do you think about the nurse?"

"If she killed him, I'd call that dumb luck, Lily. And I've learned that luck or hope has nothing to do with anything."

Violet cuts the call short, saying she has to go, and she's gone before I can protest. I set down my phone. Something feels off. It's more than being outspoken. It's like her newfound confidence has cracked open a widening fissure that's releasing something kept hidden for a very long time. I circle back to an incident a few weeks before the wedding. Mom and I were doing something in the kitchen, and Violet, who'd come over for more wedding BS, was on her phone in the other room.

"I'd have taken tin snips to his balls," she said. "Then I'd smoke a cigarette while he bled out."

Mom gave me a look.

"I hope your sister isn't smoking."

I give my head a quick shake. Inside, I wonder about a mother who picks out smoking as a concern in what we've just overheard.

"Those fucking pigs need to die, and waiting around doesn't get the job done," Violet says before ending the call and joining us. She looks agitated.

Mom does her imitation of motherhood. "Everything all right?" she asks.

My sister plasters on a fake smile. "Couldn't be better. So excited about the wedding. Let's wrap up the menu. We need a platter of iced shrimp. Lots of it."

Violet

I hear the TV when I enter the hotel room. I take a second to collect myself. I need to appear calm and empty my mind of anything that would cause my husband to doubt where I've been.

"I thought you left me," Zach says from where he's splayed out on the bed.

His tone is playful. *Good*, I think.

I sit next to him and kick off my shoes. "I went out for a walk and lost track of time."

He arches a brow. "No kidding. It's eleven. Must have been quite a walk."

He seems a little more interested in what I was up to than I'd like.

"No signal. Tried texting. Almost made it to Diamond Head but thought better of it. Had a coffee and watched the surfers. Big waves today."

"Lily sent this to me." I hand him my phone and he reads the article.

"The fucking nurse?" he says, looking up and then going back to read more.

"Yeah," I say, glad that the discussion about where I've been is done. "Talked to your mom?"

"No. She doesn't want this news, I guess, to be a distraction."

"From what?" Zach asks. "I can't see anything trumping a murder investigation."

"I can," I say, putting my hand on his moderately muscular chest and tracing the body hair that he keeps perfectly trimmed. It's a Google Maps arrow. He arouses easily, which is often not a good thing. Today, it is. He pulls me close. I know where this is going, and as we make love, I think of what I did that morning and how good it felt. When we explode together, I ride the sensation like one of those big waves I didn't really see.

I don't exaggerate. It is that good.

Truthfully, I need to get out of my head. I keep thinking about how empowering it felt to threaten and scare the bejesus out of Lewis Faraday.

That I'm becoming something I'm not sure I want to be.

CHAPTER SIXTEEN

July 2
Rose

Loneliness and despair are tricksters.

Both of which make me a worthy target.

The detective at my door is middle-aged with salt-and-pepper hair. More pepper than salt, I think. He's also handsome. I find myself scrutinizing his left hand.

Married.

I let him inside regardless. I know my husband is screwing Shondra. She practically attached herself to his hip at the memorial. *Such a good friend,* my mother said of her. Richard has so many good friends like that. Most are younger and, I suspect, more adventurous in the bedroom. I'm not interested in a battery-powered sex life. I just want to be held and loved. That hope has been vanquished by Richard's roving eye.

"I wanted to update you and your mother about where we are on the case."

"Honestly, I don't think she'd be up to it."

"That's understandable," he says. "Been through a lot."

I ask if he wants coffee or anything. I'd take a drink myself, if it weren't ten in the morning.

"I'm up to my neck in five cups already."

The detective sits on the sofa. Behind him are the family photos that now seem more like props than anything real. The frames might as well hold the images that they came packaged with—those fake memories are as solid as our own. I keep my eyes on him as he tells me very little but does so in such an authoritative way that I feel like I'm learning something.

"We received the results of the autopsy. I have them here if you feel up to it," he says, extracting some folded papers from his jacket.

"I'd appreciate it. The hospital has told us nothing."

He raises an eyebrow. "You have a lawyer?"

"We do."

"That's why. They'll communicate directly with him."

"Her," I correct.

"Her," he parrots back, adding, "sorry."

Next, he clears his throat. The detective is here for a purpose.

Here it comes: "The autopsy results were a little inconclusive."

This interests me. "How?"

He takes a beat before answering. "The cause of death was asphyxiation. We know that without a doubt. It's the manner of his death that's in question. It was either an accident or a homicide."

I look at him but say nothing.

"Something cut off your father's air supply, and he suffocated," he goes on. "Something—or someone—pinched the oxygen supply line. Or it could have been a malfunction of the machine giving him airflow."

"Something or someone?"

"Right, a malfunction of the equipment. An accident, maybe."

"You said 'someone.' You mean 'on purpose.'" I feel my stomach churn. "Is that what you are getting at?"

"I can't get into specifics."

"What can you get into?" I'm annoyed. He doesn't even know if my father was murdered or not. He's fishing.

"I need to know more about the incident that sent him to the hospital."

The collapse at the wedding.

"As I said, somehow—and I don't know how—my father's plate must have been contaminated with shellfish. He's highly allergic. He shouldn't even be in the same room with a crustacean. It's bad. It's all my fault."

"How do you mean?" he asks.

"My husband is of the mind that no reception or big party is complete without shrimp on ice. The bride insisted too."

"I have to agree with them on that," he says.

"Right. And since Dad wasn't going to be there, I didn't think twice about it."

"Oh? Was he ill?"

"Something along those lines."

The evasive quality of my reply is like a blinking light. I wish he'd wanted coffee so I could change the subject with the offer of a second cup. But he didn't. So I fill the space between us with words meant to answer without saying anything.

"I don't mean to sound so cryptic," I continue, though obscuring is what I do best. I've never been one to spill the beans. No matter how much poking by another party, no matter how relentless they are in their pursuit, I keep things tight inside. People assume I'm a "very private" person.

He gives me a look somewhere between sympathy and curiosity. Like the times a close friend confides something horrible that happened to them, and you find yourself a greedy sponge, wanting to soak in more than you should because, deep down, you're happy-dancing that it didn't happen to you.

"All right," I tell him, pretending that I will tell what I remember. "My oldest daughter—"

"That would be Violet, the bride."

I nod. "It was *her* day. And, see, Detective, her relationship with her grandfather was strained. She told me at the very beginning—and I agreed—that he couldn't come."

"Must have been a big reason."

"That's not for me to say. And yes, I hated not having my dad there. I even cried about it. In the end, however, it was her day. Violet's day. Not mine."

"I see," he says, though I can't imagine he sees all of it.

"I shouldn't have added the damn shrimp to the menu. I should have guessed that he'd show up. He was getting on in years but was still strong and stubborn enough to insist on having his way. Mom's a pushover. Guess I am too. Should have made him leave the minute he arrived."

"But you didn't."

I nod.

"And he went into shock."

"We all went into shock. Couldn't believe what was happening. It was—and still is—a nightmare for all of us. Especially for my mother. And Violet, of course. Imagine that happening on your wedding day."

I glance at his wedding band.

He ignores the trajectory of my gaze. Am I so lonely? So obviously pathetic that I'd come on to a cop in the middle of an interview? Or is this a tactic to evade the uncomfortable? I've done that my entire life. And I'm tired of that. I really, really am tired.

He circles back like a hawk. "This case is complicated, Ms. Hilliard."

"Rose" falls out of my mouth, like a schoolgirl wanting to get noticed.

"Rose," he repeats. "We have two events that converge at your father's death. We don't know if it was a homicide or not. He's rushed to the hospital with paramedics working on him the entire way. He stabilizes and the staff thinks he's out of the woods. Instead, he codes a few hours later. Could it be natural causes? Possibly. However, when there is family drama playing out in the background of a death, that needs a closer look."

"What about that nurse on duty? I heard you interviewed her."

"That's an area we're looking into."

"Her colleague seemed upset that day," I offer. "She wouldn't say why, but it wasn't because my dad died. He didn't live long enough to charm her. Though he likely would. He was that kind of guy."

Detective Hoffman stands to leave. "I don't know where this will go, Rose. I'm going to do my best."

The sound of the door shutting as he leaves is the same noise a bomb makes just before it explodes. Most don't hear it. I do.

Chapter Seventeen

July 3
Lily

A stab of sunshine through my window wakes me up, and I hear Dad talking to Mom. I scroll through my phone, checking out Twitter and Instagram. Violet posted a few more latergrams to make her friends envious of her Hawaii trip. I Like them all and reply under one of her lying in a lounge chair with an umbrella drink: *Looking good, bitch!*

I snap back to reality and listen. Good. Dad is gone.

Divide and conquer has been my approach. I like my parents better when they aren't pretending to be happy together.

Truthfully, I don't know how I felt when I first had an inkling that my mom and dad were going to split. It wasn't a surprise, of course, and I didn't feel like crying. I didn't feel much of anything. I'd heard them argue since I was six. I got used to Dad not coming home some nights when I was in junior high. Mom stayed busy teaching and volunteering, like filling up every second of her day was a cure for unbearable loneliness. Violet went away to college, and Dad and I did some father/

daughter things, which was fun. I didn't call him out on anything. I didn't want him to be mad at me.

Like he always seemed whenever it came to Mom.

In fact, we were allies in that regard. Mom was annoying. Passive. She let everyone walk all over her. Instead of making me want to protect her, it made me pile it on whenever I could. I didn't respect her for how she kowtowed to Dad, or Papa, for that matter. She went through life with blinders on.

Mom is at the kitchen table working out details on changing state requirements for the curriculum, a generous glass of wine at her fingertips. The sight is nauseatingly familiar. She's given more to the kids in her classroom than she ever did to me and Violet. She's always buying things for them. Calling their parents. Dropping off homework when the kids don't make it to school. She played heroine for everyone else in the world. People always told me how lucky I was to have a mom like her. I would politely agree, all the while wondering why it was that she wasn't that way to her own girls. Not mean. Not at all. She kept a wall up, a shell. It was as if protecting herself was more important than engaging with us.

I'm never going to have children of my own. In fact, I'm getting my tubes tied when I'm twenty-one.

She looks up at me, sets down her red pen, and tries to be that good mom people think she is.

"I was hoping we'd be able to go out to dinner tonight. Fondi sound good?"

"Oh," I begin a lie, "I made plans to meet up with Maddy and some other girls."

Disappointment eclipses her smile, and I hope she's being real. I always hope.

"Maybe another time?" I offer.

She nods and goes back to her planning for the new school year.

I text Maddy as I drive over to her place on Peacock Hill. She's been my friend forever, and while I know everything about her, I don't tell her anything about me, my sister, or my family. It's not that I don't talk about them at all, but not the deep stuff. Not the stuff that makes for good drama on Netflix. Violet let me invite her to the wedding so I'd "have someone to talk to," like I was a five-year-old. Jesus. My family has no idea how tough I am.

Maddy meets me in the driveway.

"You look weird," she announces after a cursory assessment.

"You look stupid," I shoot back.

We both laugh at our little game. We are close, nearly like sisters. But I have one of those, and everything that I am comes from things that happened to her and how my family managed them. Maddy is my best friend because she just lets me be me. She doesn't suck me dry like a vampire.

"I got some weed," she says, flashing some premade joints from a pot store in Port Orchard. "Creamsicle."

"Yummy," I reply. She hops in, and I put the car into gear. "Let's go down to the Purdy Spit and see what's happening."

"Sounds good," she says, playing with one of the joints.

We find a spot next to a rambling madrona hanging over Henderson Bay, its red bark shredding into ticker tape. The tide is low and clam diggers are out in force. The smell of low tide fills my lungs. I love it. My sister thinks it stinks. I think it smells like the earth. Maddy and I smoke and tan our legs while a Guatemalan family of four digs for geoducks—the giant clams of the Pacific Northwest.

It doesn't take long for us to get silly.

"Wonder if Zach's dick is as big as one of those, Lily."

"Gross, that's my sister."

Maddy takes another hit. "She'd be a lucky girl. Look at that fucking anaconda!"

The clam's neck is a foot long and has the girth of a bodybuilder's forearm.

I give her a look and smoke some more.

"How's she doing? She deserves a break after that shit show of a wedding."

I exhale. Can't argue with Maddy on that. "We all do."

"Yeah?"

"My family's fucked up, that's all. Always has been."

Maddy rolls up her tank top, exposing her winter-white stomach to the sun. "Because your dad screwed half the waitstaff at the Tides?"

I try to scowl, but the pot is so strong, it's hard to manage much of anything.

"Cops have been asking questions," I say. "About Papa's death."

Maddy's now red eyes widen. "Like it was a crime?"

"I guess."

"Who'd want to kill that nice old coot?"

When it gets down to it, my best friend doesn't know me at all. I could tell her everything right then. All that I know and all that I suspect. I could tell her that the nice old man was a dirtbag. Telling Maddy would make me feel better, like when I popped a zit with the sharp end of a protractor in the girls' bathroom in seventh grade. And just as it did back then, telling her would leave a mark.

A scar she would always see.

My sister's scar.

And that's not mine to reveal.

"I don't have the slightest idea," I finally answer.

Rose

Detective Hoffman has a kind face, but I've been fooled by that before. I accept apologies; I think that people mean what they say when they are sorry. I never assume a smile is a mask to hide ill intent. I feel my hands shake as I ponder the idea that he thinks my father might have been murdered. Suspects? Knows? Or just the routine machinations of a cop doing his job?

Something's coming.

I know it in my bones.

I try to put off the detective's comment about family drama.

Like a card sharp, I sweep all the fanned-out sympathy cards from Dad's memorial service into a single deck and round-file them in the can under the sink. I see no point in displaying tributes atop the mantel to a man who moved through life consuming everything in his path, leaving nothing for anyone else.

Nothing for anyone. That sums up the way things are at the moment. Mom is seeking out comfort from her old friends as they commiserate on life without their men. That almost makes me smile. Violet is with Zach. Lily's off with Maddy somewhere.

And my marriage is cratering.

Richard arrives home late, after eight. Dinner is a kiln-dried version of a rosemary roasted chicken, and I don't even care. I know he doesn't either. He drops two glassy balls of craft ice into a glass and pours himself a scotch. A double, by my calculations.

Maybe it takes a triple to be in the same room with me.

"Sorry, I'm late," he lies, ice spheres bouncing into each other. "Had a client meeting that I couldn't cut short."

I exhale. Not loudly.

I tell him about the detective's visit, and he responds with a few shrugs and useless comments. I want to ask how Shondra is doing, but I hold my tongue on the subject. I'm beyond the point of calling him out on another affair. That never got me anywhere in the past. Honestly, I don't like confronting him. When I do, he pushes back. Hard. Not physically, of course, because I wouldn't allow for that.

"Who were you with tonight?" I used to ask, with a vague word selection, in case I wanted to pretend that he was always jumping to the wrong conclusions.

He'd shake his head. "God, you're paranoid."

I didn't balk, instead, I'd lob a serve: "You're a serial fucker."

His swift return: "I wouldn't have to be if I got some around here."

And so went our anti-love match until finally Richard would end the game: "Look, Rose, don't piss me off. I'm out of here as soon as Lily goes away to college."

A threat wrapped in a promise he'd first made when our youngest was only ten. Richard is a real goal setter. I'll give him and his boomerang dick that much. The subject didn't come up in more than a year while all of us were focused on Violet and Zach. At least, I was. So when Lily graduated from Gig Harbor High, it didn't even register that he'd made it to his self-appointed finish line.

Stupidly, I thought Richard had abandoned his oft-threatened escape plan.

Delusional? Much. Hopeful? A little. Clueless? Absolutely.

My husband was always good with the preemptive strike. Gauging risks. Considering the fallout. The drama had to be contained. So once the girls were gone, he went for a sneak attack.

I was deep into my second glass of a Costco Cabernet and Richard was drinking top-shelf scotch. The conversation had centered on our daughters and the new lives they'd be making. Marriage for Violet. College for Lily. How we'd done ourselves proud as parents of girls growing up in a different time than our own.

"Glad we didn't have boys," he said.

"I thought you wanted a son."

"Maybe. What we had with our daughters could never be matched."

He was speaking of his bond with the girls, reminding me of the closeness they share—and underscoring the distance between me and our girls. More than just mother/daughter drama.

"Besides," he went on, "there aren't any flower names for boys."

I swirled the wine in my glass. "Basil," I said. "Cosmos. Ash. Reed."

"Cosmos? Really," he said, letting out a laugh.

In fact, we both laughed.

And then it came.

"I think it's time."

I played dumb. "For what?"

"You know." His face was grim, as though what he was saying was hard for him.

Inside, I was sure, he was doing cartwheels and thinking of Shondra's younger body as a holding tank for his semen.

"Time for us to end this before we suffer any more of this miserable marriage," he finally said.

Honestly, it shouldn't have been a surprise. Up to that point, it felt like one of those times when you were a kid and you messed up. You knew you were going to get in trouble, but when nothing happened, you thought you were out of the woods.

Stupid me.

Pathetic me.

In a way, I knew I deserved to be punished. The ruin of my marriage to Richard wasn't going to pay back all the hurt I was due for the things I did or didn't do. It was a start. It was a beginning.

"All right," I said.

I wasn't going to fight. Not because I didn't have the strength. More because I knew I couldn't.

I watch his mouth chew the chicken. I hate his mouth. I hate all the places it has been. He drinks more booze. I sip more wine. He finds moments in our stilted conversation to be charming even though the neck of our life together is in a guillotine. He asks how my mom's doing. If I saw the photo of Violet and Zach on the balcony of their hotel suite. He tells me that he'll miss my dad.

I wonder if that's why he's still here. Why the door hasn't shut completely on our marriage. He has something to gain yet.

That night, we have sex. It isn't farewell sex. That, I suspect, is yet to come.

CHAPTER EIGHTEEN

July 6
Tacoma, Washington
Violet

After some majorly cryptic texting, Ellie and I meet in the bar at the new McMenamins location in Tacoma. The northwest chain that resurrects old landmarks—in this case, the Elks Temple—with a mix of whimsy and zero restraint. It's a gawker's paradise. I find Ellie under an enormous art glass chandelier nursing a glass of wine. A waitress catches my eye, and I indicate that I'll have the same.

Ellie is wearing white chinos and a tank top. An infinity pendant swings from her neck.

"What happened in Hawaii?"

I stall. "Let me get some wine."

I don't know if what I did was right or crazy. I'm pretty sure it was against the law. And even with all of that bouncing through my brain, I'm certain I would do it again. I know that this is the only woman—only person, for that matter—who would understand what I did. She's the only one who knows the bottled-up rage of a survivor.

"You did all that?" Ellie asks when I tell her about the flyers printed at the hotel and the paint job I did on his car. "Kind of surprising. Kind of huge too. I like it."

She drinks while I weigh her reaction. I knew she'd be on my side.

I go on and tell her the details of Lewis Faraday's crimes. "He raped a little girl. Groomed her. Screwed with her brain until she killed herself."

I play the video on my phone. I no longer feel like I betrayed Kara by copying it. Proof of life is used in kidnapping cases. This is proof of annihilation.

She crawls her hand across the table to grasp mine.

"I'm so proud of you, Violet."

And just like that, I feel my body shake. I look around the bar to make sure no one is watching, that I'm not a spectacle. I've never felt like this before. I'm a snake shedding my skin. A pupa hatching into a butterfly. Something. Not sure exactly what. Something that I wasn't before. No. Something that was inside of me is finally free.

Ellie clasps my hand, tight. Tears stream down her eyes.

We don't speak.

She sees it.

She understands.

And she digs in.

"Did killing him cross your mind?" she asks.

I shake my head. "Of course not."

Ellie's admiration subsides. She loosens her grip, releases my hand, pushes her chair away from the table a few inches. It makes a loud scraping sound, marking the distance between us. Ellie's eyes are nearly black now.

"Why not?"

The air empties from my lungs. The space around me spins a little. I'm not drunk, but I am disoriented for a moment. This smart, strong, feisty woman is serious. She's fucking serious. I gulp more wine.

"For one thing," I say, earth back under my feet, "I'm not a murderer. I don't kill people."

"First of all, he's not a person. He's a monster."

I put my fingertips to my mouth for a second. "You're serious. Killing him? What would that accomplish?"

"It would free Donita's mother. It would free Kara's spirit. It would ensure no other girl would be victimized." She stops and waves to the waitress for more wine. She holds up two fingers. "You know how you felt when your grandfather died."

"Free. Stronger than I'd ever been."

She leans forward. "Just like I felt when I killed my tormenter."

Somehow her words don't shock. Not really.

"I thought it was a happy accident."

"Right. That's what I let you believe. There are no happy accidents when it comes to ridding the world of monsters."

I gulp the second glass of wine as soon as the waitress drops it off. I should have eaten something. I feel a little sick yet excited.

"Lu," she says, "did it too."

Lu is a woman in the group. She's in her forties, with pretty features but a straight line for a smile. She's quiet most of the time. I've only heard her story once. She was molested by the husband of her Brownie troop leader. He gave her an STD that destroyed her reproductive organs.

"My tormenter destroyed my childhood," she told the group while picking the raisins out of an oatmeal cookie. "He destroyed my adulthood too. Until he died, I just existed. I took up space. I moved from one relationship to another, trying to figure out what it was about me that could not attach. Not to a man. Not to a woman. I couldn't even bond with a dog. I had to take Chaz back to the pound pretending that I'd found a stray."

She squeezed her raisins into a ball resembling a prune and wrapped it in a paper napkin.

"And then it happened. He died. And when that happened, though not right away, I just felt a little better. About myself. About the world. I have a parakeet now."

"What happened to him?" I asked.

"Hit-and-run," she said. "He was putting out the garbage like he did every Thursday at eleven o'clock at night."

At the time, I hadn't considered how it was that she knew his routine. I hadn't a single thought that Lu, the raisin hater, had turned into a five-foot-one vigilante. But now I see it. She'd found him on the registry. She cased him. She waited until the right time—a time when no one would see her. She might have sat there for a month of Thursdays, drinking coffee, biding her time. She was in no rush. Lu's life had been ruined already. The right time would come.

And, apparently, it did.

"You took care of your grandfather," Ellie says, shifting the conversation back to me.

"I wish. But I didn't. The investigation involves the nurse. She's a hero and doesn't know it."

She gives me *the* look. The one that everyone offers up when they are being all serious. Lips taut. Eyes narrowed. Head tilted.

"You can trust me, Violet. We're sisters in this war."

I'd been gutless my entire life. When I told my mother what Papa did to me and she dismissed it out of hand, she made me feel like it was something I had made up. It scrambled my brain. Really. I never pressed the point again. I knew what he did. I knew it was ugly and wrong, but I was powerless.

"I can't take credit or I would. He ate something that sent him into anaphylactic shock, and we had the luck of getting a psycho nurse."

"Luck or a happy accident," Ellie says. "You know those never happen in real life. Not in our lives, Violet. Good girls stay quiet. Let things be done to them. Never push back. Did you tell Zach?"

I shake my head. "Of course not."

"About anything you did?"

Another no.

"About what was done to you?"

It isn't fair for her to ask.

"No," I answer anyway. "I can't. I don't want him touching me any differently. I don't want him to wonder if I'm thinking of all that bullshit."

She challenges me.

"Sometimes you do, though," she says, bangles jangling as she reaches for her purse. "Think about it. When Zach is touching you. It feels wrong."

I don't answer right away. I finish my wine.

"Not anymore," I tell her. "Not since Papa died. Like I told you, I finally feel free."

CHAPTER NINETEEN

July 8
Seattle, Washington
Violet

The offices of the Apple Commission are on South Lake Union, not far from Zach's and my place on Queen Anne Hill. In its way, the area is a glittery ghost town. Highly paid tech workers appear in flurries from high-rises with earbuds on and faces planted in devices. They spend their days holed up with desk sets from Room & Board, tapping away on keyboards and ordering everything online.

When I return, everyone showers me with congratulations and you-look-greats. I wear a white blouse to maximize the impact of my tan.

A fatherly guy in accounting says I look like a new woman.

It doesn't seem inappropriate, but it does strike a nerve. After what I did in Faraday's neighborhood, I do feel different.

The chocolate-dipped macadamias I brought back from Hawaii—truthfully, from the airport gift shop in Seattle—are gone in only an hour.

Our staff loves free stuff. Especially Maria Lopez, my partner in crime on the Apples for the New Millennium campaign that we've been assigned to manage. She's got a stash of the chocolates at her desk. She eats with chopsticks so she doesn't get chocolate on her fingers. She's a couple years older than I am. She has the most beautiful hair I've ever seen in my life, a luxurious black that she wears in a single braid every day but Friday. On those days, she lets it flow downward over her shoulders.

"You okay, Violet?" she asks me, looking up from her computer in the cubicle we share.

I'm reassessing the mountain of paperwork that greeted me upon my return.

"I was gone only a week."

"You could push it all in the recycle bin, and it wouldn't matter one bit," she says. "I took care of everything pressing. I even changed our hotel reservations. We're at the Maison now. We have to drive, though."

"That's tomorrow! Shit! It slipped my mind."

"You've had a lot on your plate, Vi. You don't have to go. I can handle it solo."

"No. No," I say. "I can do it."

It's a meeting with growers in Yakima, east of Seattle. Public relations programs are about building connections, and while Maria has roots in the community, I don't. Her family owns and operates a small orchard not far from Yakima. Her parents came to the States as guest workers and managed to flip the script to become landowners. Maria made college money picking apples and working in the cidery that the family opened when she was ten.

I plow through the teetering mess on my desk. An hour later, I scroll downward through several hundred emails. Maria is right. None of the work waiting for me accounted for much. She had my back during the wedding planning—God, I must have bored her! And then my grandfather's death and delayed honeymoon. I'm grateful.

"Lunch?" Maria reaches for her purse.

I'm starving, but too much is on my mind. "Bring me back something. I'm on a roll now."

She smiles and takes off with one of the girls from accounting.

I immediately search for any news on Faraday, but nothing shows up. After all that I did, nothing. I'd felt scared and empowered, and, honestly, I was convinced something would come of it. But nothing did. I wonder if his wife really changed the locks. If Foodland fired him. It crosses my mind that everything that I did, all I risked, added up to a big fat zero. I could call the grocery and find out if he's there, but if he wasn't fired, what good would that do?

Ellie's words echo through my brain. No, deeper than that. Through my entire being.

No one is free until the monster is dead.

The office is quiet. I look around. I'm alone.

My heart rate quickens, and I find myself searching for the Yakima County Sex Offender registry. My cursor hovers and then I click on the link.

It's the same grotesque catalog that exists in nearly every county in the country. I put my hand to my mouth. Looking at the mug shots and reading their offenses makes me sick. I won't be hungry for anything that Maria brings back. I see the same composite of blank-eyed men with droopy facial hair and slack jaws. They look like monsters. I shake my head, and, like a snow globe, the images obscure, then reform. Some look like the manager at the QFC at the foot of Queen Anne Hill. Another could be the brother of our insufferable boss here at the commission. Maybe the guy down the street who has his car on blocks but never seems to get the job done.

I see them. I see them all. The monster wears a mask. He's a chameleon. It hits me hard, and I pull some air deep into my lungs, once more surveying the empty office. If these men can blend into their surroundings, how is it that anyone could spot them. Like Faraday? He didn't look like the creeper in the mug shot. He didn't smell. Didn't have missing teeth. If I hadn't known what he'd done, I'd never have given him a second stomach-turning glance.

I cannot deny the problem or the solution. Monsters in real life are scarily average. They exist as monsters only here, only on the registry. And the only way to stop them is to make them go away for good.

Maria returns with perogies from our favorite vendor.

I flip on a smile.

"You are a lifesaver," I say.

She shrugs. "Thoughtful, maybe. Not a lifesaver."

I take the food, and as I unwrap it, I find myself latching on to the word "lifesaver." That's what I want to be. To save some girls from having to wonder if their abuser is around the corner, waiting for one more time. To give them their lives back.

CHAPTER TWENTY

Gig Harbor, Washington
Rose

The neighbor's cat meows at the door and I let her inside. The house feels empty and I'm grateful for the company. Richard's gone. He left to spend a few days "clearing his head" after our last conversation. I don't know why he continues to promote a lie when the truth no longer matters. Violet's gone. Lily isn't, but she might as well be. She and Maddy have been turning every possible day into a "one last time" adventure. Maddy's parents have a place on Anderson Island, and the girls went there for a few days. I'm glad. As the island is only accessed by ferry, I feel good about Lily's chances for staying out of trouble. It's a training day at school, and I dress casually—the same summer dress that I wore at an afternoon picnic the last time Richard and I appeared together as a couple.

I look at myself in the mirror and vow to burn the dress after today.

I'm middle-aged. I wear my hair in a bob just above the shoulders, a hairstyle that has evolved over the years as I hold fast to my vow never to be the woman with long hair and an old face. My new glasses frames came the other day. I'm not so sure about them. Lily says they are more current than what I wore before. These are blue and bold. I worry I look like I'm trying too hard to eke my way back to youth. I felt I had to do something. It is too soon for me to turn into the cat-sweatshirt-wearing schoolteacher whose life exists only in a classroom from eight to four thirty.

It's out of the way by a minute or two, so I don't feel stalkerish. I drive past Shondra's house slowly. I see Richard's car. He leaves it out like a cat leaves a dead mouse at your doorstep. To show off. To let the world see what he's been up to. Mark his new territory.

I try to put Richard out of my mind. I really do.

But then my heart stops.

I try to make sense of what I'm seeing.

It can't be true.

I park and get out and hurry toward the front door. Just as I get there, it swings open and it's Lily. She holds her hands out at my approach, like trying to hold back the sea.

"What are you doing here?" I yell.

Shondra appears behind her.

"With her!" I scream.

"Mom! Chill," Lily says.

"You bitch!" I yell over her shoulder at Shondra. "You can't take my daughter too!"

Before she can answer, I wedge myself between Lily and Shondra. Richard is calling out from somewhere in the house. Never quick to get involved in anything that matters. I give Shondra a gentle shove.

"I'm so tired of you," I say.

"Like Richard is so tired of you?"

My fist finds itself wadded and poised to strike.

"Oh, for God's sake, Rose. Get a grip." Richard finally makes it to the doorway and pushes me aside. "Get out of here or I'll call the cops." He's wearing dark denim jeans. New jeans. Not his old Levi's.

Her doing, I imagine. Make over the old fart into an image that doesn't embarrass. You can only brag about the size of a man's wallet so much.

I look at Lily. "You said you were at Anderson Island."

"I'm sorry. I knew you wouldn't want me hanging out over here. I wanted to get to know Shondra before summer ends."

"You lied to me," I say, turning away, trying to stifle my tears.

Too late.

She blathers out another apology, and I just keep going to my car. Off to school. Off to training. That's a laugh. I wish I could train myself not to get worked up, but it's not in me. It's so damn hard being replaced. By the time I get to Marine View Elementary, I'm no longer crying. I slap on a smile. It's something I've done my entire life. I don't like my face to be a mirror for others to mimic with false concern. I've seen that since I was a girl.

From my mother, mostly.

"Oh, honey," she'd say. "I'm worried about you. You've been pity partying by yourself for weeks."

I'd mostly remain mute when she did that. I knew from experience that saying anything more would get me a slap. A hard one. At the same time, I knew—or I felt—that she was trapped in this whole thing too. It hadn't occurred to me that I was being given a road map for how I'd react later in life.

Chapter Twenty-One

Seattle, Washington
Violet

Zach is working a software sprint at the office. Adderall and espresso all around. Facebook is one messed-up company, and they sprint more than a relay team at a track meet.

A phrase seizes my thoughts.

What if the worst thing you ever did was something you didn't do?

Ellie said it at a meeting, and it refuses to go away.

I pack a blue suit for the growers' meeting, then a dress for dinner, and set out an overnight bag for the sundries I'll need for the trip over the mountains. A cold beer calls my name, and I curl up on the sofa, wondering if I should wait for dinner with Zach or just make do with some cheese and fruit. The flat screen, an embarrassingly enormous intrusion in a space that I still haven't decided how to decorate, plays a reality show on mute. The sofa is soon to find its way to OfferUp. With all that's been occupying my mind, I've put off things that seemed so important before the wedding. Zach, on the other hand, wasn't about to wait for his goliath TV.

I feel funny inside. Not normal. I'm somewhere between being excited and scared. I think about Papa and how I loved him and hated him at the same time. I'm indecisive about feelings, I think. Like a politician whose head is on a swivel, and words that don't align come from one side or the other. Straight-faced. Sincere. Am I an emotional flip-flopper?

I text Zach, the one person about whom I have never flip-flopped. Not from the day we met.

Me: Hi, babe.

Zach: Hey. Still at it. New product manager is an idiot.

Me: So you've said a thousand times.

Zach: Yup. Just making sure.

Me: Going to bed. Getting up at 4 for the drive with Maria.

Zach: Crap! I forgot.

I don't snark back at him that I've told him about the trip a thousand times. I don't travel that often. Not like he does. My destinations aren't New York or London, like his. Yakima and Wenatchee are on the docket once a quarter. My biggie is a food trade show in Anaheim. I reminded him about Yakima on the flight home.

Me: Love you.

Zach: Bye, babe. I won't wake you.

I want to text Ellie and tell her what I'm thinking but reconsider. I'm not sure if I'll be able to do what is beginning to feel in my bones like the right thing to do. I leave the TV on low and make my way to the kitchen to slice some white cheddar and an apple, a fruit that I'm so tired of but get an endless supply of from my job. The knife is a small, heavy-handled blade that I keep razor sharp. It glints under the school-house pendants over the island. I pause with it poised, ready to strike.

Suddenly, I'm no longer hungry.

I'm oddly energized.

I'm also certain.

Instead of slicing cheese or fruit, I wrap the blade in a small towel and tuck it carefully between my clothes and the bottom of my overnight bag. Next, I find the sex offender registry for Yakima County. Mug shots are displayed in rows that don't allow for swiping right or left, yet in its own twisted way, it feels like a dating site.

Maybe *hunting site* is a better way to look at it.

Chapter Twenty-Two

July 9
Yakima, Washington
Violet

My phone sounds with a text—Maria is outside. I kiss my sleeping husband on his cheek. Zach stirs and murmurs something unintelligible. Our Queen Anne neighborhood is quiet at five a.m. It seems that everyone works from home or starts their routine after nine. Maria's trunk pops open, and I toss my bag inside while catching a glimpse of the three-legged cat next door as she does an amazing high-wire act along the top of the fence.

Maria indicates a coffee in the console between the front seats. Her car is a two-year-old Mercedes coupe, and I know why she wants to drive. She's the local girl who built on her family's success to create more of her own. People will see her in Yakima in that white luxury car and know that she fulfilled her promise.

They won't know, however, that the car is a lease and that we both work in a notoriously low-paying field.

"That coffee smells so good," I say.

"I needed an extra cup myself. Stayed up late going over a new PowerPoint."

I make a face. "Will you stop it with that?"

I'm kidding, but not really. Maria, the achiever, leans on PowerPoint like it's the be-all and end-all of communication tools, and is forever dinking around with its features.

"I added some amazing dissolves," she says.

"I can't wait. Got the core values in there?" I ask.

"Crisply rendered," she says back to me.

And so, it goes. Apple terms that quite literally come from the bottom of the barrel. Our clients never met an apple-related pun they didn't guffaw over. "Sweet," I say.

"Real juice in that pitch."

"Who's going to the Gala?"

"Jonathan and McIntosh."

We both laugh as we get on I-90 east to Yakima. The growers' meeting starts at ten. Our portion of the meeting is after lunch. At four, we'll have a glass of wine with Sam and Ursula Renner, two of the largest growers in Wenatchee. He'll complain about Yakima being the venue for the meeting instead of his home turf. Ursula will pretend to agree with everything her husband says while she uses the restroom at least five times in the hour we'll spend together. That evening, Maria has invited me to have dinner with her family at their orchard.

I have other plans. The kitchen knife is in my bag for a reason.

My phone pings with a text from my sister.

Lily: Missed some messed-up drama on the home front yesterday.

Me: ?

Lily: Mom came over to Shondra's on her way to school and made a big scene. Dad was there. I was there. I thought she was going to hit Shondra. Ha ha.

Me: Oh God. She needs to get over it.

Lily: Tell me about it. A train wreck.

Me: Why were you there? I can't stand Shondra. She's the worst of the bunch.

Lily: She's stupid. Kind of nice. I don't know. I was there to make nice with Dad.

Me: Suck-up.

Lily: Guilty. I can't wait to get out of here.

Me: Another month and off to Wazzu.

Lily: I know, right? Where you at?

Me: Yakima. Maria's driving.

Lily: Nice. Talk later.

Me: Okay. Later.

Maria looks over as I return my phone to my lap and sip the luke-warm dregs of my coffee.

"Everything okay?"

I swallow, then exhale. "Family."

She gives me a sympathetic glance, and I know it comes from a good place, a place of real concern, yet not one of genuine understanding.

"I get it, Vi," Maria says. "You'll love mine. Can't wait for you to meet them."

"Apples to oranges," I volley back, completely aware that I didn't stick the landing in our round of apple puns. I don't care. Thinking of my family leaves a bitter taste in my mouth.

CHAPTER TWENTY-THREE

Gig Harbor, Washington
Rose

Still reeling from the encounter with Richard and still feeling the sting of my youngest daughter's divided loyalties, I stop to see my mother on the way back from an inclusion training session. Next week, we'll take on the equity training module. In fact, I'd like to have some equity applied to my inevitable divorce from Richard. While Washington is a community property state and I'll get half of everything, I know that when I am alone, the quality of my life will drop downward. Richard's will improve.

Shondra will see to that.

I let myself in and call out, "Mom? I'm here."

She doesn't answer, and I go looking, first room to room, then outside, where I find her watering the plants in the big blue ceramic pots we gave her for Mother's Day a decade ago. Her shoulders are more stooped now, and the sight of her little, hunched-over body makes me ache inside.

"I didn't hear you, Rose." She swivels around to greet me. She looks so frail to me. Her eyes seem cloudy, like an old pet's. Her helmet hair is askew. It's never askew. She coats it in so much White Rain that she's likely a fire hazard. Her blouse is dirty, but not from dirt. Whatever she had for lunch has found a place to stay.

"I thought I'd see if you wanted to get some dinner."

"Oh," she says. "I made a spaghetti pie this morning. I know how you and your father love it."

Dad and I both hated it. It was one of the few things on which we could agree. It was neither a pie nor spaghetti. Just a bunch of pasta and sauce baked until shotput ready.

"Sounds delicious."

Mom's eyes brighten. "I have wine. Rita made it. Pretty good."

"Let me help," I tell her. "I'll get the oven going and pour the wine. Love some of Rita's wine."

Rita is my mother's oldest friend and a particularly awful wine-maker. I'm so grateful for her. I can't spend as much time with Mom as I know she needs. The girls aren't much help either. Though I know they have their own lives, I'm disappointed anyway.

Me and Mom. Together again.

As I'm en route to the kitchen, my father's face stares at me from nearly every nook and cranny in a house with an overabundance of both. Some of the photographs are a recent addition to Mom's décor. Right after Dad died, she pored over family photos, and she and Rita made multiple trips to Jo-Ann's for frames. In one of the photos with his granddaughters—a picture taken on the tram at Northwest Trek, he's got his hand crab-claw on Violet's knee while a moose roams in the background. Everyone is looking at the moose but Violet. She's looking downward where his hand is resting.

I'd seen the photo before, but not since the day it came back from the drugstore.

Looking at it now, I wonder how I could miss the abject terror in my daughter's eyes.

"Some wine in the icebox," Mom announces, joining me in the kitchen. She uses words like "icebox" all the time. Sometimes I play along, though she doesn't know it.

"I'll bring it to the parlor," I say, shooing her out of the kitchen as I fill the glasses. "Go get comfortable on the davenport."

A minute later, I settle into the big green velvet sofa. "Mom," I say, "Detective Hoffman came to see me about Dad the other day."

She tries the wine. "Mmm . . . blackberry. Rita has done it again."

I give it a try. It tastes more like blueberry to me—sweet like an ice-cream topping.

Mom dozes off before Final Jeopardy, and I help her to her room. The bed she shared with my father is made up only on his side. I straighten the other bedding and set out a glass of water while she changes into her nightgown. She laments that the wine has made her sleepy, but instead of getting into bed, she starts fussing with a pile of Dad's clothes. I help her sort them for Goodwill.

I want to say that it's cathartic for her—and for me—to rid the house of the disguises he wore to play the part of a human being. The Rotary Club sweatshirts. The team GH Kids T-shirt. The suits he wore to work. The one he wore to Violet's wedding. All those items should be burned and not given away—in case pedophilia is a dormant virus embedded in the fabric. Telling Mom that, of course, is a no-go.

She folds his shirts before setting them in a grocery bag. She says, "He wasn't all bad. You know that, Rose."

Her comment startles me a little. "I do?"

"Yes," she says, "you do." She continues folding his shirts like she still works in the men's section at the department store. "He was a good provider."

"That doesn't make what he did all right. You surely know that, Mom?"

She puts her twiglike finger to her lips.

"Shhh! Not everything has to be talked about. He's gone. That's enough. Now skedaddle to the kitchen and bring me another garbage bag."

When I return, I say, "I'll load the dishes and run the dishwasher before I go."

"Rose, sit with me."

I perch on the edge of her bed. My father's highboy looks just as it always did. On top are a couple of golf trophies and a change dish, an ashtray that I made in the second grade. Dad didn't smoke, but that hadn't occurred to me when I made it. I'd wrapped it in pink tissue and coated that with a jar of gold glitter. He made such a fuss about it that whenever I saw it—no matter what was rattling around in my brain—it made me happy.

"I want to talk, honey." Her voice is faint and sad, but I don't look at her. I stay fixed on the gift I made my father.

She notices. "Would you like to have that?"

"Huh? Oh no, Mom."

"He kept it there all these years."

I nod.

"He loved you, honey. And your girls, of course. Even Richard, although I expect he'd be whistling a different tune on that one if he were still alive."

I waited for the other shoe to drop. My mother thought that hurtful words could be weakened by a compliment given beforehand.

"It killed him that Vi didn't want him at her wedding."

Mom is spot on just then. It *had* killed him.

"Mom, you cannot control everything and everybody. Violet had her reasons, and you know what they are."

Mom reaches a quaking hand—a play for sympathy—toward the water I set on the nightstand. "That was a misunderstanding."

I can't get her to see the truth, the validity, of what my daughter said.

I get up to leave. "I'm going to go now."

"Honey, don't forget the coin dish."

I take it off the highboy, knocking over a photo of the three of us. It falls facedown. I don't pick it up.

Five minutes later, the ancient Hotpoint dishwasher is running like a steam locomotive. I'm not mad. I'm not. Just tired of it all. Tired of living in a hermetically sealed version of what my mother believes our family life was like. The photos she'd scattered around the house were like piles of slug bait in the garden. Innocuous but poisonous.

Halfway home, I roll down my window, take the ceramic dish in my hand, and summon the dormant power of my softball outfielder's arm. With one sweeping motion, I send it smashing against the roadway. I don't slow to look. Instead, I press the ball of my foot on the accelerator. I have never littered in my life, and part of me feels guilty about it. Guilt and me. Besties forever.

Chapter Twenty-Four

Yakima, Washington
Violet

Ursula Renner refuses to be denied. Just won't be. She manages to wedge her way into the booth between me and Maria, leaving her husband in a chair looking like he's squaring off with three members of a panel interview—with his wife being the hard sell of the panel. At nearly every industry event, Ursula exerts her need to share her own anecdotal market research.

She studies me. She thinks I'm her way in.

"Everyone I know agrees that we need to stop pushing apples as a healthy choice and make them a decadent treat."

I leave the space open for Sam and Maria to react, but they stay silent. God, I hate this. Ursula is excited. She's got a definite point of view. I'll give her that.

"I've never thought of apples in that way," I say.

She shoots her husband a knowing glance, and he signals for another drink.

"See, Sam?" she tells him, pointing to her nearly empty green apple-tini glass when the waitress returns.

I shake my head and so does Maria. We didn't order off the apple-a-cart menu created by the hotel for our meeting. A glass of Pinot for me. Maria, the Char.

The cavalcade of silver charms on Ursula's Pandora bracelet rattle against the surface of the table as she ticks off each point.

"Apple strudel, caramel apples, candy apples, apple spice cakes, apple turnovers . . ."

Apple Jacks cereal, I think as she goes on and on.

I tune out more when I see Maria is capturing Ursula's list on her phone's notepad. Sam is watching the waitress. I'm grateful that I can zone out about apple decadence because my mind continues to return to the registry.

I'd spent most of the "working session" that morning scrolling through the registry and searching the internet for more on the crimes of the molesters and rapists listed there. I was shopping, I guess. Looking for a local candidate that deserved, at the very least, a confrontation. A reckoning. He needed to know that serving his time didn't end his victim's trauma. It didn't stop the shame that his family endured either. He needed to know that there was no erasing the stench of what he'd done.

I selected two names in my pretend shopping cart. I'm waffling between them.

The first is Alberto Gonzalez, forty-two. He's been arrested fourteen times on charges ranging from rape to sexual assault to lurking outside a neighbor's window. He's been in prison more than half his miserable life. His tatted neck reminds me of a cross section of a tree, and I wonder if one could count the number of tattoos to determine how many years he's served. His eyes are the eyes of a predator, vacant of any emotion. It isn't because I know what he's done, so I infer there's no emotion.

I see absolutely nothing in those eyes.

Zero.

The other is older. His name is Mike Stone. He looks as hard as his name. His face is angular, and his collarbone protrudes so much, someone could hang a wet dish towel on it. Mike Stone has been a serial offender—like all of them. He molested his little brother when he was eighteen, though I suspect that's just when he was caught. After that, he's had several arrests and incarcerations in Washington, Oregon, and Idaho. Stone's victims were always boys. I know through my own internet research that molesters often beget more molesters.

That's why I select him.

For what I don't know.

Not exactly.

"Vi?"

Maria calls my name, and I shake myself back into the moment.

"Sorry. I can't stop thinking of Ursula's idea. So out of the box."

Ursula beams, and Sam gives her a woozily affectionate smile while setting down his empty glass.

"Dinner tonight, ladies?" he asks.

Before I answer, Maria politely declines for the both of us. "We're going to have dinner with my family at home. Going to show Violet what our little orchard is all about."

The Renners seem disappointed as we leave the booth. I notice them scanning the hotel bar to see what other dining partners are available.

When the elevator doors shut, Maria and I bust out in laughter.

"Out-of-the-box thinking?" she says, looking upward.

"You were writing down everything she said."

"Actually, I wasn't."

She shows me the screen of her phone.

A smile breaks over my face. "A shopping list? Wow. You had me worried for a while. Remind me never to play poker with you."

The door opens on our floor.

"Ready in fifteen?" she asks me.

I touch my abdomen. "I'll have to take a rain check. Something in my stomach has been doing handstands this afternoon."

"Oh no. Probably those awful apple pancakes."

"I think I better stay in. I was really looking forward to it."

"Can I get you anything? Tums? Pepto?"

I fish for my room card. "No. Don't worry. Have a great time. See you in the morning."

"All right, then." Maria pushes open the door to the room across from mine. "Feel better."

I shut my door, turn the dead bolt, and open my bag on the luggage rack.

Even though I really don't have a plan, I act as though I do. I won't take my phone with me because I don't want it to ping on any cell tower. I've seen enough crime TV to know that much. I write down Stone's address on a hotel pad. I'll take the whole pad with me and discard it. Again, I know what forensic scientists can do with the slightest indentation on a piece of paper.

I truly don't know what I'm going to do. Or if I'll use the knife, whose handle peers from the opening of my purse.

I change into jeans and put on a pair of sandals. I text Zach.

Me: Feeling sick. Must have been something I ate. Turning off my phone to get some rest. See you tomorrow night.

He sends a sad face and a heart emoji.

I return the puking smiley.

Phone off and out the door. A "Do Not Disturb" door hanger swings in its place.

There was a practical reason I picked this particular guy too. I don't have a car. Can't take an Uber. The address is a reasonable nine-teen-minute walk down North First to the seven hundred block. I toss the directions in the first trash receptacle I find. My landmark is the rent-by-the-hour Bali Hai Motel.

CHAPTER TWENTY-FIVE

Violet

When I see Mike Stone's house, I know what will materialize.

My objective comes into focus.

A war will be started.

The little red house behind the Bali Hai is close to what I expected. So is the Bali Hai—a dump with an incongruously exotic name—and a group of three men and two women arguing about something. I'm glad I have my knife. The pervert's home base is small and decrepit. The dried-up yard needs mowing. Better yet, a Weedwhacker and a chain saw. From the street, I can see the glow of a floor lamp and the flicker of a big-screen TV—naturally, a plasma that likely fills the entire wall. I call Seattle, possibly America's most liberal city, home. And yet as I stand there taking in Mike Stone's residence, I make assumptions rooted in bigotry toward the poor.

I pump my lungs full of warm night air and knock.

No answer.

I pound harder.

A dog barks and the door opens.

"Sir," I say, letting out the air, like I'm gasping and afraid. "Can I use your phone? Those guys over there grabbed mine. Right out of my hand. They tried to take my purse too."

Mike Stone looks nothing like his mug shot. He's a lot less scary. His eyes look kind and full of concern.

"Those assholes," he says, opening the door wide. "Tried to do the same thing to the old gal next door. Yeah, sure, come on in."

It's that easy to get inside.

His shirt, a button-down, no less, is clean. His jeans are new Levi's. The same kind that men my father's age wear.

The house is spotless.

He passes me his phone and turns down the ball game, the Mariners against Arizona.

"Who's winning?" I ask.

"We are."

"That's the second shock of the night," I say as I pretend to reach Maria.

He lets out a short laugh, and he cradles his no-longer noisy little dog, a toy poodle mix, I think.

"Can you pick me up? I got robbed. Not robbed really. Phone-napped or something. I'm on Seventh just behind the . . . a . . . ."

"Bali Hai," he says, his eyes on the TV.

"The Bali Hai Motel. I'll be outside. Right. Stupid to go for a walk, I know."

He retrieves his phone from my outstretched hand.

"My ride is about ten minutes away. I'll wait outside."

"Sure? Not the best neighborhood. Full of weirdos."

Like you, I think.

"You can say that again, Mr. Stone."

His brow braids and surprise fills his eyes.

"How do you know my name?"

Suddenly adrenaline pumps through my body like a fire hose.

"I know everything about you," I tell him, standing my ground while he steps forward and sets down his dog.

The way he regards me just then tells me everything I need to know. He's been in this moment before. Probably many times. I'm glad for that. I won't be the first to confront him. His blue eyes now seem vacant. The same light-colored eyes that rolled over victims as he sodomized them. The same eyes that didn't blink once when he told each boy they were special, that they would thank him one day for all he'd taught them.

All he'd given them.

"I want you to leave now."

He's afraid of me.

Of the knife I'm now holding.

"Look, I didn't do anything wrong. I never hurt anyone. They loved me. You don't understand. I get that. Few do. Boys need to be taught like I was taught."

His excuse is the lie that he tells himself.

"You are a destroyer, not a teacher," I say.

He segues to another approach, redemption.

"I have changed. Really. And I wanted to. I did. It wasn't because I had to. I wanted to stop."

"Stop what?" I ask, moving the knife in a way that keeps his attention.

"You know."

"Say it, Mr. Stone."

He takes a step back and slumps into a lounge chair.

"Messing with boys."

Not good enough. "Be specific."

"Having sex with them."

"Sex? That's not quite right. Is it?"

I notice beads of sweat on his upper lip.

"All right. Raping them."

I'm holding the knife in the way that cops hold a flashlight, overhand.

"Will you go now? You got whatever you came here for, I hope. If I raped your brother or something, I'm sorry. I ask for forgiveness."

I don't answer. I'm thinking about what to do. He's bigger than I am, though not by much. He's trying to show remorse, manufactured as it may be. I survey the room. The scene. I look for anything that might indicate he is a liar. I'm not sure any of that matters, but I process it all regardless. No sacks of candy. No video games. No sports gear.

My eyes land on a plush bear slumped in the corner.

His eyes land on mine.

Decision made.

CHAPTER TWENTY-SIX

July 10
Gig Harbor, Washington
Rose

Lynette's mother, Cindy Riggs, volunteers at the new senior center. I ran into her there a few weeks before Violet's wedding when I dropped off a packet of May Day artwork my class made as a community sharing project. We'd chatted only briefly that afternoon. I didn't mention my girls or the wedding. When a mother loses a child as Cindy did, it's a bit of an ugly truth that other moms, like me, find it difficult to fully reconnect. You can only say how sorry you are about her loss so many times, though you feel it every time you see her. And truthfully, deep down, you're glad you're not her. The same is mostly true of the dead child's friends. It becomes too painful. Conversations become waves across the street, then rote head nods, and finally, the pretense of not seeing the childless mom at all takes over.

I find Mrs. Riggs in the blindingly lit craft room assisting residents with an art project.

Her smile fades when she sees me.

"Jenny called me," she says.

That's probably for the best, I think. I'm not here to ambush her. "Can we go somewhere to talk? Somewhere private."

She tells me she heard about my father's passing and wondered how Mom was doing.

"Haven't seen her in ages."

"She's pretty much a homebody," I say. I know she's just being nice. Small talk. Nice people do that. "Maybe with Dad gone," I add, "she'll find more reasons to get out of the house."

"Let her know we can always use some help around here. I figure we might as well get the lay of the land; we'll all end up in a place like this sooner than later."

Mrs. Riggs gives a champagne-haired lady encouragement over tissue paper sunflowers she's making, and I follow her to a small room near the main office. We sit on hard plastic chairs that I'm certain were selected by someone who never tried them out. Mrs. Riggs's feet dangle as she's sucked backward in the seat.

I feel queasy inside, but I start anyway. "What did Jenny say?"

"The same thing she's said before. And before we go any further, I need you to know that my daughter never talked to me about anything that might have happened at your house. Not a single word of it. All I know is that she said she didn't like going over there, so we never went back."

"Didn't you find that strange? Concerning?"

"Honestly, I might have back then. I'm seventy-nine now, Rosie," she says, using the nickname that kids called me until middle school. "I'm not sure sometimes what I remember for real or if I remember it because I've heard the story so many times."

She's selling herself short. She's as sharp as ever. It's in the eyes.

"Did you ever talk to my mom about it?"

She removes her glasses and wipes them with a tissue. "Once or twice. Maybe. It was no big conversation. I just told her that Lynette wouldn't be coming around. She was uncomfortable or nervous. Your mom said she'd noticed the same thing. That was the sum of it. Really. Nothing until Jenny said a few things to me at Lynette's memorial."

I press for details. "What was that?"

"That she was molested by your father when he was showing her some baby bunnies. That she thought Lynette had been too. Even you were."

My face feels warm. "That's ridiculous."

She exhales. "I thought so too. Jenny was always on the dramatic side, and Lynette, rest her precious soul, had problems nearly from birth. Couldn't get the girl to behave. Well, you know the story."

Jenny *was* dramatic. To her, every perceived slight was intentional. Someone took her favorite spot on the bus, and she acted like it was the end of the world. For weeks. One time, our teacher ran out of metallic gold paper for a Christmas art project, and Jenny flipped out.

"My whole holiday is ruined now!"

Lynette was on the other end of the spectrum. She was quiet. I remember how I had to seek her out for friendship. I couldn't recall one time when she had behavior problems. Certainly not before the drugs. And that was long after our relationship faded away.

"Look, Rosie, no one knows why Lynette took her own life. I refused to believe your father played a part in it. Believe you me, I took a hard look for any reasons that might trace back to your house. And I admit, for a very brief time, I did think maybe Jenny could be right."

"You did?"

"Yes, when she brought up the rabbits."

"What about them?"

She puts on her glasses, magnifying her world-weary eyes. "It is silly. It is the kind of thing a grieving a mother does when grasping at straws that will save her from admitting she didn't know her own child."

Rabbits. I try to locate a memory. Even as nothing comes to mind, I feel my heart rate begin to speed. What is she getting at?

"It's silly, but I'll tell you because it will ease your mind. I know you are here to find answers about something troubling you. A little while after Lynette didn't want to go over to your place, I found her Velveteen Rabbit in the trash can. She'd loved that stuffed animal so much. It was a baby gift from her grandma, my mother. Lynette slept with it. Carried it around. Rubbed its velvet right off the darn thing's ears. Inseparable."

"Did you ask her why she got rid of it?"

One of the crafters in the other room comes looking for help.

"Not really." Mrs. Riggs gets up and gives me one last look. "She'd outgrown it. Since we were having a good day, I let it go. Good days had become harder and harder to come by at that time."

CHAPTER TWENTY-SEVEN

Yakima, Washington
Violet

The restaurant at the Maison Hotel is bustling with a horde of teachers attending a training conference. I wait for my second coffee while Maria reviews the itinerary for the morning. I hope that she doesn't want to stay and network into the lunch hour. I want to get out of Yakima as fast as I can. I didn't sleep at all. My eyes wouldn't stay closed. I emptied the minibar of all the vodka, thinking that I could drink myself into slumber. Not even close. I was wired, oddly energized. I kept seeing Stone's bewildered face, the horrified look in his eyes. Confusion too. Was it because I was a woman? Did he think I wouldn't stop him when he got up from that chair? Or did he feel for the first time what his victims felt?

Inexplicable fear.

I told him I was there to avenge the boys he'd raped.

A lie.

It was my grandfather's sagging face that I saw when the knife sliced into Stone's sinewy chest. It was Papa's gnarly hands that went after the blade as he fought me.

It was my mother's voice, however, that found its way into my brain.

Violet, you must be mistaken, honey. Papa loves you. He'd never do anything like that to you. Don't you know that?

As the hotel waitress fills my cup and Maria stays absorbed with her list of people to see, I think about how, for the longest time, I had wondered if I'd been wrong about what happened to me.

Mom insisted, stone-faced, that I'd been mistaken. She dropped toxic little excuses every now and then too.

Sometimes men get a little grabby when they drink too much. It doesn't mean a thing.

I didn't know any other girl who'd had the same experience, and there were plenty of daytime drinkers in Gig Harbor.

A medical condition? I don't know. He's old. He might have had a seizure. I'll get Nana to take him to the doctor.

That one made me believe that I wasn't a good person for not forgiving and forgetting something that hadn't been his fault.

My young brain didn't yet comprehend the concept of gaslighting. I had no idea that Mom's denial and excuses were designed to confuse reality, bury what had happened. To deny and then question my own motives, driving me further and further away from what I knew to be true.

You might have dreamed it, honey. It happens sometimes.

"You okay?"

It's Maria, snapping me away from my memories. "You seem distracted."

I brush her off with a quick shrug. "Didn't sleep well last night. Feel better now, but must have had a twenty-four-hour bug."

She signals the waitress for the bill.

"That's good. I promise to make the day a short one so you can get back home and rest. Tomorrow will be a bitch of a day with the work we have to do."

I pick up my purse from where I hung it on the back of my chair. A smear of blood on a strap comes at me like a lightning strike, a jolt of what Stone's living room had been like.

Blood everywhere.

Backstepping to the front door, I had scanned every element in the room to recall with certainty that I hadn't touched anything. I held my breath and let my heart hammer my rib cage. The molester's little dog was walking around Stone's body, leaving bloody paw prints. I wanted to scoop up the dog and take it with me. Clean it. Find it a new home.

Turning the doorknob with the bottom edge of the shirt I was wearing, I let the dog out and shut the door.

"Don't follow me," I said.

The sound of the party in the parking lot of the Bali Hai Motel snapped me out of my peculiar stupor. I grew hyperaware of what had transpired, but I couldn't fully grasp why I had risked my future in such a dangerous and egregious manner. I didn't want to get caught. I'd planned for that by leaving my phone at the hotel so I couldn't be traced. I was Carrie White after the prom, taking step by plodding step with the knife dangling in my hand.

When I got to the motel dumpster, I used fast-food napkins from the ground to wipe the handle of the knife. I smeared blood from the blade itself. Next, I dropped everything into the jaws of the receptacle.

All the way back to the hotel, I avoided eye contact with anyone on the street. I didn't want to see the horror on their faces. Everyone, I was sure, could see what I'd done. Some might understand the reasons. Some might even call me a hero for it. That wasn't me. My reflection in a storefront window belonged to a stranger. Who was she? What had happened to her?

Inside my room, the hottest water I could endure ran along my body, sending the faintest tint of pink down the mournfully slow drain.

I had been careful. I had also been lucky. I wasn't coated in blood like Carrie White, after all. At best, I had a few specks in my hair. If no one had seen me, I would be fine.

Besides, I had made it through worse things than murder.

I was, as Ellie said at that first meeting with the group, a survivor.

And an avenger.

CHAPTER TWENTY-EIGHT

Lily

Two days after the freak-out with Mom, Dad, and Shondra, I find my parents playacting that nothing happened and all is well in the Hilliard Hell House. We assemble at the kitchen table and talk about Violet's honeymoon Instagram feed and how easily she sunburns. No one mentions Papa, the investigation, or anything that truly matters. Mom offers a snack, but no one feels much like eating.

Dad flips the page on his copy of the *Times*. "Excited about school?"

It's the kind of question a stranger might ask. He knows I'm excited. He knows that I'm so ready to get away from him and Mom. If he doesn't, then he is, in fact, a stranger.

"Can't wait," I say, hoping my phone would buzz so I could hurry away to an emergency.

Mom chimes in. "Are you going to rush? Sororities are big at WSU."

"Not my thing," I say without looking like I'm about to barf at the idea of being in a sorority.

I look at my phone.

"I have to go. Maddy needs a rescue from her so-called stalker."

"Stalker," Mom repeats. "That's terrible."

"He's a junior who seems to find a way to be wherever Mad goes. She used to think it was funny, but not so much now. School's out. No way he should be running into her all over the harbor."

Dad gives me a showy hug, and Mom leans in for the same.

When I get in my car, I call Maddy right away.

"You home?"

"Yeah, and totally bored."

"Perfect. I'll be right over. So sick of my family."

"Oh goody," Maddy says. "You're angry! That always means we'll have a good time bitching about them. Hurry."

Justin Bieber blares from Spotify, and I don't give two shits who hears it. I don't care what anyone thinks because, for most of my life, no one in my family gave a fuck about me. My parents were distracted by a toxic and failing marriage. I moved my mouth, but they must have had cotton in their ears, because they never heard me. For the longest time, I thought Violet was a self-centered bitch. When I think about how I grew up, I trace every lousy thing back to Papa and how he never paid a damn thing for what he did to my sister. I am so glad he's dead. I don't care how or who did it. In fact, I hope Mom finally did something for Violet. Silence and avoidance of the truth came with too high a price for my sister.

I tried to talk to Mom about what Violet told me.

It was three weeks before the wedding. She was in her bathroom, putting on eye makeup after dressing in a school spring fling getup she'd worn, by my count, four years in a row. It was a knit twinset patterned with white and yellow daisies and teal butterflies, a style that landed somewhere between old lady and retro. Her earrings were an epic miss—oversized ladybugs—jewelry only an educator would or could wear. At least, without much warranted embarrassment. I was tired from another sleepless night, and I wanted some perspective.

Maybe some truth too.

"Mom," I said. "We need to talk."

"Money in my purse, Lily. Take what you need, but not all of it."

"That's not what I want to talk about."

She eased her goopy mascara wand back into its little tube and turned from the mirror to face me.

"Sorry. Force of habit."

"Not fair."

"Right. That's true. What's up?"

"Mom, we need to talk about what happened to Violet."

She gave me a quick, hard glance. "Nothing *happened* to her. You know it. I know it. Now stop it. We can't take on someone's drama. What's the matter with you, Lily? This kind of thinking isn't healthy."

She finished her lipstick without another word.

I stood there, feeling myself sink into a damp bath mat; a pinhole in a balloon leaking out my resolve and emptying my nerve. Mom had a way of disarming me, even when I'd promised myself ahead of time that I wouldn't succumb. I'm not some dog on the floor waiting for a belly rub.

"Mom, you agreed not to invite Papa to the wedding. You have to know Violet wouldn't have asked if—"

She put her hand up. A traffic cop. *Shut up.* Her eyes were full of anger.

"No. There is nothing to talk about. It would kill your Papa if he knew you were even entertaining the idea that Violet's story was true."

"Maybe it is, Mom."

Just then, her hand came at me like a cobra, striking me so hard on the cheek that, for a second, I lost my balance and I grabbed on to the edge of the vanity.

Her eyes weren't filled with rage but with the shock of what she'd done. Rather than say that she was sorry, she deflected her responsibility—something she'd tell her students repeatedly was the worst possible thing anyone could ever do.

"Look what you made me do, Lily. You girls know how to push my buttons."

"I believe my sister," I said, taking my hand from the sting on my cheek. "I know you do too. You just can't say it. And Dad's fucking clueless, isn't he? You make me sick, Mom. You do. You and Dad."

I got the hell out of the bathroom as fast as I could. That she would hit me was the lesser of what made me so angry. The sting would be gone. The red would fade. What tormented my sister and others like her had festered. My sister's good humor, her job at the Apple Commission, and her happy life with Zach were like a gigantic tube of concealer.

What Papa had done was always there. Under the surface. In her skin.

I park the car in Maddy's driveway, turn off Bieber, and go to the door.

She's there to meet me.

"That was fast," she says, Diet Coke in one hand, phone in the other.

I take the pop and drink.

"Some things shouldn't wait," I say, keeping the pop.

Maddy leads me upstairs to her bedroom.

"Right?" she says. "Now, tell me everything that bitch Shondra did. And your parents too. I love reality."

I tell Maddy the story she wants to hear. Shondra this. My parents that. Inside, though, I'm thinking of something else—the Instagram video that showed Mom and Nana tampering with Papa's buffet plate. I could torpedo Mom by sending it to the detective. Part of me really wants to do that.

For Violet.

For every member of that sad group of abuse survivors she meets with in Tacoma—all of them have been fucked over by silence.

CHAPTER TWENTY-NINE

July 22
Seattle, Washington
Violet

"You seem obsessed with that freak."

I turn around to find Maria, who is suddenly peering over my shoulder at my computer screen. I'm on the sex offender registry looking at the photo of Mike Stone. The county has yet to delete his photograph and criminal history.

"Maybe," I say, "a little." I don't know what else to say. I feel caught. Maria asks me to scroll down, so I do.

"My neighbor Julie came over with a list of the offenders in our area last year," she says.

"She did?"

"Yeah. Wanted us to put up posters. I told her I didn't want to be involved in anything like that."

"Why not? Seems proactive."

"I thought it seemed like a form of vigilantism. Police handle that sort of thing. And those creeps have served their time. Maybe they deserve a second chance."

I'm stunned. I don't show it. A second chance? My coworker, my friend, is a moron.

"They don't deserve a second chance, Maria. They can't be fixed. They can't stop from doing what they do."

She counters, oblivious to the passion behind my words, with a story I've heard before. It was about Cousin Rudy, now a successful business owner in Pasco. He'd served time for burglary.

"He learned his lesson, Violet. Some people can change, you know. I refuse to believe that people aren't capable of redemption. My faith won't allow me to think that way."

Your faith is stupid, I think.

"Look at these faces, Maria. Can't you see that these guys aren't like Rudy? Look what they've done."

I start spouting off phrases from the page.

"Held captive.

"Penetrated with foreign object.

"Seven-year-old.

"Infant girl.

"Serial offender.

"Disabled boy.

"Suspected of four other rapes."

I stop when I feel a hand on my shoulder.

"Vi, are you all right?"

I look up at Maria; her eyes are full of concern.

"I'm fine."

She indicates my coffee cup. It's lying on its side, and coffee is spilling onto the floor and onto my shoes. I push back from my desk.

"How did that happen?"

"You knocked it over, but you kept on reading."

I feel the eyes of the office all over me. I've made myself a spectacle. I don't know how it happened.

"You go to the bathroom and clean up," Maria says. "I'll take care of this."

As I wind my way down the hallway, I consider that there is an absolute truth at work here. Ellie told me about it when we first met.

"Only a victim knows the lasting damage of what these men do. People will mouth words saying that they care, and on some level, they might. Who wouldn't agree that molestation or rape is among the vilest things one human can do to another? In the end, the only ones who really know are those who have experienced it."

I face the bathroom mirror and splash cold water on my face. A toilet flushes, and a girl from accounting joins me. She gives me a look and compliments me on my earrings, and I thank her.

Alone again, I shed my anger toward Maria. She isn't stupid. She's a good person. Part of me is glad that she can't comprehend the reality of the men and women listed on the registry. It means that she's not been touched by that kind of evil.

I take a deep breath. I remind myself that what I did that night in Yakima was the right thing to do.

But only people like me understand.

CHAPTER THIRTY

August 15
Pullman, Washington
Lily

My parents insisted on taking me to WSU. Lucky me. The drive east over the mountains was excruciating with the two of them sitting side by side in the front seat. Dad driving and making small talk while his phone pinged incessantly. Shondra, I bet. Mom thought so too. Her muscles tightened each time the happy little sound from his phone cut through the din of our feeble conversation. We stopped for gas in Fruitland, and I bolted from the car like a kidnapping escapee. I pretended to use the restroom. Instead, I texted my sister.

Me: This is the worst.

Violet: You'll be on campus soon enough.

Me: Easy for you to say.

Me: I guess. BTW, I'm not coming home for Thanksgiving. Just so you know.

Violet: Maybe Dad will move out by then.

Me: Yeah.

Violet: Then you'd have to choose between the two of them.

Me: I know. I'll have to suck it up for Christmas.

Violet: Right. You won't be able to get out of that.

Me: How are you? Zach? Mom said on the drive over here that he's up for some promotion.

Violet: He always is.

Me: Violet.

Violet: What is it?

Me: I think I have chosen. You know, between the two of them. Dad's a pig, though a nice one, I guess.

Violet: I know. And Mom?

Me: I can't forgive her for what she did to you.

Violet: Don't let it eat you up. I'm working through things. I'm finding a way to make things right.

Me: I know that. I just think that she's as guilty as Papa.

Violet: On some level, she knows that. She has to.

Me: You think so?

Violet: I do. At least I hope so.

Me: Gotta go. I can see Dad's done filling the tank.

Violet: Take care, sis.

Me: Okay. Call you after I get settled.

I put my phone in my pocket and return to the car.

"Sorry," I say, getting into the back seat. "Line way out the door. This is sort of a last-chance-to-pee location."

Mom looks up. "I found a cool place to have dinner," she says. "The Fireside. It's close to campus."

It didn't sound cool to me, but I nod as I pop in my earbuds. "Sounds good."

I know I can't have them drop me off at the curb, though I would prefer it to a protracted meal of goodbyes and parental advice. Dad will tell me about boys. I won't tell him that I haven't been a virgin since I was fifteen. Dads think their little girls never grow up.

Mom will tell me to make sure I watch what I eat so I don't get the dreaded "freshman fifteen."

Mom refuses to deal with anything above her limited emotional pay grade. She doesn't have the temerity for confrontation. She's simply unable to summon the fortitude, the inner grit, to stop someone when it would be clear to a total stranger that intervention was needed.

"Her teaching six-year-olds all these years is a good fit for her," Violet said on one occasion, assessing our mother's mental and emotional abilities. "She can't deal with older kids who might challenge her with problems bigger than a broken crayon."

"Little kids have big problems," I reminded her, thinking of our family. Thinking of her.

"Right. But they can't always articulate them. Not unless you really listen. Really see. Mom perfected the skill of looking the other way, Lily."

The thought passes, and I loosen the seat belt as much as I can without undoing the clasp to bring my legs up onto the seat. I curl up and feign sleep, listening to a podcast that I've already played. Dad drives twenty miles over the speed limit so he can scare Mom and hurry the day along at the same time.

Rolling hills planted with endless acres of wheat stream by my window. We finally climb the hill to campus and park in the lot behind my dorm. A hot wind pelts the hood of Dad's Lexus with acorns. He cusses under his breath in that manner that is supposed to be unheard but is meant to get attention. Out of seemingly nowhere, an overly cheerful girl pushes a big hospital laundry cart at us like she's on a shopping spree show and introduces herself. Katie is full of energy and laughs at every other thing that comes out of her mouth. She's either on drugs or nervous. I make a mental note about the drug potential. Katie rapid-fire welcomes me to a get-together in the dorm at five.

"Sounds good," I say.

My parents help load up the cart—new bedding from Target, a Krups coffee maker, boxes of clothes, a full suitcase, my laptop, and a few items from my old room, including an acrylic photo cube Nana gave me, which I consider something along the lines of loaded dice. No matter what side faces you, you see a member of a family of liars and pretenders.

I know Dad doesn't want to have dinner at the Fireside or anywhere else. He wants to get home. He needs this part of his life over.

I let him off the hook.

"Dad, do you mind if I get a rain check on dinner?"

Mom is suddenly deflated but doesn't interject a word of disappointment.

"I guess so," he answers, as though he's unsure.

I hug him tightly, then put my arms around Mom. "I can take it from here," I say, grasping the handle of the cart.

"Don't you want us to help you unpack?" she asks. "I want to see your room."

I think she might cry. Sometimes it's hard to tell with her.

I insist that I can manage. "You can see it when it's all decorated when you come next time."

She fishes for something in her purse and pulls out a small silver-framed photo of the four of us, taken on the beach at the wedding.

"Oh, Mom," I say.

Oh no, Mom, I think. Why give me another example of her not standing her ground? She had only one job to do—keep Papa from coming and ruining everything.

Later in my dorm room, I plop down on my new Target comforter, a pink-and-orange abstract print light-years from the Vera Bradley florals Mom foisted on us ever since I can remember—lilies for me, violets for my sister. The wedding photo stares in my direction. Taunts me. I reach over, and with one clean flick, it tumbles into the wastebasket with the photo cube Nana made.

Suddenly, I feel a whole lot better.

I flip through the videos on my phone until I come to the short video I took at the wedding. More and more, I find myself thinking about it. It could be used as leverage to make sure Mom pays. Or maybe the opposite. Proof that she's sorry for what she's done.

In the end, I know just what to do with it. I don't know the real why behind my reasoning.

A game?

Retribution?

Justice?

Any of the three will suffice.

CHAPTER THIRTY-ONE

September 7
Gig Harbor, Washington
Rose

My stomach is doing summersaults. Nervousness pummels me in the gut. I can't shake it. I survey my classroom. Everything looks fresh. Colorful. Happy.

*I s*hould be happy.

The first day of class was my favorite day of the school calendar, though, with each passing year, less so. First graders are far more worldly than when I started teaching. They're savvier. Entitled. Devious. My peers blame the rise of the digital tablet instead of TV like my generation did. The issue, colleagues insist, isn't merely the device, but rather the proliferation of content that gives every user the digital drug they need. For most kids lately, it has been *PAW Patrol*. Judging by the backpacks and shoes I can see as I look out the window, it appears more of the same this year. I greet the happy and wary new faces as they line up outside the door. I note one clinging mom and two criers.

An improvement over the previous class when I had four clingers. Extricating a little boy or girl from their mother is a delicate task.

I study the printed-out roster. It's an even split of eleven boys and eleven girls. While they are all individuals, they will represent specific archetypes. That's just the way it is. Leaders will be apparent today. So will the attention seekers—we used to call them "brats"—and they'll come with a diagnosis, oppositional defiant disorder. One or two kids will undoubtedly latch on to me like mussels on a pier. At least one kid will be evaluated and sent to the resource room on a semipermanent basis. And every year, there will be a girl or boy who will tear at my heart. I'll worry about him or her. I'll watch them closely. As a mandatory reporter of child abuse, I'll make the call. I will. I promise. So far, in my twenty years, I haven't had to.

I'm the only teacher I know who hasn't. Every teacher has a story. Sometimes more than one.

I think of Jenny and Lynette when they were in the first grade. Had anyone noticed anything? Did either of them tell a teacher? Back then, my generation was woefully unaware of our own bodies. Or how the mere fact of being a girl could bring devasting, unwanted, horrific attention. I couldn't switch from saying "privates" to "vagina" until I was in the sixth grade and they separated the boys from the girls to show us a film about our changing bodies. When the lights went up, the school nurse asked if we had any questions. No one had any. Mary Gilbert, who routinely sat in the back of the class covered with a protective shield of baggy clothing and long hair that hid her face, however, bolted from the room. I wonder about that now.

Was she remembering something done to her?

While the kids are at recess, I scroll through my text messages to find the one Lily sent me that morning.

Lily: I got a call from the detective working Papa's case. He wants to talk to me.

Me: Oh. That's good.

Lily: Is it?

Me: Why wouldn't it be?

Lily: You know why.

Me: I don't. Call me.

Lily: I'm in class.

Me: When is he coming?

Lily: Not sure. Soon, I guess.

Me: I see.

The roll of antacids in my drawer beckons. I feel my chest tighten. I don't know how to take this exchange with my daughter. It comes off like a threat.

It *is* a threat.

I look at the clock. Four minutes until recess is over. I hurry out of the classroom to the staff bathroom. I thank God no one is in there. It is the only place in the school that has absolute privacy. I turn the lock and, for good measure, go into a stall and latch the door.

I dial and wait for Lily to pick up, but it goes to voice mail.

"Honey," I say, "I have no idea what you are talking about. I'm sure that I'm reading more into your text than you meant. Frankly, it felt a little hostile. I've told you that I'm sorry for things I did or didn't do in the past."

One minute before the kids return.

"I will do better. I will."

As I end the call, I see a video pop up on my phone. It's from Lily. I press Play.

It's me and Mom at the wedding. The plate. The shrimp. The whole ugly thing.

CHAPTER THIRTY-TWO

September 12
Seattle, Washington
Violet

"Are you okay, baby?"

I sit up in our bed, releasing my damp neck from the hot pillow.

"Bad dream," I tell him.

Zach turns on the light by his beside. It's after two in the morning.

"You had one last night too," he informs me as though it is something I didn't know. "What was it, Vi? Let's talk it out."

And just like that, my husband's eyes are no longer heavy-lidded. That's Zach. He falls asleep and awakens with the speed of a jack-in-the-box. He shifts his body and, now lying on his side, strokes my arm gently. So gently that it feels like the breeze of a faraway fan. Zach loves me, and not telling him everything makes me sick, as though I'm betraying his trust.

I slide out of bed and get a glass of water.

"I can't remember it," I call out from the bathroom.

If I told him, he'd think I was a monster. I know it. It is easy for people to offer up a comment that they'd kill someone if they had a chance. Line up for it. Flip the switch. Make him wish he was never born. All of that is talk and posturing. It's in the abstract. If some creep murdered a child, the parents would say they'd kill the son of a bitch with their own hands. Make him suffer. Make him feel everything they'd felt and everything, more importantly, that their child had.

That's a fantasy, albeit a dark one. It's the kind of revenge game that people play when doing it safely is impossible.

"You've been distracted lately." Zach lifts the comforter as I crawl back under the covers. "Something going on? Is it work? Your parents and their situation?"

I pivot away from work, which, of the options suggested by my husband, is the closest to the truth. Not work itself, rather what I did at the conference.

"Work's fine. Busy. I guess my parents and that up-and-down marriage of theirs. I wish Dad would just make up his mind. I don't see it working out."

"It's done, right?"

"He's back with Mom. Sort of, I guess. Shondra dumped him." As I'm saying it out loud, I realize I completely blocked this out after Dad texted me the news the other day. I tucked it away to mention to Zach, and it slipped my mind.

He's surprised. "Wow. Why didn't you say something?"

Even though that was not the truth of my nightmares, it wasn't a lie. Neither was what I was about to tell Zach.

"I don't want you to feel like you've made a mistake."

"I don't follow."

I let his words have space before I answer.

"Marrying me. Marrying into this clusterfuck of a family."

He pulls me closer, so close that all I can see are his eyes.

"Violet," he says, "you are my dream. You are all that I want in this world. If that means I have to put up with the seesawing relationship between your parents, no prob. I got it. I have my own strange family quirks."

Zach takes a pause and lets out a sigh.

Good. Here comes a deep, dark secret. I wait for it.

"My parents filed for bankruptcy," he says, clearly embarrassed. Next, he drops the bombshell. "Twice."

I already knew that thanks to Dad. He made it a point to inform me what he'd found on the internet when Zach and I first got engaged. I didn't care about it then, and I don't care about it now. Now, however, it's a welcome diversion.

"Oh. I had no idea."

"Just wanted you to know. No one is perfect. Except you."

Zach kisses me and dims the light. In no time at all, his faint snoring resumes. I lay there in the dark, remembering my dream, frame by frame. The look on Mike Stone's face when I inserted the knife into his chest. Testing a cake with a toothpick comes to mind. One of Nana's cherry Jell-O-filled poke cakes, I guess. I think I speak to the man, but I'm not sure. The dream that unfolds is a silent movie.

And then he slumps over and tumbles backward.

I see my own face from his perspective.

I am as confused as he is.

What did I just do?

The little dog jumps up onto his chest, then slides off, slipping on blood shooting from where the knife has plunged. The canine's unclipped paws smear blood on the checkerboard floor.

Potato prints like the ones Mom made us test for her class.

My mouth, tight with horror, loosens.

In my silent dream, I read my own lips.

Papa.

CHAPTER THIRTY-THREE

Pullman, Washington
Lily

The lobby bulletin board of our dorm is plastered with neon-colored flyers of two kinds: requests for new roommates and counseling services for my fucked-up generation. I read them as I wait for the new key to the laundry room to be handed off by the resident aide. The notices spark the memory of my attendance—awakening, really—at my sister's support group.

Violet had asked me a couple of times to accompany her to her sexual abuse survivors group. I thought most forms of therapy were bullshit. Never helped me much. At least, not in the way that good weed did. I resisted her invitation as long as I could by telling her I'd found something better to do.

Or an excuse that seemed to have merit.

"Big test tomorrow. Have to study."

That was the gold standard of excuses in the Hilliard household, one that was falling apart under the crushing weight of my parents' butterfly-wing flimsy marriage. School was important. That was all the two of them could agree on.

Violet was deep into dealing with Mom and Nana with her wedding, and she was making noises about how the support group was helping her deal with the past and insisted that I come.

"Family ties are important."

I pushed back on the invitation. "Family ties are what got you to need therapy in the first place."

She looked at me skeptically. I could tell she was unsure of whether I supported her just then or was mocking her constant angst over what happened when she was six.

Get over it, I thought. *Move on.*

"You feel that way?"

"Yes," I admitted, trying to dig myself out of the divot in the floor that was beginning to swallow me. "I don't need to go to a meeting to convince you that whatever you've gone through, are still going through, is real or whatever." I stopped, thinking that I'd said too many whatevers and was going to be gulped up by the floor. "I love you, Violet."

That was a good way to end it, I thought. Making it all about how much I loved her—the period at the end of the sentence in my attempt to mitigate the harshness of my words.

"We won't have much time together for a while," she said.

I gave her a mock glare. "What? You're going to drop me once the ring goes on?"

Violet laughed and tilted her head, her hair moving like the softest breeze over one of those wheat fields near campus.

"Maybe I will."

She was teasing me. At least, I thought so.

"Okay," I finally said, "I'll go."

The group congregated in the back room of a Tacoma used bookstore and coffee shop that had been dealing with an ongoing water line leak. It smelled like wet sneakers accented by Nana's mothballs, but heavier. When we arrived, Violet was immediately surrounded by a dozen women. Younger. Older. I stood away, watching them embrace her, asking if she was all right.

"You know you can call me, Vi," one said. "Day or night. I'm always home."

"Vi, me too."

When the swarm of supporting hugs ebbed, she introduced me.

The other women were welcoming, although admittedly a little wary. At least, that's how I took it. They wore the armor of politeness. They let the moment fill with silence as if I were going to disclose something dramatic.

"I'm here to support my sister," I said, catching my sister's gaze.

"Well, then," the leader, Ellie, said, "let's go to circle."

I hadn't been "to circle" since kindergarten.

One of the group, Patrice, opened a box of white wine and filled plastic glasses. When she got to me, I pointed to my water bottle. She's about forty, with a pleasant round face with lips that protruded from her mouth—new braces were my guess. Another member of the group lifted the covering from a Costco cheese tray. I wondered if this was like a book club.

Without a book.

Without the admission by most attendees that they hadn't read the whole thing.

It wasn't.

It wasn't like that at all.

"I'm in a battle," puffy-lipped Patrice announced. "I'm taking back what that bastard took from me."

I liked getting high listening to true crime podcasts whenever there was nothing better to do, which was more time than I cared to admit.

I knew about all the horrible things men do. I read crime books. I watched forensic shows too.

Yet inside the so-called circle, I was bombarded with stories from real women. Victims. I placed my water bottle on the floor when I felt it slipping from my fingers. I was glued to each, as one after another described things that seem a million times worse than fake reenactments on TV or the overwrought narration of a podcaster.

"I don't want you to judge me," Patrice went on. "But even now, thirty years later, I still have a hard time with my feelings. Yes, I hate him. I hate him for what he did to me. How it ruined my family. How it made my mother cry every night, and my father . . . it made him look at me like he didn't trust me even when I got older."

"Didn't trust you?" asked Ellie. "How do you mean?"

Patrice had probably told her story a hundred times, still the question gave her pause.

"Not that he blamed me for what happened," she said. "That he didn't trust me to not allow it to happen to me again."

"Like you were asking for it? You were only a kid."

Patrice tightened her lips over her braces, and a droplet of blood oozed from the corner of her mouth. She held her hand up like she was stopping traffic.

"Not that," she said. "That I was somehow damaged and would succumb to some other man. Not that I was asking for it, but that I wouldn't be able to stop a predator."

"That's victim shaming," Violet said.

Everyone nodded in agreement.

I saw things a little differently, but I didn't say so. I thought about what Patrice was saying. Her father couldn't protect her on every date, every encounter. He couldn't be a fly on the wall. He had to let her go out into the world.

A woman with short salt-and-pepper hair was next. Her name was Ruth. She was in her late fifties. She had on black pants and a white top.

No makeup. No jewelry. Her mouth was a flat line. Her eyes moved like a pendulum as they swept over each of us.

Just as Ruth opened her mouth, she began to cry.

Oddly, no one said anything to comfort her.

She stretched out her hand. Patrice handed her a box of tissues from the floor, which were likely set there specifically for such a moment. Ruth was a crier. The others sipped wine and listened to what I gathered was something they'd heard before.

"He wasn't my uncle," she said quietly. "After my dad died, there were quite a few uncles coming and going. None of the men she brought into the house were related to us. What Uncle Ted did to my brother was the worst thing that a man could do to a little boy. Clarke was only four when it started."

She stopped speaking to blow her nose.

Leader Ellie broke from the group to get more wine.

Intermission, I thought, in a familiar story.

As I looked around, I wondered why it was that Ruth was given such a cool reception. Had her constant hot stream of tears annoyed the group? Was she a bad example because she was still struggling with what happened all those years ago? Was it that she wasn't the victim herself?

My answer came from Ruth herself.

"I know you all think I should have done something, but I didn't know what to do."

Aha. She hadn't protected her brother.

She didn't stop Uncle Ted.

A woman named Caroline from the other side of the circle jumped into the conversation. "It was a different time. You didn't know what would happen to you if you did tell. If anyone would believe you?"

Ruth sniffed into her tissue. The others nodded.

It all seemed so sad and strange.

She was an outsider in a circle meant to provide support for survivors and their families. She hadn't enabled her brother's molester. Nor had she facilitated it like Ruth's mom. She was guilty, though none said it, because she hadn't done anything to stop it. She hadn't told her mother or anyone. Her life had been one regret after another, and everyone in the supposed safe space of the circle didn't reach out to make her feel better.

Only Caroline.

Violet passed on telling her story next. Instead, she leaned close to me.

"My sister is everything to me," she told them. "She's younger but wiser. She's here to support me because that's what a real family member does. My mom won't budge from the fence she's sitting on, even though I know she has to believe me. And I don't want to lose every connection to my family because of what my grandfather did."

All eyes were on me. I was supposed to say something, but it took me a minute to pull something out.

"I'm here for you, Violet," I began. "You know that. You are the best sister a sister could ever have." I found myself repeating the speech I'd been writing for her wedding. I backed up a little. "I've watched you struggle with so much. When I was younger, I didn't know what it was that made you so angry."

Her eyes were wet, and I knew that the faucet had been twisted.

"It was because you always hid what happened to you so well. I probably couldn't have helped you then, but I'm here now."

Violet was full-on sobbing at my mix of wedding and group confessional talk.

Ruth handed my sister a used Kleenex. She mouthed, "Sorry." The box was empty.

Violet took a moment and composed herself.

"This isn't a club that any of us wanted to join, right?" she asked. "It's pain, secrets, humiliation, and a thousand sleepless nights that gets you a membership card. No one would want one. You wouldn't wish any of this on your worst enemy."

The group gave a small wave of applause, and my sister hugged me from her chair.

"Thank you for coming, Lily. It means everything."

And just like that, it was over.

Violet followed Ellie into the office of the bookstore while the rest of us collected the cheese plate and plastic cups. Patrice picked up Ruth's half-full cup of wine and downed it like a pro. I was embarrassed for her, and I quickly averted my eyes.

"I used to go to AA," she told me. "I learned that I didn't have a drinking problem. Not really. My problem was what happened when I was a girl. Drinking to forget. That kind of stupid move. You know?"

"I guess so," I said.

She checked me out, assessing.

"You don't know, do you?"

Her manner was confrontational.

"Don't know what?" I asked.

"You never forget."

✄

I fish my phone from my pocket and finally return Mom's voice mail from the other day. I've ignored a dozen texts since then too.

"Lily," she says, "I've been trying to reach you."

"I know, Mom. Just super busy with classes."

"I know. Lots to do."

"How's Nana?" I ask. "She's been through a lot."

"Trying to adjust. Having you gone has been hard on her."

She doesn't mention Papa. Or the video. So I do.

"You saw the video, right?"

"Yes. Not sure I got the whole thing."

"You got the part I wanted you to see."

"I don't understand."

"You do, Mom."

"It isn't what you think."

I figured she'd play it this way. It is her style completely. It makes me sad, though. Part of me had hoped, more than anything, she'd say she'd finally done the right thing. Not her. Not my mother.

"You won't show it to anyone, will you?"

"Violet's seen it. Maybe Nana should too. Dad. That detective." I lied about hearing from him, and it seems clear he's not interested in our family, but keeping up the pressure now can't hurt.

Mom doesn't say anything for a long time.

"Mom, I know you believe her. I know that you had to have known. Maybe you thought you could fix things by killing Papa—"

She cuts me off right there.

"I would never kill anyone. You know that, Lily."

"I don't. Not at all. I believe my sister. I just don't understand how you could be such a fucking bitch and not believe her. Everything points to her being truthful. Look at her. Tell her."

"It didn't happen, Lily."

With that, I've had enough. I hang up. Nothing will get her on the right side of reality.

Chapter Thirty-Four

Seattle, Washington
Violet

"Papers or junk mail?"

Maria divvies up the future contents of the office's recycle bin, and I place my coffee cup on my desk. "Aren't they the same thing?"

"Don't I know it."

"Junk mail for me this time. You can have the pleasure of reading what's new in Selah this week."

"Next to nothing," she says. "Same as last week."

While I pick through press releases and assorted direct mail pieces promising SEO and market research, Maria huddles at her desk and sifts through the daily and weekly newspapers that the commission receives to keep tabs on a region that hasn't fully caught up with the digital media age. The weeklies' online editions only carry ads and a story or two. Paperboys still have a job in Apple Land.

Every now and then, Maria will read me a line or two in mock sincerity about a cow that's missing or a stolen birdbath.

I admire her for that. Most people from the coast—as the Eastern Washington contingent calls us in Seattle—find plenty of things to ridicule about those who live on the other side of the Cascades. Maria keeps it classy. In turn, so do I.

Most of the time.

The junk mail is a far easier task, so I finish first.

I slip past her desk on my way to the break room. "Coffee?"

Maria doesn't answer.

"New apple weevil?" I joke.

She shakes her head and looks up.

"Remember your child molester?"

The ceiling drops down for a moment. "Huh?"

"The guy in Yakima," she continues. "You researched him on the sex offender directory after we came back from the conference."

My heart plummets to my knees.

"Vaguely," I say as I keep moving.

Maria isn't done and I freeze to catch every word.

"Guy got stabbed in his own home."

"Jesus," I reply.

"A woman came forward and said she saw someone that night coming from his place toward the Bali Hai where she and her fiancé live."

"Fiancé? More like a pimp," I say.

She makes a face. "Hey, you don't know that."

Maria gives everyone the benefit of the doubt, another of her many good qualities.

"Just putting it out there. The place was a dump, right?"

Maria goes on. "She said that the woman put something in the motel dumpster."

"What was it?" I ask, my heart now somewhere in the vicinity of my calves.

"Police don't know. Garbage service came the next day. They're picking through the dump now. The witness said that the woman was white, well dressed."

I pull my feet from the floor where they feel stuck and start for the break room.

"Hey, I've been wondering about something," Maria calls after me.

The glue trap floor stops me and I turn to her.

Here it comes. She'll say something about the blood on my purse. She'll say that she knows I wasn't in my room when she came back from dinner. Or that I wasn't sick. That I'm a liar. That she's going to call the police and tell them that I've been acting strangely since our trip.

All of which is true.

All of which I will deny.

"What?" I ask, willing my heart to stop beating so rapidly.

Her eyes meet mine.

I don't blink.

"Can you see if Cami's stashed away any of her Earl Grey with lavender? Cabinet next to the fridge. I can't face that coffee. Just the mention of it makes my stomach hurt."

I nod, and finally breathe.

✻

That night, I find myself searching for more information on Mike Stone's demise on the *Yakima Herald-Republic*'s website. I see a photo of his little red house and his now familiar mug shot. I scroll to a photograph of Tommy Nealon, twenty-two.

Under his name: *Victim.*

Tommy's brother is quoted:

> "I'm glad Stone got offed. I was seven when he raped
> me and my little brother. I got over it best I could.

Tim didn't. He killed himself when he was thirteen. I blame Stone for that. He messed up a lot of lives. Good riddance."

Next, I click on the registry and scroll.

Mike Stone is no longer listed.

Good riddance indeed.

CHAPTER THIRTY-FIVE

October 20
Gig Harbor, Washington
Rose

While my students press maple and poplar leaves collected at recess between sheets of wax paper with the assistance of two parent volunteers, I survey the classroom. The familiarity of the scene calms me in the way I think a service animal helps a person with anxiety. The smell of wax scorched by a hot iron fills my nose.

I'm in my safe place.

I'm in charge.

I'm trusted and adored.

I am everything that I should be, but that's only here. Never at home. At home, I am a failure as a mother and wife. Dropped by Shondra, Richard sleeps in Violet's old room. Lily is at college and volleyed a preemptive strike in my direction: she's going to have Thanksgiving with a group of other kids—kids who live in another country and have a decent excuse for not going home. Violet and Zach will be with his parents this year—an agreed-upon arrangement that leaves me with Christmas.

Me, Mom, and Richard. What a trio.

I focus on the kids in my classroom.

Ivanna's two sheets of wax paper refuse to adhere. She starts to cry, and her mom, one of the volunteers, goes over to her.

That always happens. Kids will cry at anything if their mother is within earshot. If Ivanna's mom hadn't been around, the girl would suck it up.

Solomon pounds the table, sending crayon shavings all over the floor.

"Need help?" I ask from the front of the room.

"No," he says. "I can fix it."

My eyes zero in on Piper, the smallest of my students. Adorable too. She has big brown eyes and dark-brown hair so thick that from where I'm standing, it looks like yarn. She's squinting at her leaves, carefully deciding what leaf should go where. She is the quietest of this year's group. Has been since the first day when her mother dropped her off on her way to work at a bubble tea café in the Tacoma Mall. Mom smelled like smoke and a gallon of Scope.

"How's it going, Piper?" I ask her.

She looks upward, but not exactly at my eyes.

"My eyes are here and here," I say, a reminder of what we've agreed to work on in class.

"I don't want to make a mistake, Ms. Hilliard," she says, catching my eyes for barely a second before looking back down at her project.

"You can't make a mistake. Whatever you decide to do is the right thing."

She's not so sure and it shows.

"I can help her," says Briana, whose mother is the opposite of Piper's. She's Lululemon and Tesla to the core.

Gig Harbor is peculiar in the way it separates the haves and the have-not-so-muches. Waterfront access is the key. You'll find leaky manufactured homes at the start of a long-wooded driveway leading down to the water, where there are homes that would be the first choice of any Vrbo renter—if they can afford the nightly rate.

Our school draws a cross section of the population, which I prefer. At least in the beginning when I believed being a teacher could alter the course of a young human's life. Not so now. I've picked up enough about each child to have a pretty good idea of where they are from and where they will go. I keep it to myself, because to say the words out loud wouldn't alter a path that is preordained. Not for all. For most. I can see who is going to make it to college and beyond—that's easy. I can tell, even now, who doesn't have a fighting chance to graduate from high school. I can tell who will get pregnant at a young age, who will get caught up in drugs.

Piper is one of those kids that I will pass off at the end of the year to another teacher, who, in turn, will do the same. And so on. A pre ordained path.

Briana finishes instructing Piper on the best way to place the foliage.

"I like it like this," she says.

Piper tilts her head. "Okay. I like it too."

When she stretches her arms to press the paper together, the sleeves on her pink shirt rise and I notice a red mark on her wrist.

"How did that happen, Piper?"

She looks at me, again only for a flash. "What?"

I can't be sure, but I think she's stalling her answer.

She pulls down her sleeves. "Joey scratched me."

"Who is Joey?" I ask.

"Our cat. He's a mean old tabby."

"I like dogs," Briana offers.

"Me too," Piper says.

I stand there observing the girls until my phone pings with the time for recess. The kids know the subtle alarm and immediately stir.

"Five minutes. No one is going outside until everything is put away, guys."

The rumble of the classroom goes silent as the space empties itself of kids and parental helpers. I sit at my desk thinking of Piper and the red mark on her wrist. I look up the number for the bubble tea café where her mother works, and as I get ready to dial, I stop myself. It dawns on me that my reluctance to get involved isn't that I don't really suspect child abuse, it has to do with the fact that I know ringing that bell is a beginning to more trauma. Not an ending. I don't call Piper's mother—or any other mother—because my own mother instilled deep inside me that family secrets told are family secrets that destroy.

Whatever happens inside the walls of our home is solely our concern, she'd said more than once. *No one else's business. We live and deal with our own shame. Telling a stranger your business only gives them power to hurt you even more.*

CHAPTER THIRTY-SIX

October 27
Pullman, Washington
Lily

My head is a bass drum from the Washington State University marching band. Thump. Thump. I breathe in more frigid air, thinking that oxygen will help. Katie and I trudge across the parking lot to the Bookie. Down the steps of their big white sorority house, I notice the girls coming toward us. Chi O's run in a mostly tight pack like beautiful gazelles. I spot the weakest of the herd. Her name is Darby, and I have the distinct feeling that she's part of my sister's pack, not theirs. I've seen her lurking in the back of the frat parties that are as stupid as I imagined when Shondra talked about how "cool and cray" they were back in her day. Darby alternates between hanging all over a drunk and pushing him away when his hands go there.

Or there.

The guys deride her as a cock tease with such anger that the transgression is worse than being a serial murderer.

I take in more air. I drank and smoked too much last night.

The trees are bare, and their jagged skeletal branches frame a lead sky in a tattered lace that conjures up a doily on Nana's coffee table and the summer when Violet and I stretched it onto a wire coat hanger to make a butterfly net. Nana was so mad at us for destroying a family heirloom. To make matters worse, the net we'd fashioned was an epic failure. We didn't even catch a moth.

Katie's in my tribe. That was clear the second I saw the map of parallel lines on her arm.

Just like predators have the innate ability to spot the perfect victim, a victim—or one as close to a victim as I am to my sister—can see another with 20/20 clarity.

"You're stone silent today," Katie says.

"'Stoned' is a good word. Last night was too much of everything."

"Really extra. I noticed."

"Of course you did, Katie. You notice everything." My tone is a little off-putting, which was not my intent. "I mean that you are very intuitive."

"Thanks, Lily. I think."

The gazelles file past as we go inside the bookstore. I make a beeline for the Tylenol while Katie wanders around the magazines. I decide on Advil instead and stand in line to pay. The guy in front of me gives me a look. I've seen him around. He wears dark-framed glasses, which I am almost certain are for affect only. He's good-looking, with a strong chin that doesn't need the shadow of a stubbly beard to enhance or conceal it. He's likely more boyfriend material than hookup.

If I wanted a boyfriend, that is.

He says hi and I say hi back, then almost as quickly, I look at my phone.

My sister and I drunk texted around midnight.

At least I was drunk.

Her: They are going to arrest that nurse for killing Papa.

Me: Seriously? Shit. That's big.

Her: Yeah. Someone leaked an interview she did with the police.

Me: Wow. What did she say?

I barely say "wow" in real life, at least, I hope so. Here I am using it like it's my go-to word.

Her: I'll send you the link.

I end the conversation with a heart and a beer emoji.

Katie's still over by the magazines. The faces of the confessional squad stare out from the rack. Ellen. Padma. Queen Oprah. All of them—and others, too—have spoken out about things that a generation ago would never have been mentioned. Not to anyone. People think the world has changed because of the "courage" it takes to speak out. They also think that saying it, posting it, screaming it out to the world changes something. For some, maybe. But there are still women everywhere—they are sitting on a bus, speaking in a boardroom, dropping their kids off at school—unable to say what was done to them and unable to let it go. I learned that from my sister and the women in her support group.

I forward the link to Mom and Dad as we head out the door to class, imagining Mom's simultaneous relief and worry that I could still interfere by sharing that video with the detective. My mother doesn't live on her phone, anyway. It's partly because of her job at school. It's also "a generational thing," as she says every time some social-media-driven fad finally makes it to her awareness. She thought TikTok was a Kesha song, which, I admit, it was—when I was, like, twelve. She told me that Tide Pods were for lazy people anyway and eating them was probably better than using the product to actually clean clothes. And planking? She thought Violet was talking about flooring. It was only last year that she mastered the hook-arm-on-hips pose for photographs.

As Katie and I go our separate ways—she, to a music appreciation class, and me, to a philosophy class that I shouldn't have enrolled in—I think about Mom's denial and Violet's support group. I decide I'll ask Katie tonight to tell me the story of her scars. Not why she cut herself—everyone knows that's a form of coping with severe emotional pain.

I want to know who did what to her.

CHAPTER THIRTY-SEVEN

Seattle, Washington
Violet

I am drowning, but a lifeline at this point could become a noose.

Zach and Maria make matters worse by asking why I'm distracted. I've called in sick twice now, purposely selecting days when Zach is away so I can lie in bed or drink without judgment.

Judgment.

That word seems ironic just now. I stood in judgment when I went to see Mike Stone that evening in July.

I am not myself. Really, I'm not.

I don't want to be myself.

Yesterday, I went to my stylist and had her color and cut my hair. I went too far, I think, as I stand in front of the bathroom mirror studying my self-inflicted disaster. Who is this? Do I even know her? My hair is almost black now, and the choppy cut looks like a Liza Minnelli wig from the back pages of Nana's old *Woman's Day* magazines. It didn't look great then, and it looks even worse now.

I am a mess and can't talk to anyone about it. It's a matter of trust, of course. I hate all the labels that come with what Papa did to me. "Survivor"? Really? Is that what I am? "Victim"? Is that what I want myself to be? My grandfather molested me. Even that word bothers me. "Molest"? He raped me. I was raped, and the weight of that word stays true to the reality. No guessing. No explaining is needed.

The reason I can't speak to anyone about it is a matter of trust. Until I told Ellie, I had only told my mother. Lily and I never talked about it because we didn't need to. She is my sister. I didn't need to turn her against Papa, though I watched his every move when we were with him. He and I knew why. Lily didn't understand until later.

My secret was a million pounds on my back. My secret made me into a liar. It made me unable to trust, to let anyone get to know me. Even Zach, to some degree. How much, I don't speculate because it hurts too much. Zach loves me. I know that. I can't help wondering sometimes, what would he think when we made love if he knew what had happened to me when I was a girl? Would it change the way he touched me? Would he think twice about the intimacy between the two of us? Would he hate my mother? My father? Nana? The family that looked the other way.

And Ellie. She would understand why I did what I did. Her group gave me the impetus to scroll through the pages of the registry to see the faces of those who'd left their permanent mark on girls and boys like me. And yet, I don't tell her anything about Mike Stone. I don't mention it.

I don't trust anyone.

CHAPTER THIRTY-EIGHT

November 11
Gig Harbor, Washington
Rose

I can hear my husband or, maybe, more appropriately, my on-again, off-again husband.

Husband of convenience.

Booty call, if the kids still say that.

He's in my daughter's bedroom snoring so loudly that I feel the wall between us vibrate. I lay there, the wetness between my thighs mocking me and reminding me what an idiot I am. I let it happen tonight like I did a week ago when I—and I'll use the excuse that is just that, an excuse—when I drank too much wine and fell for the tried-and-true "old time's sake" line.

I use the shirt he left behind and wipe him away, though avoiding the dreaded wet spot isn't an issue anymore. He literally came and went, leaving me to sleep alone in our bed.

How did this all happen? How did we start out so good and end up so bad? It all changed. I still don't know why. The girls, maybe?

He wasn't the center of attention anymore. He'd wanted boys, so that might have played into his growing aloofness. At first, I just accepted it. Chalked it up as a phase that would pass. It wasn't as though I didn't ask, but Richard's not the kind of man who digs deep into his feelings. I was always left to connect the dots. Nor was he an astute observer of what was really going on here.

Maybe that's why I married him, after all.

I want to bang on the wall just then to get him to stop snoring. His obliviousness, which I once put up with, now rankles me to no end.

I fling Richard's shirt to the floor and retrieve my phone from what used to be his nightstand.

I find the text Lily sent and click on the link.

It's not a transcript but a video. I recognize the players right away. It's Amy Woods and Detective Hoffman sitting across from each other in a bleak, tightly confined interview room. He's got his hands folded on the table. She's pushed herself back against the wall, so much so that her head touches it.

"Am I under arrest?" she asks.

Detective Hoffman lifts his hands from the table and waves away the suggestion. "No. No. Just an interview." He pauses a beat. "Do you think you should be under arrest?"

Amy shakes her head. "No. Of course not. But I've told you everything about that night. Yes, Mr. Bradley was under my care, but I didn't do anything wrong."

"Yes," he says, "you've told me that. But you've also refused to take a polygraph."

"Isn't that my right? Are we at the point in this country where the police can just round people up and force them to do whatever they say?"

"Whoa," he says. "That's not what's going on here. It would clear you, wouldn't it? And we could get this all done right now."

She folds her arms against her chest. "I'm in the medical field, Detective. I'm on medication for anxiety. I'm not about to take a polygraph. Can we move on?"

A fly lands on the camera lens, and I instinctively want to shoo it away. It flies away and I hear a swat. Detective Hoffman comes back into my view. Exterminator and detective. They go hand in hand, I suppose.

"I didn't ask you to come down for the poly," he says.

"Then why bring it up?"

Nurse Woods is angry, and I suspect whatever dosage she's on for anxiety isn't working for her.

The detective slides a file folder closer and taps it with his fingers. It's a light tap. Not a sound. Just an indicating gesture.

Her eyes move to the folder.

"Fair enough," he says. "I wanted you to come here so we could talk about Oregon."

She puts on a poker face and says nothing.

"Eugene, specifically," he adds.

She knows what he's talking about. It's been on the news. One of her coworkers told the police about the suspicion that followed her from a previous job.

"You were Amy Atkinson back then, right?"

"You know that already. Why are you asking like you don't already know?"

"Just confirming. Confirming," he repeats.

He draws the folder upward like sheet music. His fingers shift around the contents until he takes out a photograph of a woman. She looks to be in her thirties. Maybe younger. Hard to tell on the tiny screen of my phone. Attractive, I think.

Amy Woods brings her hands to her mouth.

"Do you know who this is?"

Again, it's hard to view. I dim the bedside light to see if darkening the room improves things. It does enough that I can tell she's crying.

"Who is this?" he asks.

Her hand stays over her mouth and she bends forward, leaving her tears to puddle on the metal table.

He gives her time.

"Jade," she finally answers. "Jade Shelton."

"You were her nurse. Isn't that right?"

She clamps her eyes and lets out a forceful, jarring cry. Loud enough, I think, that it might wake snoring Richard. She's inconsolable. Mucus drips downward from her nostrils, and Amy frantically searches for something to wipe her eyes and nose. Detective Hoffman gets up and opens the door, and someone hands him a box of tissues. He gives it to her.

"More than that," she answers, pulling out another tissue. "She and I were kindred spirits. And no, we were not lovers, as everyone seemed to think."

"Live and let live is my motto," Hoffman says.

"Good for you, Detective. The fact of the matter is that Jade was like a sister to me. I took care of her, first on the ward, and then at her parents' home as a private nurse."

"I spoke to the police down in Eugene, then had a call with Jade's mother."

She's no longer crying. Her face has morphed into stone.

"Of course you did. All cruel roads lead to Charlotte. She pushed a false narrative that I ended her daughter's life."

"Something like that," he says, once more selecting a sheet of paper from the folder. He puts on a pair of readers and runs his finger down the page. "Says here that Jade died of asphyxia."

Amy pushes back. Her face is calmer, as though she's told herself that being upset makes her look unhinged. Which it did and does.

"She had cancer," she says.

The glasses come off and the paper goes back in the folder.

"Says that too," he volleys back, "but says it was operable."

"She didn't want the surgery. Jade was Christian Scientist. Devout. She was sure that God would heal her. It wasn't my job to get her to change her beliefs."

"You were a trained nurse," he says. "You knew better."

She bristles and shakes her head. "That's Charlotte's take on things. Not Jade's."

"And the investigators from the DA's office?" he continues. "They said you and only you could have killed Jade."

Over the shock of seeing the photo and the very direct accusations coming at her, Amy fumbles around for her purse, trying to collect herself.

"What does any of this have to do with Mr. Bradley?"

I know the answer. So, I suspect, does Nurse Woods.

Detective Hoffman lays it out plainly and succinctly. "He died in the very same way as Jade." He takes a sip of coffee. "With the same person in charge. That'd be you."

Amy's having none of it. She starts for the exit. "If you want to talk to me again, call my lawyer." She's out of the range of the camera's lens, but not the microphone, when she hurls her final words.

"If you talk to her again, tell Charlotte to fuck off. Her daughter hated her as much as I did."

The video done, I put my phone on the sleep setting. Richard continues to snore in the other room, and I struggle to find a way to get away from the noise by covering my head with a pillow. I feel myself sinking. I'm trying to find a way to quiet the mistakes I've made. With my girls. With other kids probably. I also feel sorry for the nurse in the video.

Her past is catching up to her.

Mine might be too.

CHAPTER THIRTY-NINE

November 23
Rose

My mom is deep into her eighties, and I give in to doing things her way as I prepare Thanksgiving for three in her kitchen. Frozen this and that. A turkey that she'll insist should be stuffed—which is fine, but I still remember the year that I got sick. The smell of sage takes me right back there every time. Richard, who is taking a break from Shondra and has nowhere else to go, takes a bottle of Jameson, sits by the TV, and digs into a Hickory Farms cheese log.

"Honey," Mom says, "can you start the rolls?"

I smack a silver tube on the edge of the countertop.

"Crescents," she says. "Pillsbury."

"The best," I say.

The electric can opener sputters as she unzips the lid of the olives.

"Rose, remember how you used to put the olives on your fingertips? All ten. So darned cute."

"All kids do that," I say. "It's kind of a holiday rite of passage."

She smiles. "Your girls did it too, as I recall."

Mom's elderly, but she's mostly steady on her feet and moves with purpose. From the corner of my eye, I watch her pour herself some of Rita's wine, topping it with a splash of 7Up.

The rolls go onto the baking sheet, one by one. I am exact with the placement of each. Mom chatters more, but I barely listen. I'm thinking about those olives and how my father put them on my fingertips. It's a hazy memory, one that I haven't revisited in a long time. Libby's olives were the only olives Mom ever purchased. Brand loyalty was nearly a second religion. Cranberry had to be Ocean Spray. Fruit cocktail was always Del Monte. Coffee? Yuban.

I look at the can on the counter.

"How come they aren't Libby's?"

She drinks more of her spritzer and stirs her famous canned gravy.

"I stopped buying that brand years ago."

"Oh? I didn't know."

"Got a bad batch once." She stops stirring and wipes off her glasses, fogged by steam rising from the saucepan. "Remember? Made you one sick puppy."

I'd thought it was undercooked stuffing that had made me ill that year.

"Rose?"

It's Richard suddenly standing right next to me. I didn't see him come in, so I step back a little.

"Are you all right?" he asks. His eyes are funny. *Peculiar.* Not drunk. He looks like he cares and that surprises me.

"Fine," I say, snapping out of the memory. "Just lost in thought. Mom, when do you think we'll be ready?"

She puts down the wooden spoon and looks over with a smile. She sees something in us, I'm sure, that's not there anymore.

"Five minutes," she says with a note of triumph. "Gravy's bubbling, and the rolls should be out lickety-split."

It was the olives that made me ill.

I think back to a dinner, years and years ago. I've retold the story of how my mom's cooking made me ill one Thanksgiving and she never once pushed back. Dad and I laid it on thick too. It was family lore. When *Worst Cooks in America* first came on TV, Lily insisted Nana should apply to be on the show.

Mom was a little defensive about it.

"I never claimed to be Julia Child," she said.

Richard revs up the old Hamilton Beach electric knife—which tears rather than slices—and attacks the turkey. I grab a memory of Dad putting glossy black olives on each of my fingers and then eating them one at a time, his eyes never straying from mine.

We both laughed at the silliness of it all.

Chapter Forty

Pullman, Washington
Lily

For our dorm-room Thanksgiving, Katie and I drink bottom shelf whiskey we got from a girl from Mercer Island with great access to alcohol through a boyfriend who always goes super cheap. We can't be choosy. And honestly, we didn't recognize any difference between various brands anyway. My goal isn't to get her drunk, just a little loose. I imagine what I'm doing is like what the frat guys do all the time. However, I'm not going to try to have sex with her.

That's a big difference.

Katie sits on the floor with her legs crossed and only speaks when asked about something. Her dark-blue sweats are loose and baggy. More to do with hiding than comfort, I think. The girls on our floor think she's weird. I think Maddy and I would have shit-talked about her behind her back.

"You don't talk about your family much," I say, thinking that'll open a door.

"You don't either, Lily."

She's right. *I don't*. And I don't want to go there now. "You know everything about Violet and Zach and their careers."

"Right." She reaches for the bottle and pours us another.

I wonder if she's trying to get me drunk.

Now that would be funny.

She continues, "Well, you never talk about your parents."

"You know I can't stand them half the time."

"Yes," she says, taking a big, throat-burning gulp. "I don't know why, though. You've never really said."

I let her turn the tables.

"Okay. Fine. My dad was the best dad ever when I was growing up." I lean my back against the bed. "I gave him a mug with that written on it."

That brings a sad smile to my face.

Katie pounces. "Sounds like he gave up the best dad title at some point."

"Yeah."

"What happened?"

The smell of burned popcorn slips in from the hall. Sienna next door still doesn't know her way around the dorm's temperamental microwave.

"Lily?"

"Okay," I say. "When she was little, something happened to Violet. I didn't know for the longest, I mean *longest*, time. And it fucked up our entire family."

Her eyes penetrate mine.

"Did your dad do something to her?"

"Yes," I say, quickly adding, "I mean, no, if you think he messed with her. He didn't do that."

"Someone else?"

I've never spoken to anyone outside of Violet and my mom about it. I used my dad's affairs as the reason for tears when I needed a release.

I just couldn't say the words, because by doing so, I knew that my relationships would all be tainted by something I didn't do. I didn't want that. I refused to consider myself a victim.

Which, I know now, I am—a victim of living in a house of lies.

"My grandfather."

"Seriously?" she asks. "That's fucking horrible."

I let the fact that I've told someone sink in. Then I tell her about what that was like growing up in that house. How what happened was treated like a ghost story that no one ever told. It was buried so deep, so we'd never have to confront it. Our age gap kept me on the periphery of whatever had been going on with her.

Inside our home.

"The funny thing was once my sister told me what he did, I found myself looking back at our family, every holiday, conversation, gathering . . . whatever. Things that didn't mean a thing to me at the time, seemed, I don't know . . . like they weren't real?"

Katie is listening intently, and I know that she's not thinking about how she's going to text this out to a bunch of our friends.

Like I probably would have.

I want to flip the topic of the conversation to her, but I can't.

"You mean," she asks, "like the good times weren't real?"

"Not at the time, only when looking back," I say, wishing that my minifridge made more than eight ice cubes at a time. I drink some more whiskey and let it burn. "How could they be?"

"Was it your dad's father who abused her?"

I shake my head. "No. Mom's dad."

"Then why do you hate your dad? I don't get it."

"I don't know if I really hate him. I'm so pissed off. He was so fucking clueless. It happened right under his roof. So messed up. He still doesn't know. Violet doesn't want him to know. She's screwed up about that. Says that he'll see her differently, and at this point, why bother?"

"Why don't you blame your mom?"

"My mom is weak. She's not capable of standing up to anyone. Never has been. She doesn't like conflict. Period. I've seen my dad, however, fight for something a thousand times. You know, all big and tough. Yelling at the TV. Telling someone to fuck off when they cut in front of him on the freeway—or telling someone to fuck off if they are out of line. He liked to right a wrong. I grew up believing that."

I think I might be drunk now. That's got to be why I'm spilling my guts to Katie.

"So, you forgive your mom?"

"Kidding, right? I don't forgive her at all. I just don't think she has the ability to do what needs to be done when it comes to making a stand. Even her own kid. Or her kids in her classroom. She's so wrapped up in what people will think."

"Think?"

"Of *her*."

"Your family is more fucked up than mine."

"You can say that again."

I ask her the question that I've wanted to since I first laid eyes on her.

"Tell me about that?" I indicate the scars on her arm.

She looks down and smiles. It's a slightly boozed-up smile, but there's something real about it.

"This has been a subject of great interest since I got here," she says.

"Yeah."

"I know what some of the girls call me. Katie the Cutter, right? I've heard it before and I really don't care. So, as far as I can see, what's carved on my arm is more of a reminder to me than a sign to anyone else. Everyone has a secret or two. You do. I do. My secret has a visible indicator—one of my own making."

"We all have something, Katie. You know about mine."

She pushes her hair back. My eyes remain on that scarred-up arm of hers. I can't stop looking. Crime-scene photo. Car crash. Horrendous outfit. Some things glue to your eyes. You practically have to break your neck to turn away.

"Why, then?" I ask.

"You already know why. Everyone that's ever been around girls our age knows."

"Control," I say.

She rolls her eyes. "That's what they say, right? I saw a counselor, and she tried to get me to see that's why I did it, and I couldn't argue against it because it's like I didn't know why when I'm doing it. I only know it feels good. Crazy, right?"

The whiskey bottle is nearly empty, and that's probably a good thing. I manage to get up from the floor and retrieve some string cheese sticks from the fridge and a box of Wheat Thins. I buy the low-fat kind because that's how I was raised, though no one in the Hilliard household was overweight.

"You're expecting that I was raped or molested like your sister, right?"

"Yeah." I offer her some cheese. "Something awful like that."

Katie makes a show of pulling it apart, making a fringe of cheese.

"I'm going to disappoint you. After your drama, mine seems silly. In fact, it makes me feel even more stupid about what I did. Like anyone would mutilate themselves for such an insignificant reason."

"I won't think that," I say. "Promise."

"It's fine," she says, shrugging. "It is what it is."

She runs a fingertip over the scars like she's tracing a tissue overlay.

"I think I was just born this way," she confides to me. "Something always there telling me that I wasn't good enough. Maybe I was jealous of my siblings. Probably I was. My older sisters were A students. My brother, the same. Also, they were athletic, and I don't mean just good at sports—lettered in varsity all three years. I was clumsy. Still am. I had to study my ass off to get Bs, and the rest of my family just skated through win after win."

I immediately counter and tell her how smart she is. She gives me a nod. No smile. Just a kind of appreciative look.

I ask if they picked on her.

"Not really. Maybe not until my sisters told my mom what I was doing to myself. You think that the girls here were the first to call me Katie the Cutter? Having a last name like Sharpe made things even worse."

Now she lets out a laugh.

I do too.

"My family, all perfectly good people, were handed a pile of shit to deal with when I started cutting. I know that now. Not then. Then, I thought that it made me feel better. It was a hurt that was real, not something in my head about being not enough. For my family. For boys later. Even for coming here."

She stops and looks at me.

"You think I'm crazy, right?"

I answer right away. "Not at all."

The truth is I really don't know what to think about Katie Sharpe. Part of me wants to tell her to get over herself. Cutting didn't really make her feel better, but the truth is, I don't really know that for sure. Just like when my sister told me that she only felt better when Papa died. I didn't see how that could fix things.

The scars look old, but I ask anyway.

"You still do it to yourself?"

"I think about it every day. Maybe ten times a day. Or more. I had a flash of wanting to leave your room when you started telling me about your family. It kind of—I don't know—made me hate myself for not being good enough to even complain about my life."

"That's messed up, Katie."

"I know, right? But that's how it goes. I start spinning, and the only way to stop is to go off somewhere where no one can see me and do what I do."

"Cut."

"Yeah, but I don't really think of you that way."

"Then how?"

"Release the poison that's hurting me inside. When I'm doing it, I feel better. Really good. It's like all the bad feelings just seep out. They're just gone."

Like my sister felt at her group, I think. Disclosing the truth in front of strangers made her feel better. Stronger. Talking about it released some of the poison Papa left pent up inside.

"I can almost breathe now," Vi had told me on the way home from the meeting.

The only thing keeping her from breathing in more oxygen was the fact that her abuser was still alive.

My thoughts travel back to the chaos at Violet and Zach's wedding. The plate. The shrimp. Then the collapse by the buffet table. Papa gasping for air. Nana on the floor, whispering something in his ear. A neighbor rendering medical aid. It plays in my thoughts at fast-forward speed.

Katie's passed out now. I get a blanket and put it over her, then flop onto my bed. My thoughts rewind, then fast-forward again, stopping on a final freeze-frame.

Violet, in her wedding dress, leaning over to pick up something from the ground.

She hid Papa's EpiPen.

My sister made another invisible cut to excise more poison.

CHAPTER FORTY-ONE

After Everything Happened
Violet

I drive past an elementary school in Gig Harbor and catch the sight of a grandmother and her granddaughter. The girl, about six, is stomping her feet in an old-school tantrum. She whips her ponytail in a fury, lashing at the grandmother like a lion tamer. Roles reversed. She is in charge.

A line from a presidential debate not long ago comes to me.

"I was that little girl."

I am that little girl.

And now I am in charge. Out of all of us. It's me.

I turn the corner, and the fence with that frilly razor-wire ruffle looping over the top comes into view. I have visited my mother at the Washington State Corrections Center for Women every other week since her incarceration. I talk to Rose on the phone or on video when I can't make it down to Gig Harbor. I actually prefer those electronic visits. They go fast. There's a half-hour time limit imposed by the prison.

Our family has become one of those candles that Nana stuck into the neck of a Chianti bottle from Gino's. We've melted down into a congealed mass. Some drips are fragile and fall from the stem of the bottle. Some are more rigid and, in their tortured mass, cling on for dear life. Our family was one of the good ones. Everyone thought so. And despite what happened to me, to my mother, I thought so too. A lot of dirt stayed under the rug that was our family. When you don't see the dirt, just the small lumps under the rug, it's easy to set it all aside.

When your mother goes to prison for murder, no amount of looking the other way fixes things. No sweeping. No shaking. No nothing. It's there. The world sees it. And really, who cares about the world? What you care about, what you know in the moment of your family's demise, is that the only people who can really hurt you are those who know you. Friends and neighbors stop coming by. Calls go unreturned. The worst are the whispers among people that aren't really whispers at all. I've caught Maria a time or two at work, but I don't say anything. I don't want to make an enemy of someone who maybe has an inkling about what I did when we were in Yakima chatting up the apple growers.

For all I know, she might have seen the blood on my purse.

So, I keep her close.

When I park, I note the time. Early. I imagine Rose waiting in line with other inmates as they are processed for today's visit. She bends over and they check her anus for contraband; something they will do again when the visit is over. They'll examine her vagina. They'll have her open her mouth like a baby bird. She'll do all of that with a practiced humiliation. To see anyone inside the walls, she must relinquish her modesty. She confided to me that, the first time, it was difficult and that she nearly cried, but crying is something that works in neither baseball nor prison.

"I call it a dance in my head," she said after a visit early on. "I do all the steps. In a way, it helps me. After doing it dozens of times, it's a routine that seems so natural that you don't have to think about what the officer is thinking as she peers inside your body."

A light rain starts to fall, and I hurry across the parking lot to the door to be processed. The officer at the desk is stoic. I have never seen a single glimmer of emotion as he says the same words every single time.

"ID? Inmate?"

I answer, though I'm thinking that he's seen me dozens of times and should know all of that by now. He probably does. It's procedure. Procedure rules all interactions. This isn't Starbucks where an employee gets bonus points for knowing a regular and writing their name on a cup.

A man in jeans and a blue hoodie stands behind me and adjusts the little girl hooked onto his hip. Her hair is in crooked pigtails and the new pink sweatshirt she's wearing still has its tags. She's there to see Mommy. She's got shiny black hair and brown eyes. She smiles at me. It's the only joy in the reception area. A dozen of us wait in line, not many for this time of day. The officer hands each of us a key. We stash all personal belongings in lockers on the opposite side of the reception area. Through metal detectors, then a wand over our private parts, and finally the noise of the gate being unlocked. We all file inside.

No one speaks. Except the girl. She's excited about getting a candy bar from the vending machine.

I'm trying to find myself back to forgiveness. Of my mother. Of myself.

Chapter Forty-Two

December 13
Gig Harbor, Washington
Rose

It's almost four and it's already dark. Decembers in the Pacific Northwest are like that. My classroom is starting to get cold—part of our principal's edict to turn off the heat the second the kids leave for home, which means his teaching staff is left to freeze in the winter. He drives a brand-new Escalade (black, of course), which none of us think is ironic since he's such an ass and we know damn well he doesn't really care about climate change or even saving money for the district. Not this guy. For him, it is purely a strategic move. It's about showing the superintendent that he is a great leader.

No.

An amazing leader!

I peer up from the next day's lesson plan, satisfied that I've whipped it into shape, in time to see Detective Hoffman approaching from across the parking lot. His warm breath sends out puffs of steam. He's a train coming forward. Puff. Puff. Puff. He's wearing a hat and dark overcoat that makes him look more like some nefarious character from a Marvel movie. Before I decide on which one, he's at my door and I let him inside.

"Cold as hell out there," he says.

"Not great in here either. Cost savings."

He removes his hat and runs his fingers through his clamped-down hair.

I wait for small talk, but he doesn't offer any.

"I have some news," he says. "You aren't going to like it."

I don't care for the sound of that at all. My blood pressure rises a little, and I sit down. He sits across from me on the other side of my desk.

"Shoot," I say.

He jumps right into it. "We're closing your father's case."

I don't know what to do with that. I drop my jaw and shake my head. "But I thought you'd arrested his murderer?"

"Not exactly," he says. "I mean, yes and no. Sorry. Let me back up."

"Okay." I study those kind eyes of his, searching for more than I see.

"Amy Woods and her lawyer have negotiated a plea deal. A complicated one."

"She's confessed?"

"Not exactly," he repeats. "She's taking what's called the Alford plea. That's when a person says that they think there is enough evidence to convict them, but they don't want to go to trial, and they don't want to admit guilt."

I'm confused and my face shows it.

"Think of it this way—she's not saying she's guilty, but she's saying she'll do the time."

"Sounds guilty, then."

"To me, it does too. It's a conviction. She'll go to prison."

"Did she say what she did to my father?"

"She doesn't have to say anything unless the judge says so."

"What about Oregon?"

"That's the key to all of this. She says that she killed her patient there following the woman's wishes."

"Assisted suicide?"

"Yeah. So, in Oregon, they allow that sort of thing now, but not back then. The law is sticky there. Our prosecutor and the one down there hammered out a deal where Woods will serve the bulk of her time here, following three months or so down there."

"Three months for a murder? Are you serious? And what kind of time for my dad's?"

"Not murder. Negligent homicide. She'll be warehoused for seven years—less for good behavior. It's the best we could do."

He's expecting an argument. Some pushback on the feather-light sentence. That I'll insist the sentence is bogus and my father's life was worth more than the punishment doled out like a game piece.

I gather papers in front of me. And then, the unimaginable falls from my lips. I find myself defending him. A reflex. "My father wasn't perfect, but his life was worth more than seven years."

"Understood," Detective Hoffman concedes. "It was, as I told you, the best we could do. The case was dependent on a confession. That's the truth."

"You didn't get a confession. You got some kind of legalese deal that sends a killer nurse to prison for less time than most kids spend in college these days."

"Understood," he repeats as he follows me to the door, and I turn off the lights. "I hear you."

I heard me too.

And I loathe myself for what I said.

I sit silently in my car. I don't turn on the ignition. Just sit. Thinking. She didn't kill my father. I rationalize that her admission, or quasi-admission, about her soul mate in Oregon, is worthy of some kind of punishment. But it's messy now. Too hard to unravel. Too hard to explain what I know.

What is wrong with me? I am such a goddamn coward.

CHAPTER FORTY-THREE

December 14
Seattle, Washington
Violet

Maria jack-in-the-boxes from her chair the instant she sees me in the office. Her eyes are twice their normal size.

"God, I saw the story, Vi."

All eyes turn in my direction. I know it isn't my new hairstyle that interests them.

Maria puts her arms around me and lowers her voice. "That nurse bitch killed your grandfather."

I step back from her and set my coat and purse on an empty table between our cubicles.

"Yeah. We're all in shock."

Maria rapidly taps a pretty red nail against her computer screen. A gallery of Amy Woods at various stages in her career carousel by.

"Look at her," Maria says. "Smug. Self-righteous. One of those who thinks rules only apply to other people."

"We all know the type, Maria."

I am the type, I think.

"Your grandfather wasn't terminal like the nurse's girlfriend. Some Angel of Mercy."

"Angel of Death is a better name for her," I say, adding, "although I'm struggling with the angel part."

Maria puts her hand on my arm. "This must be so hard."

"I'm fine. My mother thought it was coming."

"She must be devastated."

"I don't know. Yes and no. She's funny. My mother has always been good at holding her feelings inside. I think all of us Hilliards are that way."

"Not my family," Maria says, turning the conversation back to herself. "They never hold a thing back. I always end up knowing way more than I want to know. I wish they kept their feelings inside."

Trying to make me feel better. I get it.

In order to feel better, however, you need to feel bad in the first place.

CHAPTER FORTY-FOUR

December 19
Gig Harbor, Washington
Rose

The news of Amy Woods's plea bargain brings only a nod from Mom as she picks through Christmas stuff for her first holiday without Dad. It is her favorite time of year by far, so I accept her focus on decorations. Her sewing/craft/storage room looks like the North Pole and all its glory exploded. Red and green. Gold and silver. Everywhere. I help her to pick out some, as she tends to ignore things that were the first out of the box.

"What about the Santa cookie plate?"

She blows off the surface dust.

"You can have it, honey."

Honestly, I don't want it. Why would I? Kids are gone. Husband has one foot out the door half the time.

"Your father liked it," she says, putting it back. Not gently but dropping it into a mound of decades-old tissue paper. "I never did. There's not a lot that I like here."

Her remark surprises me. My mother's voice seemed different. Not her usual "oh fiddlesticks" lilt.

I ask what she means.

"It was his thing. Christmas. I'm really tired of all of it."

"It was your thing, Mom. Remember?"

She takes me in with those faded eyes of hers. "I'm not senile, Rose. I don't need a prompt to remember anything. What I don't remember is a choice that I make. And I never liked Christmas. I really didn't like any of those holidays."

One of her oft-said chestnuts came to mind.

You could have knocked me over with a feather, honey.

"You can't mean that."

"Sorry to burst your bubble, honey, but yes, I do."

I scoot some boxes aside to give her more room. Some contain Dad's clothes, old books, and even Mom's beauty operator's uniform.

I follow her into the living room with the sole item she deemed worthy to display—a ceramic tree with multicolored lights. One of her friends had a kiln, and I remember Mom painting the glaze on the greenware. Her attention to detail was remarkable.

She plugs it in and fiddles with the switch. All but one light illuminates, and she rotates the tree so that the burned-out bulb is in the back. Even though it's only four thirty, it's dark outside. Rain clouds have rolled in and sprayed sloppy drops all over the windows. The lights glow. It's a corny decoration. My girls loved it because of its distinctly vintage vibe.

"Mom, you just can't leave it dangling there."

"What?"

"Saying you never liked Christmas. That's not the way I saw things at all."

"Good," she says, focusing a stare on me. "I'm glad you have some happy memories. I wasn't sure if you did."

Her joints are knobs poking under her tissue skin. Her mouth loosely frames her teeth, all her own. I take another deep breath. She's opened the door for me to ask the question that I never could.

"Did you know, Mom?"

She stirs, thinking. I'm wondering if she's been ruminating along the same lines. Did she open the door on purpose?

"Knowing of something and believing it aren't the same thing, Rose."

I feel disoriented and sit down. "You need to unpack that."

"Unpack what?"

"What's behind what you are saying."

She attempts to brush it off. "Isn't that enough? I've kept all that ugliness inside for most of my life. Saying it will make it worse. It will all come back. I'm surprised that I didn't get cancer from carrying this all these years. That happens, you know."

I know what she's doing. She is in that same space all of us have been. Telling your truth might feel good; finally letting go of something dark often is. That's why counselors are in business. That's why confiding to a perfect stranger next to you on an airplane sometimes does the trick. The flip side is that sometimes when you release a dark secret, it comes back, a boomerang trimmed in razor blades.

You put it out there and it returns to hurt you again.

I guess I don't care if it hurts her. I'm not happy about the prospect. Not sad or sorry either.

"Not enough, Mom."

She adjusts the ceramic tree some more and leads me into the kitchen for more of that god-awful wine.

"Honey," she says, tears in her eyes, "what do you want from me?"

"The truth, I guess. Why didn't you stop him? Stop Dad."

Her tears match the rolling rain outside. Heavy, relentless.

She finds the hanky from under her bra strap and sinks into a chair at the kitchen table. I bring the glasses she filled and set them down.

She starts to talk, never really making an excuse. Always saying that it was her fault that she'd failed me as a mother. That it was easier for her to push it aside than to really deal with it, head-on.

"Back then, no one talked about this kind of thing, Rose. That's not my way out of my responsibility or my failure. If you don't have the script, don't know who to talk to, or what it really means, you freeze. You pray. You look the other way."

I push for more. "Even when I tried to tell you?"

"Especially then," she goes on, refusing to look directly at me. "I didn't want to allow those words, that ugly stuff, to be part of you. We had a neighbor when I was growing up, and something terrible had happened to him. Something that his uncle did. We didn't know what it was, but we somehow turned him into the problem. If we saw him, we went in the other direction. I'm talking about the boy. Not the uncle. The uncle we stayed away from too, but the boy, he became an outcast."

Mom moves her eyes further downward, wadding her hanky into a ball and clenching it in her palm. Over and over.

"I've thought about that little boy over the years," she says. "Your aunt Helen said that he killed himself when he was in his twenties. You think I would ever want that for you?"

"But I wouldn't," I tell her. My tone is resolute. "You know that."

Her hand trembles as she drinks some wine. "Honestly, I don't. And you don't either. You don't know what it would be like if every girl in your class called you names, or boys acted like you were a dime-store floozy and they could do anything they wanted to you. I can't change what happened, Rose. I hope you will forgive me. I did what I thought was best. And now he's gone."

"Right. Gone. He didn't ever have to face any consequences, did he?"

Mom finishes her glass. I haven't touched mine.

"He didn't go to jail, if that's what you mean."

"No, he didn't."

"He didn't drag our family into a cesspool of public humiliation either."

"Really, Mom?" My throat constricts, and my anger is just on the verge of lashing out. "You think that he gets to leave the earth with his memory untarnished? The guys at the Eagles think he's a great guy. All my friends told me how lucky I was to have a dad who was so successful but still nice to everyone. Never too busy to help out."

"I know all of that. You aren't telling me anything new, but I need you to know that I did tell him what I thought of him. I gave it to him, and I didn't mince words."

I think I know what she's talking about.

It was at the wedding. The wedding that he was specifically told not to come to.

"We were down on the floor . . . and he was trying to breathe. I told him then. I whispered I hoped he'd choke to death. I leaned right into that smelly ear and said what I wanted to say the day Jenny came over and stirred things up."

I had seen her say something to him when he was writhing. I thought she was trying to comfort him. He turned his head and whispered back to her. It looked so beautiful, a lifetime couple, the wife helping to ease her husband into the next world.

Mom says bitterly, "He told me I was a lousy mother. Lousy in bed."

I push away from the table and gulp the wine. Suddenly I want to defend her.

"He's dead now."

"Yes," she said. "The nurse finished what I started."

"Started?"

"He wasn't supposed to be at that wedding. He had no right to be there. You know what I did. You were right there."

"The shrimp?"

She wraps her arms around her ever-shrinking frame, literally holding herself together.

"I was so mad at Dave for making us go to the wedding when Violet didn't want him there. Or maybe she didn't want me either. I told him that it was a mistake, that it was an important day, but he railed about being embarrassed around his friends. *My granddaughter disinvited me to her own goddamn wedding. I fucking paid for most of her college. And this is what I get? For some unknown reason, I've been cut out of her life.*"

She shrugs. Or is it a little shoulder spasm? Hard to know for sure.

"It wasn't a plan," she says. "It just came to me. Like a vision. I saw that beautiful plate of pink shrimp, and it just drew me over to it. While your father was crowing about something or another, I took one and rubbed it all over his plate and fork. I did it fast."

She stops.

"And you clean freak, you, almost ruined it. Wiping the plate."

I don't disagree. I don't know how to respond.

"It wasn't my intent to kill him. When he died, though, I assumed I was responsible. At first, I thought, uh-oh. Then after a day or so, I thought, who's going to care about an old man? Pretty soon, by the time of his memorial, I thought, well, if I get caught, who'd care about a little old lady? They'd let me go, wouldn't they?"

I leave for the bathroom, passing those photographs, wondering why Mom felt the need to put them up. Was she atoning for what she did at the wedding? Personally, I would never want to see the face of someone I'd tried to kill. Too much constant self-reflection.

"Mom," I ask when I return, "why all the photos?"

She doesn't answer right away. She's thinking. Remembering something.

"Mom?"

She snaps to attention, no longer lost in thought. "A game, I think. An act of defiance, possibly. After all the ugly he brought to our family, I think I just wanted to show him I could stare him down. That he didn't scare me anymore. His being dead fixed that."

My mother. When I was a girl, I wanted to be *her*, which seems ludicrous now. Looking at her through my adult eyes, I don't view her as that beautiful creature who floated through the house and made everything smell so nice. So clean. All of that was an apparition.

Now I see an elderly figure sitting at the kitchen table, an empty glass of shitty wine in her knotted hands. She's a crumpled and weak version of what I knew when I was growing up. She was pummeled. She let my dad do whatever he wanted to her.

To me.

She never pulled me aside and told me that we had to escape.

To what?

And from what?

We were the perfect family.

"Why didn't we just leave?" I ask.

"You're looking for something that isn't there, honey. You're looking for a sliver of character. Maybe even something righteous. It isn't me. I survived by learning to look away. We're a lot alike, Rose. You and I."

I know she's right.

Silence fills the space between us.

"You better go home," she finally says. "Lily's home from college. She'll want time with you. I'll see you on Christmas. Pecan pie all right? Apple too. I ordered both."

I sit in my car for the longest time. Engine running. Defroster failing to clear the condensation separating me from the outside world. I know in my heart that I am the same person as my mother. I looked the other way too. I want to blame her for modeling such destructive behavior, but how can I? I didn't even know what was going on in our beautiful home with the view of the harbor. I knew what happened to me, but only as though it were a memory told by someone else.

My mom and I are alike, after all.

CHAPTER FORTY-FIVE

December 20
Rose

Like the students of today, the teacher's lounge has changed over the years. When I was student teaching in Olympia, the ratty couches smelled of cigarette smoke and coffee burned all day long in a Bunn carafe. A literal hot mess. At Marine View, we have a Nespresso machine and Febreze-fresh furniture from IKEA. One thing that hasn't changed, however, is the players. Different faces. Different names. Same people.

The instant I enter, the room falls silent, which tells me that the other teachers were talking about me. And the news that came out recently.

I spare them feigned embarrassment.

"I guess you all heard?"

"On the news, Rose," says Maureen Lockwood, who teaches fifth grade and dresses like a member of her own class. Today she's wearing her ironic graphic tee. It reads: "Graphic T." Skinny jeans and Converse sneakers complete her look.

"That nurse . . ." says Pete O'Hara, a stocky figure over by the creamer. "What a piece of work." Pete teaches fourth grade and coaches the morning intramural teams. He wears shorts every day. Even today, as clouds threaten snow.

"We're glad something's come of the investigation," I say.

"Give us the deets," says Maureen.

"Sorry," I tell her as I sweep my eyes over the others. "Police say we aren't supposed to talk about it."

Detective Hoffman never said anything of the kind.

Everyone looks disappointed, and I know the second I leave, they'll all say how they are worried about me or some such. I know how it goes. I make my coffee and return to my classroom.

Later that morning, Piper tells me her tummy hurts.

"Do you need to use the bathroom?"

She shakes her head.

The nurse isn't there that day. She only comes twice a week. I think about sending Piper to the principal's office, but that won't do any good. Her mom works in Tacoma.

"I don't want to go home," she tells me.

"All right," I say, reading her eyes and not liking what I see. "Let's see how it goes. Do you think you could sit in the reading cubby?"

Piper brightens. "Okay."

She doesn't want to go home.

That can mean a lot of things. Some kids love school. It's fun. It's where they get lunch. They have friends.

However, I know that's not the case with Piper.

The walls are closing in. I feel it. I suspect it's not her tummy at all. I suspect something far worse. Something familiar too.

Reporting an abuser is the first twist of a can opener on the proverbial can of worms. I find it impossible to separate my own experiences from others'. Women like me are delusional and cowardly. We have chosen to stay silent. We do that for many, many reasons. Some of us manage to find a way to blame the child—that it was all his or her fault. Some simply think that it will go away. Or if they tell anyone the truth, their marriage will be over. Or they think it is possible that their child made the whole thing up.

Piper reads a book, and I allow myself to believe she's feeling better. I scan the room and take in the rest of my students—those living closest to the water and those far down a rutted dirt road. Any one of them could be victimized by a stranger or a family member. As far as I can tell, however, only one of them is showing the signs.

I reach for the bottle of Xanax I keep in my desk drawer. I take two. I think for a second. And take another for good measure.

The rest of the day flies by. Before I know it, the kids are gone—including Piper. I sift through the Christmas cards and little gifts my students left on my desk. Six Starbucks gift cards. One for Nordstrom. A plethora of candy canes. Some chocolates too.

The one from Piper tugs at my heart.

It's a photo of her with a mall Santa. She looks so happy. Tears fill my eyes. On the back of the card, she's written a note in her distinctive printing—letters follow a path upward as they move across the paper.

I love you, Mrs. Hilliard. Don't forget about me.

—LOVE, PIPER

CHAPTER FORTY-SIX

After Everything Happened
Rose

I've started seeing a therapist and I'm not embarrassed about it. My girls don't agree, but I believe talking helps—especially when you have kept things inside for as long as I have. Ironic, I know, when a huge part of the rift between us was because I never wanted to talk when they did.

My counselor has been on the job longer than I served as a teacher by at least ten years. His name is Vance Henderson. He's in his sixties, with a bald pate and a brown curtain of hair that is so long, it looks like the fringe on the Western jacket that Richard once borrowed for a costume party—Wild Bill Hickok to my Annie Oakley. Vance, as he insists I call him, has an eager countenance. Everything I utter elicits such enthusiasm that I wonder if I'm saying something either crazy or insightful.

His office is stripped down in its décor, though that word itself is a bit of an overstatement. The desk looks government issue, same with the seating. Behind him is a framed photograph of the balloon festival in Albuquerque. How many others have pondered that image, thinking of its intended message? Rising to hope? Crash and burn?

I suspect it simply came with the office.

"Rose," he says, "how are we doing today?"

"*We* are fine," I answer as the scent of his licorice tea fills my nose. Inwardly, my eyes roll like a pair of dice. It is always "we."

He leans back in his office chair, the signal for me to start blathering about whatever subject he selects.

Today is all about my husband and the reason that I cannot accept that he left me.

"I've told you, Vance, already. I'm over it."

"But are you? Really?"

That's the less-than-helpful response that Vance should simply record and play like an Easy button.

"Rose?"

I give in. "All right. I'm not over it. I'm still angry. I just think that when Richard finally did leave me, it was the worst possible time. It made me look terrible to our family."

"What someone else does to move on with their own life doesn't always reflect on another party."

"You believe that, don't you?" I lob back, keeping my voice calm. "You haven't lived my life, Vance. Because I know without a shred of doubt that what another party does comes right back at you."

He folds his arms behind his head, and the motion moves the cowboy fringe of his hair.

"Again, the actions of others aren't your concern or responsibility," he tells me like it's some great truth. "You have to let go of all of that."

"I know," I say, giving in, because Vance has no idea what he's talking about.

We talk some more and the bell rings.

"I better get back now," I say.

"Next week?"

I nod. "Yes. It's really helping, Vance."

"That's why I'm here, Rose."

"Me too," I say as though I truly mean it, which I don't. I've learned that agreeing is the only way to survive.

Later that evening, I sit on my bed looking at the letters I keep to reread in hopes of finding something new. I've folded and unfolded the one Lily sent so many times that the paper threatens to break into thirds.

Mom,

If you are looking for forgiveness, you will have to wait. Maybe a super long time. I'm not saying that I'll never find a way to that point, but I don't see it in the stars anytime soon. You cannot understand what it was like growing up in our house of lies. What happened to my sister impacted me too. I watched Violet struggle when we were growing up. I heard her crying and vomiting and saying she didn't want to live. I didn't know for sure what was going on with her until a few months before the wedding when she took me to Tacoma for a meeting with other survivors. Doesn't that break your heart, Mom? Violet had to rely on strangers to help her!!! Do you even understand how that must have felt? That her own mother didn't do anything to stop Papa? Don't tell me you didn't know. Mom, you were never stupid. You were, however, a total fraud. A good mother would never have let Violet get abused like that. You knew. You always knew. Just writing this to you is making me angrier. One day I will try to find a way to come to better terms with everything. I just think that we need to pause our relationship until I do.

Your daughter,

Lily

I tried to call Lily when I first received the letter. By that time, she'd blocked me. I spoke to Violet about it, but she was at work and couldn't really talk. So now, I sit here on my bed and try to accept every word that Lily wrote. I deserve her anger. I do. Pleading that I didn't know about some things Violet did doesn't address the root cause. Or my role in it. I let my tears roll down my face without wiping them away. I don't deserve to dry them. Let them fall in a flood and drown me. I am not a monster. What I ignored, however, is something that can't be undone.

It seems there are no do-overs for bad mothers.

I make origami of the letter and press it to my lips. A kiss. I will survive long enough for Lily to see that I'm sorry. Repentant. Worthy of forgiveness.

I check the time. Time for work. Growing up with a mother who couldn't make anything that didn't come prepackaged, I always excelled at cooking.

❦

Tamale Pie Night is a favorite here—second only to Chow Mein Night, which requires three cases of those La Choy fried noodles. The girls love crunch. We follow a recipe that, despite being printed on a plastic card, is so stained from grease and tomato sauce that it's barely legible. Before I came to work in the prison kitchen, a girl misread the recipe and used four bottles of cayenne. I'm told the bathrooms were very busy that evening.

I give the task of making the corn bread to two other girls, and I have Sheila—who's in for raping a teenager with the handle of a fishing pole—help with the rest.

"My mom made something like this," she tells me, putting a hairnet over her salad bowl–styled haircut as she pours vegetable oil into the bottom of a huge stainless-steel pot. "Used Fritos corn chips for the topping instead of corn bread."

"Sounds good," I say. Of course, anything crispy and salty sounds good. The cost of such snacks is so steep at the commissary that few can afford them.

Sheila studies the recipe, then looks up.

"We need a ginormous can of black olives."

"We're out," I tell her.

"You're wrong," she insists, turning away from the pot to the walk-in pantry. "I saw some yesterday. I'll get them."

I take her by the shoulder, and she reacts by clenching her fist. "No. Please."

I'm agitated and angsty, and she knows it. She's good with teenagers, after all.

"You okay?"

"Can we just leave it alone?"

"What? The olives?"

"Yes. The whole subject."

"I don't get it."

My eyes are suddenly wet, but I will no tears to fall.

"Please."

She looks at me like she can read me. I'm not sure about Sheila. Her life choices have been terrible, or she wouldn't be here. I say nothing more, and she backs down.

"Olives are overrated," she finally says, stirring the big pot.

CHAPTER FORTY-SEVEN

December 24
Gig Harbor, Washington
Violet

Lots of talk about triggers these days.

It can be a word. An image. Even a particular smell.

In my case, it's Andy Williams's voice.

The singer's classic holiday tune plays in the background. I wholeheartedly disagree with the sentiment. It is not the most wonderful time of the year. At least, not in my parents' house, where we go through the motions of festiveness. Zach is a good sport. He accepts the strange pretense of this awkward family gathering with my father back in the fold. Dad says this time for good.

Right.

Rose, Nana, and Lily are in the kitchen with all burners and the oven going. The smell of a prime rib roast fills the air. Zach sits across from my father valiantly trying to be interested in the merits of tying your own flies. I know where this is headed, and I'm right. The two of them, drinks in hand, leave the living room to check out my father's fly cabinet in the garage.

We've all been there. My sister and I used to sit on a bench while Dad showed us the fur and feathers that were irresistible to the hungry mouths of trout and steelhead. Lily was always bored, but I didn't mind. I liked the idea of catching and releasing fish. I liked that my father didn't kill anything. A neighbor girl's father was a hunter, and it made me retch the time he had me come over and look at the dead bear in the back of his pickup.

"Do you guys eat that?" I asked.

"No. Gross. Daddy's making a bearskin rug out of it. The head and everything."

"That's so disgusting."

The girl disagreed. When I went home that afternoon and caught my parents yelling about something, I could only pick out the words that came from Rose's voice. Dad's voice was too low. Too deep. All I could hear was her saying he needed to stop.

Stop what?

I never knew.

※

I join my sister, Nana, and Rose in the kitchen. Lily is acting like it's a real treat to have a glass of wine, and Nana is scolding Rose for allowing it.

"Violet," Lily says, giving me a sheepish look, "I'm told we'll be ready to eat in a half hour."

Our mother could never get everything ready on time. Or at the same time. We always added an hour or two when it was a holiday to-do, like today. By the time we sit down, Dad will be drunk and Mom will be exhausted and cranky.

"I have two daughters," she'd say before slumping into a dining chair, "but zero help."

No joke. Rose liked control. She was a teacher during the day, helping kids learn new things. At home, though, she was an autocrat who pretended to welcome help but didn't trust anyone to get it right.

"I'll make up the relish tray," I tell her, getting a clean cutting board and pulling a knife from the wooden block by the stove.

Since the task merely involves slicing and arranging raw vegetables, Rose acquiesces to the offer. My sister and I go to work, listening to Nana and Rose talk about how difficult it is to find fresh chestnuts for the stuffing.

"Have they heard of the internet?" Lily asks.

"Guess not." I open the can of black olives that I brought along with a pumpkin pie from the Dahlia Bakery in downtown Seattle. "Rose, do you have any banana peppers for Dad?"

She looks over and sees the olives.

That look on her face! Weird!

"Uh, no, honey," she snaps as she turns away.

Lily

After a fairly drama-free Christmas Eve dinner, when everyone either has gone home or is drunk, I text Katie from my bed. I type while facing the mural my sister and I painted one spring when our parents were away on an Inside Passage cruise to Juneau. Its palm trees framing a scene in Hawaii, which we thought was a much better choice than Alaska as a destination. It's on the garish side. I told Mom to paint over it when I left for college, but I'm glad it's still there. It reminds me of a happier time.

Katie: How's Christmas Eve? Sucked here.

Me: Pretty much the same.

Katie: Remind me not to come back for spring break.

Me: Ditto.

Katie: I almost did it tonight.

Me: What?

Katie: You know.

Me: You didn't. Did you?

Katie: No. Just all those old feelings come up when I'm here.

Me: Yeah. I get it.

Katie: How's Violet?

Me: Good. Zach's good. Everyone is good. Really the same. If you consider that good. You know?

Katie: I think so. Thanks for being my friend, Lily.

Me: You might think differently when you get my bill.

Katie: Oh.

Me: Kidding. I'm beat. Talk later.

Katie: Night.

In that last-minute cleanup whirlwind earlier in the day, Mom relocated a bunch of her school stuff from the kitchen to my room, which I now figure is the storage room. I move everything off the end of the bed. The contents of one box catch my eye. Like the tropical mural, the laminated and comb-bound books her students made remind me of a good time. I pick through them. Always so interesting to see how children share the same artistic flourishes. Bold, thick lines, filled in with color. Big smiles on faces. Printing varies, but the tendency to seesaw over the lines is gone by the middle of the school year. More control. More self-awareness. Mom always said every kid enters a race when they come out of the womb. All begin at the same starting line. Any one of them could be something amazing and wonderful.

"If, and only if, they have the right circumstances in their family," she insisted one time. "Some don't. And, honey, that's the way life is sometimes. You can't lift everyone. I see my job as trying to give those lagging behind a boost while keeping the others from running as fast as they can."

Looking back, the irony is glaring.

Piper Beckman's face peers out at me from under the sheen of Office Depot's educator-discount lamination. She has big, sad eyes like one of those vintage Keanes in Violet's room.

Inside Piper's book are the same items as the others—spelling tests, drawings, and an about me. It's the "About Me" that brings me closer:

> I live with my mom and her friend. I had a cat. She ran away after I did something bad. I like chocolate pudding and Wheat Thin crackers. I have my own room, but sometimes Mom's friend stays overnight. I don't like that. I love Marine View, and Ms. Hilliard is the nicest friend I have.

I turn the page to a drawing of a girl, small as she can be, on the far side of a bed. She isn't smiling like other classmates in their about-me portraits. In fact, she wears a straight line, almost a frown. In the corner of the bedroom, she's colored what looks like a big green Christmas tree, which I think is weird. When I look closer, I can tell that she's made an alteration to her portrait. Colored over something. I would have asked for more paper. I hated messing up.

What did she draw first?

If the artwork hadn't been laminated, I would scratch off the green to see what's hidden underneath. Instead, I twist the gooseneck of my bedside lamp and shine the light through the page.

Sasquatch?

The figure under the green is large and would have loomed over the entire scene. So strange that Piper would cover that up. Kids that age love Bigfoot and dinosaurs. They wish both were available for adoption at Petco. When I was a little girl, I wanted a real unicorn.

As I'm closing the book, the air rushes out of the room.

It's right there. I see it. I can tell what Piper has tried to hide.

CHAPTER FORTY-EIGHT

December 25
Rose

Lily is already in the kitchen drinking coffee and flipping through the pages of *O* magazine. She looks lovely in the blue-and-white Lanz of Salzburg nightgown my mother bought for the girls. Women, now. I wonder if Violet wore hers last night. This is the first year I won't have a photograph of the two of them together in front of the tree on Christmas morning.

"Excited?"

"What?"

"About your presents?"

"I guess, Mom."

I turn on the oven for the strudel I made after everyone went to bed and pour myself a cup of coffee. I top off Lily's gargantuan Starbucks New York mug and start another pot. Richard is in the shower and will be out soon. We had sex last night, and, like every time now, I wonder if it is the last time I'll ever have sex. No pillow talk. Not even a kiss. For

Richard, I'm sure it was only a release or a means of inducing slumber. As if all the booze weren't enough.

Lily is quiet, and I'm not sure if I've done something wrong or she's just waking up.

"Honey," I ask. "What is it?"

"I was looking through your students' 'About Me' books before I went to bed."

"Seem familiar?"

"Yes. Very much, Mom."

Her words hang in the air.

"What's wrong?"

I hadn't noticed until now, but under the magazine is Piper Beckman's "About Me."

"Cute girl," I say. "Smart too."

"Tell me more about her."

Her interest scares me a little. I haven't done anything wrong.

She opens the book to Piper's drawing and points to the big tree.

I furrow my brow. "Christmas tree?"

Lily rotates the book so I can see it more clearly.

"She colored over something, Mom."

Her eyes stay fastened to mine.

"I thought it was a Sasquatch or a bear or something. It's not, Mom."

I fetch my reading glasses and try to see what my daughter sees.

"It's a man, Mom."

"It could be, I guess," I say.

"Look here, Mom."

It's hard to see through the plastic and under the green of the tree, but I see it.

A penis. An erect penis.

"No little girl is drawing something like that without having seen one. Look at how she's cowering in her own bed? Mom, someone is hurting her."

I don't let on that the thought has crossed my mind.

"Mom," Lily says, her voice becoming more urgent, "you've got to do something about this."

"I know."

"What are you going to do? What are you going to do to stop whatever is happening to that little girl?"

"Everything all right in here?"

Richard comes in like he always does, completely unaware. He acts like he cares, but that has been so spotty, I usually shut him out.

This time, I don't.

"I think one of my students might be being abused."

"Shit," he says. "That's terrible."

"Mom's going to take care of it, Dad," Lily says, then looks over at me. "You can count on that."

Violet

My phone pings just as we arrive at Zach's parents' house in Bellevue for Christmas morning. Manfred and Clarice live in a boxy, contemporary home perched above Lake Washington—it's a house that people who have claimed bankruptcy twice probably don't deserve. Manfred works as a banker, of all things. Clarice is a buyer for a regional chain of retail stores. Zach is their only child. He could have been spoiled and entitled.

Yet somehow, he's managed to take on none of his parents' ideas about money. He's frugal. Not cheap. He buys good things that last. He's ethical too.

I find my phone in the dark pit of my purse. The text is from my sister.

Lily: Need to talk.

Me: Not now. Just got here.

Lily: Serious. Now.

When we get inside, I make a beeline for the bathroom. I overhear Clarice ask Zach if I'm sick. Her tone is hopeful, like maybe she's hoping I'm pregnant. The woman has become relentless in her pursuit of grandchildren even though we've only been married six months—to which she always counters: *You've been together for more than two years.*

I sit on the toilet and answer Lily.

Me: What is it?

Lily: Mom has a kid in her class that's being abused. I don't trust her, Violet. I don't think she'll do anything. Should I call the police or what?

Me: Don't do that.

Lily: What, then? Call Ellie?

Me: It's Christmas Day.

Lily: Right. Getting raped is okay because it's Christmas.

Me: You know what I mean.

Lily: This is fucked up. You of all people. She's six. Want to be like that woman in the circle that didn't do a fucking thing? Just let it happen.

Me: Give me a minute. Send whatever you can find out about him.

When I return to the living room, Clarice is serving bacon-wrapped chestnuts.

"Zach's favorite," she says.

Zach gives me a sheepish grin and reaches for another. As much as I roll my eyes and tease him about his folks, I know that they are genuine in their affection for him.

They would never let him down. Every family has to deal with bullshit of one kind or another. In my family, the bullshit could overflow a landfill.

And send me to prison.

While Manfred opens a gift Zach and I got him—a pair of new-with-tags Prada sunglasses we got on eBay—Lily sends me information she gleaned from Mom's class roster and her students' emergency contacts. Piper is the girl's name. There are two numbers listed for her mother, work and home. I type the address into Google.

"Something to drink?" Zach asks.

I look up from my phone. "Whatever your mom is having, please."

"Spiked eggnog," he says, which he knows isn't my favorite. "Coming right up."

I look back at the results of my search, and I hold my breath while I scroll downward.

In addition to Piper's mother, another name is associated with the same address: Daniel Grayson.

I type the name into the registry.

There's only one Grayson.

Not Daniel.

Leonard Grayson.

Address is the same.

Rotten pervert, I think. Not supposed to use a different name. And not supposed to live in a household with a child.

Leonard Grayson, forty-two, was convicted twice of sexual abuse of a minor. I know that it is nearly impossible that figure reflects the true number of the crimes of a middle-aged offender. These guys are serial offenders. They hunt for victims they can manipulate into silence.

Zach brings the nog.

"Looks good."

"You gonna be on your phone all day?"

He's not mad, chiding me like that.

"Helping Lily with something," I tell him. "Just about done."

He rejoins his parents, and I search the internet to see what kind of media coverage there was on Grayson's cases. Very little. One small mention of Grayson being arrested for masturbating in his car in front of a Kitsap County park. The report didn't say "masturbating," of course. It said a "lewd" act upon his own person. A longer article, this time in the *Peninsula Gateway,* has his mug shot. He looks normal—clean and neat. His hair is cut. His face clean-shaven. Even the clothes he wears in the photo are crisp and fresh looking.

Like Mike Stone, he doesn't look like a slobbering cretin.

He's the guy next door.

A man Piper's mom might have thought was some kind of a catch—if she hadn't seen the headline:

Child Rape Charges for Key Penn Man

I read as fast as possible. Grayson was sentenced to three years after a plea deal that included undergoing psychiatric evaluations and some experimental treatments to stop behavioral proclivities. Experimental? I wonder if he was in the chemical castration program that had been hailed as a potential solution by some criminal justice advocates. Ellie and I talked about that over coffee one time. We both believed that shrinking a man's gonads into raisins might yield many worthwhile benefits, but it wouldn't necessarily stop the true driver of sexual violence—power over another person.

I text Lily.

Me: I'll take care of this.

Lily: How?

Me: I'll be in the harbor tomorrow.

CHAPTER FORTY-NINE

After Everything Happened
Rose

My prison counselor, Vance, can't be trusted. No one here can. Girls are always looking for a way to gain something, and besides drugs and sex, nothing trades at a higher value than information. There's no risk involved with information. No contraband to send you to the hole.

I have nothing to offer the traders of secrets. That's one of the benefits of pleading guilty to a crime. No one here has anything to hang over you. You do your time. Stay away from the girls you know are trouble. Never be dismissive of them, of course. Be firm.

I pled guilty because I was. Not for the murder of Piper's tormentor but because I'd let my own daughter think that I didn't believe her. It was even worse than that. I decided my own shame over what had happened to me was more important than the abuse she was experiencing. I forgave my mother. I thought my girls would forgive me too. The times are different today. I realize that now. My mother couldn't even say the word "sex," let alone deal with the very idea of a grown man forcing himself on a child. She was a product of her time, and I misguidedly—stupidly—adopted her way of coping. She was twenty-five years out of step with a changing world. If it seems like I'm blaming her, I'm sorry. I blame myself.

Vance leans back, removes his glasses, and wipes off greasy residue left by his fingertips.

"Rose," he says, slipping his glasses back on, "I understand that you've been tutoring some of the incarcerated here. How's that going?"

"Fine," I answer. I don't tell him that, as a schoolteacher for almost three decades, I cannot for the life of me figure out how our system allowed so many to slip through the cracks. Kitty, who has started working with me in the kitchen, has the reading ability of a fifth grader. She's one of the smarter ones too.

"How does it make you feel when you're teaching here?"

How I feel all the time is hopeless and full of self-loathing.

"Being able to help some of the girls brings me purpose, Vance," I say, giving him what he wants. "And I'm grateful. It makes the time I'm serving of value."

"Wonderful," he says, looking through his notes. "Now, we haven't talked about the reason you're here at WCCW."

"No." My body tightens. I put my hands under my thighs to keep them steady, out of view.

"We don't have to, you know. It is up to you. All of this is up to you, Rose."

Suddenly I want to laugh out loud. I'm in a place where nothing is up to me. I'm parked here like a used car, kept clean, rolled out into the yard with the others, and brought back inside. I have no control over anything.

"If you think it will help," I say.

He nods. "You killed Mr. Grayson."

"You know I did. I said as much."

He gives me a sympathetic look. "Right. I want you to take me through what you did. You don't have to, of course, but it has been my experience that this kind of therapy will be beneficial as you chart the rest of your life."

He makes it sound as if I'm embarking on a cruise.

I tell him anyway.

⚓

The day after Christmas, Lily and I drove to the mall in Tacoma. She had a sweater that didn't fit properly, and she wanted to return it. I never returned anything if it had been given as a gift. If I hated the sweater, I simply didn't wear it often.

My mother insisted it was bad manners to return things given as a gesture of love.

"It's like telling the giver that you don't care one thing about them. All you care about is you. Put on the jacket that your aunt gave you and wear it with a big smile. That's the nice thing to do. We are nice people."

The entire way there, Lily harangued me about calling CPS on Piper's behalf. She told me that I had been a terrible mother to let what happened to her sister happen and that she was glad Papa was dead. She wished that he'd died sooner and suffered more. Anything I offered as an excuse, or an apology, was met with a harsh and swift attack.

"You can't do anything for Violet, Mom. Can't erase what happened. You can't save your marriage. You have to do something for the girl in your class."

I admitted that I'd made mistakes. She wouldn't listen. It was painful. My hands sweated on the steering wheel. My jaw was clenched so tightly that I thought I'd crack a tooth. And truthfully, I wanted to slap her. Hard. She had no idea how heavy the burden of my lies had been. I did my best to shield both my girls. I really did. And now, Lily was like a feral cat that I thought had been tamed.

And I was her scratching post.

"The law says you have to report child abuse, Mom."

"I'm not sure if that's what's going on."

"It doesn't matter. You don't have to be sure. You can just do it."

I stop talking, and Vance takes a break from his incessant note-taking.

"Go on," he says.

"So, I waited in the car while she went inside Nordstrom, and I knew she was right."

"Is that when you searched Leonard Grayson's name and found your way to the sex offender registry?"

"After that, but yes. I did eventually find that information."

"All right. Go on."

I tell him how I decided to go check on Piper.

"To be sure she was all right. Nothing more."

"Why did you bring a knife, then?"

I don't have a good answer for that. I never have. It's a piece of the puzzle that must be shoved into its ill-fitting spot.

"I don't know. I just did."

He writes something down, and I do my best to read it, but his fish-and-chips lunch has spotted the page with grease, and I can't make out what it says. I know it's a judgment that he's going to share with the superintendent later.

"Grayson answered the door wearing a white undershirt and faded Levi's. He was handsome, but I knew that the beautiful skin and his even white teeth were camouflage. I'd read his profile on the registry. I knew what he had done."

"And then what happened?"

"I said that I had something for Piper, and he said that she was napping. That bothered me. Piper was too old for a nap. I didn't challenge him on it. Instead, I handed him a candy cane to give to her when she woke up."

I take a breath. "This is the hard part, Vance. It happened so fast that I find it difficult to describe in exactly the right sequence."

"Fine," he goes on, pen poised for some more scribbling in his little book. "Nothing can be retrieved from the mind exactly as it happened.

You can only see from your eyes, your perspective. That doesn't allow for one hundred percent accuracy."

"Right. I told him that he wasn't supposed to be alone with a child."

"Then what, Rose?"

I close my eyes to try to picture how it all played out.

✳

Grayson took a step backward.

"What are you talking about?" he asked me, his eyes marked by confusion.

"I know who you are and what you've done, and I'm going to go back to my car and call the police. I'm going to wait here until they come."

Then he grabbed my wrist with his grotesquely soft, smooth, doll-like hands.

"You will not be calling anyone," he said. "I'm not that man anymore. I've been cured."

✳

I don't disclose the next part. I don't because none of this really happened that way. The phrase about being fixed was something Lily told me when she talked about the support group her sister had taken her to before the wedding. She told me how all the women there had suffered horrendous abuse by family members, boyfriends, neighbors. How the men who'd hurt them had been sent to prison or to counseling and that neither approach solved the problem.

"Mom," she said to me, "these creepers can't be fixed."

I think about how when I was seven, my father went away on a two-month business trip. It was sudden and strange. He looked so upset and sad that it didn't seem like he really wanted to go. Mom was the one who called a cab and set his bags out. He hugged me goodbye and said he'd be back soon.

"Better than ever," he said.

Later, when I was older, I knew it hadn't been a business trip that my father had been on, and I figured that he'd gone to rehab, because Mom left me with her sister on the weekends so she could see Dad. I asked her about it one time. When I look back now, I know that it was the closest thing to the truth ever spoken between us.

"No, he wasn't on a business trip, Rose," my mother told me. "He had a problem that needed to be fixed."

"What problem?"

"I don't want to say it. I don't think it is good to relive every little ugly or give voice to each of the rotten things that has been visited upon us."

I was fifteen, almost sixteen, at the time. Dad was teaching me how to drive a stick. When he touched my hand to guide me into the gears, a vague feeling came that reminded me of something from the earliest parts of my memory.

"What had to be fixed, Mom?"

"You know, Rose. Now let's drop it."

Her tone was hard and final.

I knew.

"I reached into my purse for my phone," I say to Vance. "Instead, my fingers somehow found the knife."

"And then what?"

"And then it happened. Like I said in court, like you can read in all my paperwork. I stabbed him."

"Seventeen times," he says, as though the number means something. Stabbed is stabbed.

"If you say so," I answer. "I wasn't counting. I was out of my mind. Terrified. Traumatized. I stabbed him many times, yes. And I ran out of there as fast as I could. I barely remember driving home."

"What were you thinking?"

"That's just the thing. I wasn't. Not really. I was reacting. I was fleeing the scene and trying to make sense of what I'd done. I was a first-grade schoolteacher. I wasn't a violent person. I told the court that I snapped."

"You cleaned the blood from your car."

"As much as I could. As you know, I missed some."

"Right. You left the knife behind."

"Yes. Though I don't remember that part. As I said, it happened so fast, my memory didn't capture it all."

He scribbles some more. I look at the clock. Only a few more minutes. I hope that this is the last time I'm required to revisit that story. I think of the headlines and how they have been fused to my memories.

Teacher questioned in slaying

That was the first one. I was alone when I read it online. Detective Hoffman and some other detective I didn't know had come to the house a couple days after Grayson was murdered. My car was photographed by Grayson's security system—ostensibly, they said, used as a game camera. Mr. Grayson liked to hunt with a crossbow and, according to neighbors, was known to hunt in his own yard.

The Schoolteacher and the Sex Offender

That one was an attempt by *Seattle Magazine* to do an in-depth piece that would give its readers *Vanity Fair* vibes. The writer was no Maureen Orth, that's for sure. And my life and Grayson's life were far, far from Dominick Dunne territory.

Friends recall teacher's 'peculiar' behavior

I didn't expect this kind of story. I had thought that I'd lived—at least to the outside world—a decent, even exemplary life. I'd tried to. Apparently, once one is accused of murder, your life gets a thorough reexamination as everyone you knew takes but a breath before reassessing everything you did. Teachers at Marine View were mostly silent. That hurt. If I was anything, I was a good teacher. I cared about all of the kids in the class.

"She had a way of classifying the potential of her students," said one teacher, who didn't want to be named. "I thought it was a little mean. I can't say if that was her intent. Otherwise, I think she did a good job here at Marine View."

All my years teaching had been boiled down to doing a good job, with my former colleague's little mean caveat tacked on as though my life could be assessed like a Yelp review.

Plea deal for vigilante Rose Hilliard

My lawyer said by pleading I'd avoid the risk of something going haywire in a jury trial. Even though Grayson was a convicted sex offender, and so as far as victims go, he was deep in the dark bottom of the basket of undesirables. It was still risky. I felt I could survive a sentence mitigated by the compulsion to protect a little girl from the worst kind of a predator. Lily and I had watched *Orange Is the New Black*. With good behavior, I could be out in half my sentence. Knowing that was a comfort. If I could stay off the radar like the women who move about the background of each shot on the Netflix series, then I'd be fine.

"Time's up for the day," Vance says.

I stand and start to say something but think better of it.

"Are you all right?"

I come out of it. "Yeah. I'm fine."

I will never be fine.

CHAPTER FIFTY

January 3
Seattle, Washington
Violet

I have a sixth sense. I understand the ebb and flow of the energy of emotion. Most abuse victims are that way. We can spot another one of us in a crowd. We also pick up the energy of pretense because we have perfected our own.

Maria saunters into work in a gorgeous new outfit.

"Wow," I say. "You look amazing."

She gives me a smile. "One of the advantages of being single. I can get myself the Christmas present I want. Wait until you see me tomorrow."

"Already waiting," I say.

Maria laughs and sets down a new handbag. I compliment that too. She drinks it all in, of course. She has a need to show the world that she's made it. I understand. And I don't mind being her cheer squad.

"You?" she asks. "How'd you make out?"

"Zach is more of the 'let's give experiences instead of tangible gifts' kind of guy. We made plans to buy a boat."

She gives me an exaggerated side-eye.

"I know. It seems like buying a boat is a gray area in the scheme of things."

"Hey," she says, changing the subject. "Heard about that murder in Gig Harbor. A sex offender. Just like the freak in Yakima."

I think quickly about how to respond. I'm unsure about Maria. Is she dangling suspicion or merely pointing out a coincidence?

"Yeah, that was pretty messed up," I say.

Maria nods. "News said his girlfriend's kid was at Marine View. Isn't that where your mom teaches?"

Suspicion. That's what she's dangling.

"Right," I answer, reaching for my phone. "Mom told me that. Got to take this."

Lily

Katie and I meander over to the Coug to get coffee. She returned to campus early too. Family drama. She talks about not wanting to go home again, and I tell her that I feel the same way. Our boots leave deep tracks on the not-quite fully trampled snow.

"College is always promoted to help us be independent," she says, puffs of white coming out as she speaks.

"I think it's more like to help us escape."

She agrees. "The weird thing about that is that only once you're away from home do you fully understand the magnitude of the harm that's been done to you."

I can't even think of all that I'm feeling—and hiding. I think that's the one thing that I've learned most from living in a family that pays attention to the trivial but ignores the things that really matter. Good grades, so important. Child rape, not so much. That's my take on things now.

That same cute boy from the Bookie holds the door to the Coug open. I give him a quick smile of encouragement as we go inside. He smiles back. I know that my smile is a fraud, not because I don't think I might like him but because of what I'm hiding. I wonder if his is fake too.

Later, I head for the computers in the Holland Library. I can't use my phone to look up things. I can't use my laptop. I'm clearly in paranoid mode.

Violet didn't want us to bring our cell phones the night she stabbed Grayson. Violet told me to turn on my phone in my dorm room.

Cell towers record locations.

Computers record keystrokes.

No log-on is required on university library PCs. Students are free to view whatever they want without any fear of judgment or reprisal. Or arrest. Porn is discouraged, however. So are alt-right sites. Everything else is a few clicks away.

I search for Michael Stone in Yakima. I read about the unsolved murder of a man who—by the latest count—had molested and raped sixteen boys. One of the mothers of a boy who had been in and out of rehab since being abused said that whoever killed Stone should be lauded, not arrested.

> "The night after I learned Stone had been murdered was the first time I had a good night's sleep for the first time in ten years. I don't care if it was a drug deal that went wrong or what, I'll call Stone's murder a blessing from God for the rest of my life."

Violet was a hero.

I had been nothing but a bystander.

I look up the Grayson murder, and there is only the mention that it's being investigated as a homicide. Nothing more.

When I get back to the dorm, I call Mom. My head is spinning. I suppose I've been traumatized by what happened. Who wouldn't be?

"Why didn't you believe her?" I ask right away.

"On some level, I always believed her."

"Did Dad know?"

"No. I thought I could fix it on my own, and I figured your father would blame me."

"Did Nana know?"

"Yes."

The admission stuns me. "She *did?*"

"I told her that I'd never allow your grandfather to be alone with either of you girls. Ever. She agreed."

"So, I guess what you're saying is Papa was more important to you than Violet?"

"It wasn't that simple, Lily."

"Then why? I need to understand how it was that you didn't do more."

"I did what I could manage."

"You fucking failed, Mom. You destroyed her. Look at what she did. How are you going to live with that, Mom?"

The line stays quiet.

"I know, Lily, I have a lot to answer for."

"You fucking got that right."

"Please, honey. Forgive me," she says before dropping the words that will never make sense to me. "Violet has."

"Bullshit. That's a survival game she's playing with herself. I don't have to play that game, Mom. I won't. Not ever."

"Don't talk like that, please."

Her voice is ragged, choked with emotion. It feels good to me. It feels like a payback that I didn't know I could even make. I hang up and call Violet.

"Mom says you've forgiven her," I say right out of the gate.

"I'm trying to."

"Why in the fuck would you forgive her?"

A long silence fills my ear.

"You still there, Violet?"

"Yeah. I am. I forgive her because she's a victim too."

"Victim of what?"

"Papa."

"I don't get it," I say. "What do you mean?"

"The same thing he did to me he did to her."

I think back on the woman in the support group, the one who was received with such coolness because she'd let her mother's boyfriend molest her brother. I had felt sorry for her. Now, not so much. She'd made a choice.

I can make a choice.

"That bitch," I say. "I fucking hate her."

Violet does her best to calm me. She points out that the world has changed, and society accepts that the cycle of abuse can only be broken by direct action.

Call the police.

Tell a grown-up.

Kill the abuser.

"It's easy to hate Rose," Violet says. "I go back and forth on it. I think what I did that night in Gig Harbor and in Yakima was necessary and right. I'm not sorry I killed those perverts. Vengeance was my motivator. Forgiving Rose is my way of stopping the anger."

"I won't ever forgive her."

"You don't have to. No one should tell you how to feel. Or who you can trust."

"You really trust her?"

"I do. I think, in the end, forgiving will save me."

CHAPTER FIFTY-ONE

December 26
Gig Harbor, Washington
Rose

Violet dried her hair, and I sat alone at the table listening to the tumbling sound of the clothes drier thinking of what to do, thinking of what to say. Richard texted, and I texted back to tell him the girls and I were having a movie night and he ought to stay at Shondra's. I'd tell him later that Lily and I had a fight and she went back to school early.

Richard: What will Lily think?

Me: About what?

Richard: Me not coming home tonight?

Me: She knows our reunion was temporary.

Richard: Oh.

Me: Bye.

The teakettle whistled, and I slid it from the red-hot burner just as Violet, dressed, returned. She was wearing one of my now too-small outfits that I'd set out for her. A white sweater and black jeans. She looked better than I ever did. I knew this was the opportunity for my reckoning.

But I was so ashamed.

"You need to leave now," I said.

"I'm not leaving you with this mess."

"I can handle this," I told her. "You go. Zach's going to be worried."

"Mom," she said. "I'm not sorry for what I did."

I take that in. From the moment I'd laid eyes on her in the delivery room at Tacoma General, she was the most precious thing in my life. A perfect little baby. She even smelled wonderful, a scent that I still remembered. When she looked up at me with big blue eyes that would never change color, I knew that nothing would compete with that moment.

Right now, Violet's blue eyes were red. Her skin, blotchy. She had the haunted look of an addict.

All of which I owned.

"I've got this handled, honey. But before you go, I need to tell you something."

✳

The front door shut, and I heard Violet's shoes crunch the gravel of the path to the driveway. I watched from an opening in the drapes. She was walking fast, wanting to get away from me as quickly as she can. I didn't blame her. How could I? Her car started, and she punched the accelerator like she was leaving the scene of a crime—which, admittedly, wasn't all that far off. The lights of the Christmas tree streaked like falling rain through the tears in my eyes as I watched her leave. My heart was beating so fast that I was all but certain I would die. And if I did, my girls would be better off for it.

I gathered up Violet's and Lily's bloody clothes and wadded them into a small kitchen garbage bag. Gig Harbor has always been the proverbial small town that rolls up its sidewalks at seven p.m. In the darkness of winter, it might even be sooner. I walked down Sound View to the harbor, chilly air blasting my face and drying my tears. My head swiveled right and left with each step.

Will someone walking a dog stop me? Will I run into someone I know?

A pickup truck passed, and I followed the smear of red from its taillights down the hill to the parking lot of a strip mall.

A single car sat in the hazily illuminated lot, engine running, windows opaque with condensation. I kept moving, the bag of cold, wet clothes pressed against my chest like a baby. I thought better of tossing it into the harbor. My idea had been to weigh down the bag with a heavy rock. I abandoned that plan. There were no rocks along the water, and the bag could become undone from its makeshift anchor.

The dumpster behind a Japanese steak house was my default destination. I lifted the lid and dumped the bag inside, on top of a chaotic nest of vegetable trimmings and holiday gift wrapping, the remains of a family's celebration. Right. It was Christmastime. Not my mother's favorite holiday anymore.

And now, certainly not mine.

Back at the house, I packed the tree ornaments, wrapping each in tissue paper that had been used so often it felt like chamois. I lingered on a few—the ones the girls made when they were small. Popsicle sticks wrapped in thick red and green yarn, glittery pine cones, little plastic globes filled with fake snow and a school portrait—all were precious to me those many years ago. Even more so at that moment.

Chapter Fifty-Two

December 26
Violet

After Lily drove off with a dazed look in her eyes, Rose asked me to stay. *To talk.* Before she said a single word, she started sobbing. When the words came, they fell out of her mouth one at a time. She left me to piece them together.

"This is all my fault, Violet," she said.

I held her. I wanted her to know that the part she'd played in setting everything in motion was small.

"I own what I did," I said. I felt fierce and invincible. Stabbing Stone had scared me a little, but killing Grayson had been different. It wasn't euphoria, although there was kind of a buzz running through my body as I watched him stagger and melt to the floor.

"You wouldn't have done what you did if I had been a good mother."

I eased her into a chair. She seemed to shrink before my eyes. A suddenly tiny, rolled-up version of my mother, Rose Hilliard.

"Even though you didn't believe me, once I told you, it stopped," I said. "How could you have known before then? Papa only touched me when we were alone. And that never happened again. That was your doing, wasn't it?"

She tightened her frame and rocked back and forth in the chair. I dropped to my knees and wrapped my arms around her.

She stayed quiet.

We both did.

Finally, she spoke. "He did it to me too, Violet."

The admission came at such force, a blast, I couldn't breathe.

"What?"

"I'm so sorry, honey. I didn't . . ." She shut down. Rose could be like that when trying to tell a difficult story, finding herself unable to retrieve the appropriate words.

I loosened my grip on her and stood up. "Didn't what?"

"Didn't think he'd ever do it again."

The unexpected charge that I'd gotten from stopping Grayson had been yanked away from me.

"He didn't after I told you."

She didn't say anything else for the longest time. The schoolhouse clock on the mantel ticked. The drier down the hall tumbled. Wind scraped a vine maple's naked branches against the living room window.

"I'm talking about *before*. Before you, he molested me. He molested me when I was a girl."

I took in the room as if I were standing in a foreign place and needed to get my bearings.

I heard her. I understood. Yet, I asked for clarification.

"What are you saying?"

My mother could handle a class of twenty squirming, noisy, out-of-control kids. She couldn't handle herself just then.

Neither could I.

She started wailing. "Papa did it to me too. I let him in this house! And look what he did to you. Look what has happened. To you. To all of us. I'm so sorry."

My tears dripped hot on my cheeks. My throat closed so tightly, I had to cough out my words.

"Then why? Why did you leave us alone at all?"

She was mute, thinking. "Don't have a good answer. I thought that he stopped doing things like that. I really did."

Shock suddenly became rage. Everything around me became a blur. If I had that knife in my hand, God help me, I would have cut her.

"Fuck you, Rose. Fuck Papa. You let him get away with it. Like I was nothing to you. How could you? How do you sleep at night?" I grabbed my purse off the table by the Christmas tree and went for the door.

"Does Dad know?"

Her look told me he didn't.

She was the only one.

"I made a terrible mistake," she said.

"A mistake?" I spat at her. "That's what you call it?"

"Sorry. I'm so sorry."

The words were all wrong. They didn't, *couldn't*, even scrape the edges of the magnitude of what she'd done to me. It was like running over some kid's dog and telling him not to worry.

That he could get another dog.

Everything will be all right.

Then I let her have it. I picked words that would sicken her.

"Are you serious? He raped me! He stuck his nicotine-stained fingers inside me. He made me suck his cock until he came in my mouth. He fucking made me scared inside every relationship I've ever had. He made me doubt myself. So did you. You knew what he was capable of this whole time? Well, then, fuck you!"

"I'll make it up to you, Violet. I promise."

Promise? I was so done with her.

Her arms flailing to stop me, I pushed her away and I slammed the door. It hit the frame so hard, it sounded like a gunshot.

A bomb.

I wish it had been.

My mother, my betrayer, had kept a secret all those years.

Which, to my way of thinking just then, was the same thing as telling a big, fat lie.

I don't know how I made it home that night. I was so angry and distraught as I drove over the Narrows from the Peninsula to Tacoma, I thought of ramming my car into the bridge guardrail. My hands hurt as I tightened my fingers on the wheel, fighting the urge to crash and tumble over the edge.

I was over the edge.

I could have killed Rose. At least throttled her for her weak, pathetic apology. I'd killed Stone and Grayson for the side of right. I was a blooming flower, or maybe a snake shedding its skin. Changed. I was stomping a boot on the cycle of abuse. Ending those men. Freeing others just like me. To try to reconcile that with my mother's fucked-up nothingness was futile. She was the opposite of me. She had purposely locked away critical information and perpetuated an evil.

There could be no denying she did it to save herself. Plain and simple as that. In doing so, she'd sacrificed another little girl.

Me.

CHAPTER FIFTY-THREE

After Everything Happened
Rose

In prison, waking hours are consumed by revisiting the past. I'm sure some girls think about where they went wrong, the fatal mistake they made. I'm the opposite. I think about what I did right. I play back the last conversation with Violet in the living room the night of Grayson's murder. The anger she aimed at me was soul-crushing.

And completely deserved.

I lie atop my blue bedspread and close my eyes. The sounds of my unit float through the air. The girls across the hall, both in for drug trafficking, are talking about a letter one received that afternoon from her boyfriend. Not a happy letter. A corrections officer is bragging about her ski boat. Again. I hear the girl pushing a squeaky-wheeled cart with the usual spate offerings of self-help and hobbyist books.

No crime. True or otherwise.

Plenty on crocheting and gardening.

I revisit my arrest.

◆

Detective Hoffman was at the front door three days after the murder. He was as handsome as ever. Any idiotic thought that I had about him evaporated the night my girls killed Piper's attacker. He wasn't alone; a woman he introduced as Detective Carol Smith stood right behind him. She was about Violet's age but with an impassive face that didn't betray any emotion.

"We're here with a search warrant, Ms. Hilliard."

He used to call me by my first name.

I skimmed the paper.

"Car is in the garage."

I directed them through the kitchen to the door to the garage.

A minute later, maybe two, I heard Detective Smith's voice.

"Blood. Passenger's side."

Then Detective Hoffman's. "Tech's on the way."

The rest of that day was ill-fitting pieces to a puzzle that I'd created with every mistake I'd ever made. Grayson's security camera had recorded my car at the murder scene. The plates were blurred, and it took the forensic lab in Olympia to decipher the last three digits. Other teachers, former friends, said they were worried about me. *Really?* None had said so to me. Richard said I'd been acting strangely ever since my father died. *Maybe I am?* My life had been upended, and things that I didn't want to think about wouldn't go away. My own mother said mental illness could be a factor.

Later, my lawyer told me that the detectives' interviews with my girls yielded little for the prosecution. That was the saving grace. They weren't in Gig Harbor when it happened. Both said, however, that I had talked about Piper at Christmas and had promised I would do something to help her.

That something, both suggested, was that visit to Grayson's place with the knife.

The only one who thought I might not have killed anyone was Hoffman.

When the jailers brought me to court for sentencing, the detective and I met one last time. It was in the corridor outside the courtroom. I thought he'd keep going, not really looking at me, the way people avert their eyes from the homeless. Instead, he planted his feet.

"One thing bothers me," he said.

"What's that?"

"Blood on the passenger side."

"Oh?"

"How did it get there?"

I repeated the answer I provided when he and Detective Smith mentioned it. "I threw my coat over on that side of the car."

"As you know, we never found that coat."

We were toe to toe then. "You took ten coats and jackets from the house."

His stare was unblinking. Either he was no longer trying to charm me, or I was immune to such things now.

"Right, but none had a single spot of blood."

Of course, I hadn't told him about the dumpster behind the Japanese restaurant. Violet's and Lily's bloody clothes were likely still there. If the police recovered them, my daughter would be put away. Maybe both of them. I couldn't let that happen.

"Luminal lit up the passenger side of the car like fireworks over the Commencement Bay on the Fourth of July."

"So you've said."

"Seems remarkable that no blood was found on any items of clothing in your house. And certainly not any coat."

"Sounds like a real mystery."

The jailer with bad breath tugged on my shoulder. "Got to go."

I gave Hoffman one final look. Maybe he knew the truth and let it slide. Maybe he would do the same thing for his daughter. I know from letters from strangers that flood my cell that, as brutal as Grayson's murder was, no one wanted to lock me up and throw away the key.

They thanked me, lauded me.

For something I didn't do.

CHAPTER FIFTY-FOUR

After Everything Happened
Violet

Rose insists court-ordered therapy with her prison counselor is helping. I hope so. She has a lot to process. We all do. She keeps asking me to come for a family counseling session, but I keep putting it off. I have a life separate from her. Separate from everyone but Zach and Lily.

Lily.

She alone is the reason I'd ask God for a do-over of what happened that night. It is all I would ask for, because to erase everything Papa did to me and what I'd done to Mike Stone would eliminate the good I'd done for others like me.

It is in my head, locked tight.

It is always there, just below the surface.

I just have to close my eyes and I see it.

I was a Rorschach of blood when Lily and I sped from Grayson's place. I let her drive. She barely said a word the whole way home. I did all the talking, filling up the space between us with a rambling dissertation on why I'd done what I'd done. The heater blasted me, and the drying blood crackled and pulled at the skin on my forearm.

"We freed that girl," I said. "We did what had to be done, and it felt good. After all the fucking things he's done to little girls over a lifetime, he thought he was invincible. Like the sickness that could never be cured was a shield. Delusional. Fucked up. Dangerous."

My mouth ran. I told Lily about Stone in Yakima, Faraday in Hawaii. How I'd learned that letting these men go on only served to continue the disease. They were a virus infecting the children they touched.

"Some victims will be predators," I went on in a kind of stream of consciousness that kept her rapt and my lips moving. "Some will be fucked up for the rest of their lives, afraid to love and trust. Some won't even know they are fucked up until it comes back to them in a fever dream that loops continuously."

Even with Lily's silence, her eyes fixed on the road and not in my direction, I could tell she understood every word I was saying. I didn't need a response. She knew from what had happened to me how the act of an abuser—sexual, physical, emotional—leaves an indelible mark on its target. It implants a GPS code that leads a life where it tells it to go. To keep secrets. To never reveal too much about what was done to you because, by doing so, it only invites another abuser to step in. Not always sexual, of course. Some abusers are those who listen and pretend to understand.

"No one can understand. Not even you. Not completely. You know that, right?"

She was crying.

"This is going to be all right, Lily."

Mom wasn't home when we arrived back at the house. She was on a walk. Dad, who'd left before breakfast that morning, was probably back fucking Shondra under her fake Christmas tree. I'd bet money on that one. On Christmas Eve, I'd gone into the master bathroom looking for some Advil, and noticed Dad was still using his black leather shaving kit. He hadn't really unpacked. His place at the table on Christmas was likely just another example of the way our family dealt with reality.

I calmly instructed Lily to open the passenger door. The less I actually touched, the better.

"Easier cleanup," I added.

Still quiet, I followed Lily to the side door that led inside from the garage.

"Get me some newspapers."

She did what I asked and retrieved them from the recycling bin.

"I need you to spread them out so I can undress on top of them."

"Okay," Lily said.

She had spoken. Finally. Good, I thought. That meant she was taking this in and was fine with it. I knew she would be. Sisters know things about each other. We share a bond that can never be undone. What happened had been a secret of the highest order. One I hoped, after it was over, we'd never mention again.

I'd lock it inside. So would she.

Our family was adept at that.

CHAPTER FIFTY-FIVE

After Everything Happened
Lily

The gummies from We're Just Buds on Bishop Boulevard are kicking in nicely. I've been overdoing the cannabis lately, so I'm trying to leave that indulgence for weekends only. From my bed, I watch as rain licks the windowpane. Stormy weather almost always fits my mood.

Violet texted me last night about Mom's continued plea for family counseling. What a joke. For one thing, we were never a family. I don't know how my sister can forgive her. I can't and I won't. Counseling? Seriously messed up. I don't need to go over things that happened the day after Christmas.

I remember it all.

Buzzed or drunk or some combination of the two, I will always remember.

When we got to Grayson's house, Violet told me to wait in the car.

"Mom doesn't have the guts to do this." She opened the door and faced me head-on. "But I do."

Now, when I look back on that exchange, Violet's words take on a different meaning. I thought she wanted to go see Grayson to just talk with him. Threaten him. The knife was only for show. I thought she was going to tell him that he'd better get as far away from Piper and Gig Harbor as possible. I realize now how stupid that might sound to someone—like a nosy counselor—now.

My sister was working from a completely different reality.

My first clue should have been that Violet told me not to bring my phone.

"We don't want any interruptions."

I told her that I could put my settings on silent.

She wouldn't budge. "No, we need to focus. No distractions."

I remained in the car, listening to the radio and thinking how boring life was without a phone. Ten minutes later, I caught sight of Violet winding her way up the walkway. The parking lights were dim, so I couldn't really see her face.

"Open the door, Lily," she said. *Commanded*, I think now. Her voice was lower than normal, and white puffs of warm air escaped her mouth with each syllable.

"It's not locked."

"Get out of the car and come open it from the outside."

I didn't get what she was talking about.

"Now, Lily."

As I opened the door, the dome light illuminated the black coat she was wearing. Blood spatter covered the front like a shiny appliqué. Droplets of red mottled her face and hair. Her bare hands looked as if she'd put on red gloves.

My heart nearly exploded.

"Holy fuck, what happened?"

She ignored me. "You're going to drive."

"Are you all right? You're bleeding. We have to get you to a hospital."

She got in the car. "Now shut the door."

I did as she asked—*commanded again*—and got behind the wheel.

"Just drive."

"St. Anthony's?"

"Home. Right now. I'm fine, Lily. He's not."

"What did you do?"

"I cut out the cancer."

I stayed quiet the rest of the way. I wondered how doing the right thing meant going off somewhere to kill someone. In my silence, I knew what Violet had intended from the minute I texted her. My sister and I grew up in the same house. Yet we were nothing alike because Papa never touched me the way he touched her. It poisoned her. Changed her. Maybe modified her DNA. She wasn't acting on a compulsion for which she had no control. She'd been rational. She'd planned it.

She didn't want us to bring our phones.

Cell towers recorded user locations.

She said we'd need to mix bleach in water to clean the car.

We both stared straight ahead as she talked about what she'd done on her honeymoon and during a work meeting in Yakima. It was a flood of information—little pieces that neatly fit into a puzzle I hadn't even known that I'd been putting together. How Violet had changed. How she looked. I just nodded. My heart was thumping so hard that I thought I might have a heart attack. I wished I would.

It would save me from whatever was going to happen next.

CHAPTER FIFTY-SIX

December 26
Rose

As soon as the door to the garage rumbled open, I saw Lily kneeling next to the passenger door of the car. Beside her was an orange Home Depot bucket—of something. In her hand was what appeared to be a pink cloth. My nose filled with the scent of bleach.

"Close the door, Mom!"

Terror filled her eyes.

"What's going on?"

"Shut the door!"

I pushed the button as though I'd been gored with a spear. My stomach dropped. Adrenaline pumped through my body. My brain raced.

"Were you in an accident? Where's Violet?"

Lily wrung out the rag she'd been using. "She's fine. In the shower now."

The water in the bucket was tinted red. The cloth was not a pink one but white and stained with red.

"What's going on?"

My youngest daughter kept cleaning. Vigorously so. I put my hand on her shoulder to get her attention.

"Talk to me, Lily. What happened?"

Her focus stayed on the carpet on the floorboard of the passenger side. She started dabbing at what I knew were specks of blood.

"Lily, talk!"

She gave me only a brief look. "Violet did what you couldn't, Mom. What you could *never* do. She stopped Piper's molester. She saved Piper. Mom, she fucking killed him!"

What I could never do.

Her eyes were a wild animal's. Scared.

I lost my balance, and my right knee smacked the concrete. Pain surged through my body. Disoriented. Confused. The garage spun around me. Lily went about cleaning with quick, manic movements.

I crawled toward the door to the house, hoisted myself up, and managed to get inside. I slid down the wall by the bathroom door. When the shower stopped running, I heard Violet open the door.

This was my fault. Mine and no one else's. I couldn't blame my mother. Richard. Papa. The watery blood in the bucket was all mine.

I'd done this.

An eternity later, though likely but a minute, Violet emerged with a towel around her body and another one on her head. She appeared like she did when she was sixteen. No makeup. Beautiful. Sad eyes.

I spoke first.

"I'm sorry."

No answer. Instead, she sat down next to me and put her hand on my throbbing knee and leaned her head against my shoulder.

"Are you okay?" I asked.

She gave a little nod. "Mom," she said, "I killed someone."

"You snapped."

She shook her head. "No. I didn't. I've done it before."

I owned more than that bucket of bloody water.

"Before?"

"I killed a sex offender when Maria and I were at that conference in Yakima."

Air escaped my lungs in the quietest gasp I could manage.

"Did you hear me?"

"Does anyone else know?"

"No."

"Did anyone see you tonight?"

"No."

I pulled my daughter close. "Did Lily help?"

She shook her head. I felt the dampness of the towel as I leaned in.

"She waited in the car."

"Tell me everything," I said. "Everything you did. Everything you touched."

Lily

Mom and Violet were in the kitchen when I emerged from the garage. Violet was wearing Mom's favorite robe, pink with roses, of course. Her shortened hair was nearly dry. It could be a scene from any Saturday morning. It wasn't, though. They weren't talking. Just sitting there. The air between them was calm.

"Lily, get showered. Leave your clothes on top of Violet's in the bathroom. You're going back to school tonight."

"Violet needs me."

Violet grabbed me by the shoulders. "She's right. You can't be here."

"I'm here now."

"You went to the dorm this morning," Violet said, her tone firm. A command. "Do you understand? *This morning.* That's all you have to do. Just one lie."

I noticed five twenties were on the table.

"Do not use a credit card for gas," Mom said, handing me the bills. Her affect was the same as Violet's. "And if you can make it all the way to Pullman, don't stop at all."

My sister grabbed my shoulders again. Hard. "Your phone is already turned off. Keep it that way. Don't power it up until you get to your dorm room."

I had earned a spot here. They were treating me as an outsider again.

"I want to stay," I said. "No one is on campus, anyway. Why would I go home before the end of the break?"

Violet offered an answer.

"You and Mom had a big blowout over something."

"Like what?"

"Like Dad and Shondra? Anything. I'm sure you can think of something."

"I'm not going when you need me."

"You're going. I shouldn't have brought you along."

"I wanted to go."

"You didn't want to kill Grayson. I did."

"I'm glad you did, Violet. I am. I just don't want you to get caught. I want to help."

Again, Mom told me to get cleaned up.

I was so mad at her.

"Mom, this is your fucking fault," I said. "You know that, right?"

Her eyes were glossy, and her pupils eclipsed her irises.

"I do."

An admission, but no explanation. I didn't know for certain I'd believe her anyway. Mom had spent her entire life denying what happened in our home. She let a monster come and go freely. He was at all our birthday parties. He watched us play soccer. Papa was free to hide what he was, while we were forced into a charade. It was like we were a family in witness protection with a false narrative surrounding who and what we were.

So, yes, it was all her fault.

I said goodbye right there. I hugged my sister. Tears ran. I didn't hug Mom. She cried softly, muffled like the sounds of Nana's old percolator coffeepot. Mom didn't reach out for me because she knew me. She knew that I couldn't hold her. I could barely look at her.

The black screen of my phone sat next to me as I drove. I wanted to call Violet. I wanted to tell Maddy that I wouldn't be around for the New Year's party. Part of me felt glad for this escape. Most of me. My eyes hurt, and I squinted as oncoming cars used their headlights for target practice. I told myself that I'd hold on to this secret no matter what. It would eat at me. It would challenge me to reassess what it meant to do the right thing.

The bridge over the Columbia River came into view. The moon, diffused by clouds, sent a faint pathway over the water and across the craggy sagebrush-stubbled terrain. It was both desolate and beautiful. A wet snow fell on the windshield. I reached to turn on the wipers and a thought came to me.

Mom and Violet were totally in sync about what to do. I hadn't seen them behave like that. Ever. They'd always been at odds about nearly everything. Even small things of no real consequence like how to do a simple chore were debated. Big things too. Mom had hired a photographer for Violet's senior portrait. Violet wanted someone else. As payback, Violet dyed her hair black the night before. Her portrait, now next to mine in the family room, looks like a stranger.

But they had been in sync tonight.

As more blurry memories came into focus, I wondered if the two of them had been that way at the wedding. If the shrimp had been ordered at the last minute because Mom knew Papa would crash the wedding. If

Mom knew he was coming because Nana had already told her. If Violet did her part by ensuring Papa's EpiPen would never be found.

The coroner's report was one of at least two pieces that didn't fit the puzzle. Papa hadn't died from toxic shock associated with his allergies to shellfish. He'd been asphyxiated. And Nurse Woods had been arrested and pled no contest.

Why would an innocent woman do something like that?

Chapter Fifty-Seven

After Everything Happened
Rose

The joke in prison is that having sex with another woman doesn't make you a lesbian. It simply passes the time. I'd never tell my daughters, but I have experimented a little. And the truth is, it does help pass the time. Passing time is essential. A few of the girls have had sex with male correction officers, but those trysts have faded as lawsuits and behavior training have taken a foothold.

Prison isn't supposed to be easy. It is, after all, *prison*. Yet, personalities aside, it isn't that difficult either. Some of the girls here are happier inside than they'd ever been before in their lives—except for the freedom part. Many incarcerated have close relationships with each other, maybe the tightest they've ever had in their lives. For some, the assigned routine provides more comfort than resistance. The idea that every day is nearly the same in cadence and activity seems to help those who are there because their lives were out of control—victims of men who used them to sell drugs.

Like Colleen, my cellmate.

She's in for the murder of her drug-dealing boyfriend in Omak, a small town on the Canadian border.

"How'd the visit go?" she asks, lifting her head from her bed and away from the TV her father sent her for her birthday—one of the first flat screens in our unit.

"Fine," I say, purposely cryptic in my response. "She's doing great. Job is good. Husband's nice."

I don't bother painting a picture in anything other than the broadest of strokes. It isn't because I don't remember every word Violet said. It is because Colleen hasn't seen her own children since she took up residence here nine years ago.

She and I work in the kitchen together. Tonight is pizza night. We head to the kitchen, where two officers drink Cokes and watch our every move.

I pride myself on making a pretty good dough, even though it's from a twenty-pound premixed bag. I knead alongside Colleen. She has tiny, almost baby hands, but she works them like a machine and barely says a word. I like that about her. We can stand side by side in the warmth of the kitchen as we work the gluten in the flour into elastic.

"Ready to cut and weigh for the proof?"

Colleen nods. "Ready, Rose."

She looks at me in an odd way.

"What is it?"

"New girl came today," she announces. "Assigned to Red pod."

The timbre of her voice is scratchy, an old LP spinning around a turntable.

"Really?"

"We had three newbies yesterday. If this keeps up, they'll have to parole you."

We roll dough into thick ropes and begin to cut and weigh on twin food scales.

Colleen adjusts her hair covering with a floured finger, leaving a white patch on her forehead.

"That'll be the day," she says. "Anyway, she knows you."

I drop a perfectly sized ball of dough onto the scale. "What's her name?"

Colleen stops what she's doing.

"Amy Woods."

Despite the warmth of the kitchen, a prickly chill comes over me. I don't say a word at first. I don't have to. Instead, I cut another piece of dough and knead with amplified vigor.

"I can't believe they brought her here," I finally say. "Thought she was at Cedar."

"Was at Cedar. She asked about you."

"Did she?"

"Says she didn't kill your father."

I drop another ball onto the tray. "She pled Alford. She can say whatever she likes."

Colleen goes back to weighing dough balls. "She wants to talk to you."

My knife slices into the belly of the fat snake of dough. Hard. The sound of the stainless-steel counter underneath comes through.

"Can't see any point in talking. She killed my father, and it doesn't matter to me or my mom or my children what she says now."

Colleen finishes filling a tray, covers it with plastic, and passes by me to the proofing oven.

"She's pretty convincing, Rose."

I stay quiet. It seems that every day when I wake up, I tell myself that this is the day when all of this becomes routine. This is the day when I learn to live without thinking about my life on the outside and the turn of events that landed me here. Today, however, won't be that day.

On my way back to my room, I pass the bank of phones with crying girls, sexy girls, girls who are still figuring out how to use their twenty minutes on the phone most effectively. They want attention. Contraband. They want that information feed coming into their ears to be of value. Tradable value. A male officer we call Pocket Pool, because he has his hand jammed into his trousers adjusting himself nearly every time he's watching us, stands guard over the phones.

"Back off, Frobisher," he says to an inmate aggressively crowding baby-killer Merri Capp, who is next in line for a call.

Diane Frobisher has the body of a linebacker and a tough attitude that aligns perfectly with her muscular frame.

"Yeah, whatever, Officer," she says, taking a step back from Merri.

Diane is in here for beating the crap out of a business associate—a meth cook who double-crossed her. She's been in admin segregation, the hole, longer than anyone here. No one messes with Di. I don't even make eye contact with her.

I pick up my pace to skirt any drama. In here, I'm one of the good ones. I'm not like the baby killer or the drunk driver or the meth-head killer. I'm looked on as a woman who committed a forgivable crime. Those are the crimes for which few, if any, mourn the victim. It isn't about shifting blame. It's about killing someone for all the right reasons.

Peggy Walker gives me a cautious smile as I make my way down the long corridor to our unit.

I used to share my room with her. Peg cried herself to sleep every night. She's only twenty. I tried my best to make my time with her useful. It's the teacher in me. I'm still working with her on reading and math. Peg needs a GED. I want to get her to the finish line.

"You look upset," she says, stopping me for a beat. Her eyes are big and brown, full of cocker spaniel sadness. "You look like something's bothering you."

She's a good kid. Perceptive too.

"No," I lie right to her face. "I'm good."

I *am* good. Good at lying.

CHAPTER FIFTY-EIGHT

After Everything Happened
Lily

People know me. At least, they know my mother. When I rushed sororities at WSU in the spring, there was always some other girl saying something about my mother in a loud whisper. I tried not to react, but sometimes it just couldn't be avoided. I could have pledged at any house. In fact, they all wanted me. Even the Tri Delts. I guess I'm a great conversation piece, something they could trot out when beer pong no longer captivates.

I passed on all invitations.

So now I sit in my room, scrolling TikTok in search of something to make me smile. My only other release is the occasional blunt with the guys in the dorm closest to mine. They know about my mom and what she did, but they don't ask about it. They don't talk about it behind my back. They don't act like it's even of interest.

I don't talk to Mom. I don't visit her. She writes me little notes and decorates the envelopes with hearts and flowers. I get one every Friday. She must mail them on Wednesdays when she's got a free day from her job in the prison kitchen.

The latest arrived yesterday.

> *Dear Lily,*
> *Violet came to see me. She and Zach are up to their*
> *eyeballs renovating their million-dollar condo. Wow. Such*
> *a place it will be! Have you been helping with the design*
> *choices? Remember when we painted her room while she*
> *was away at camp? You should be an interior designer.*
> *She cried tears of joy. That was a happy time.*

I notice the period at the end of the last sentence. It's larger than the others. A long pause as she reflected on that memory. I think about it too. Violet was obsessed with the color that shares her name, so we just went for it. With the bedding. On the walls. We even painted her desk chair. It was, I think now, way too much. She loved it, though. Really did.

Katie knocks and pokes her head inside.

"Want to get some food?"

"Just a sec."

She says she'll meet me downstairs, and I return my attention to Mom's letter.

> *I hope school is going well for you. I know that WSU*
> *has a reputation as a party school, but I know you. I'll*
> *bet you have your nose to the grindstone and are doing*
> *your very best. Your best is always leaps and bounds above*
> *others. Sure would like to hear from you. I know you are*
> *busy. I know you are hurt. You are my precious daughter.*
> *You and Violet are all I have left in this world.*
> *Love,*
> *Mom*

It strikes me that this is the third letter in which she doesn't mention *her* mom. I call my sister.

"Hey, Violet."

"Hey back. Doing okay?"

"Yes," I snap at her a little. "Why, do you think I only call when I'm mad about something?"

"More like pissy. Not mad. There's a difference."

My sister is a know-it-all who doesn't know a thing about me.

"What's up with Mom and Nana?"

"Huh?"

"I got another letter. She doesn't talk about Nana anymore. What's up with that?"

Silence echoes in my ear.

"Nana had a stroke. She's okay. She's at Cottesmore. Recovering."

My face goes hot. Now I *am* pissy.

"Why didn't you tell me? And what do you mean she's okay? She had a fucking stroke and no one bothered to tell me?"

"You were getting ready for exams, Lily. There was nothing you could do."

"I have a right to know."

My sister lowers her voice. She's still at work. "Really? Do you really care?"

I think carefully before answering. "Maybe. I guess. I do."

"Sounds definitive."

"Don't be such a bitch, Vi. I'm stranded here in the middle of nowhere, and you're off buying new furniture with Zach. It's like everyone has moved on to something better. Dad has Shondra. You have a husband. I don't have anyone."

"You told me you needed the solitude."

Now I'm beyond pissy. "That's not the point! And Nana? I don't know if I love her or hate her, but she's still my grandma, and I don't want to be left in the dark anymore, Vi."

"Copy that."

"I hate it when you say that. It's like Zach's taking over your brain."

"Copy that too!"

I hang up and start composing a letter on my laptop.

> *Dear Mom,*
>
> *I wish you would stop writing me. Your letters are useless. They are all surface and no substance. I'd get an F if I turned in anything like them for class credit. I am so angry at you. I don't know if I will ever get over it. You were so busy focusing on keeping up appearances that you never even saw me. Denial is funny. I think people let it spread over everything in their lives. It's a disease. And it kept you from knowing me, Mom. I had sex with a boy when I was fifteen. I used drugs for the first time when I was fourteen. Maddy and I used to steal money out of your purse to get high. Dad came and got me after the Gig Harbor Police picked me up for being drunk in the park. We made a pact not to tell you. We were always tiptoeing around making you upset. I never knew why until Violet told me about Papa. At first, I felt so sorry for you. For how you must have felt when Violet told you. So dumb of me. You didn't believe her. That's what you said. And you said that to me too. Such a liar. You knew all along because it happened to you too. Papa raped you too. Violet told me. That's where I draw the line. You don't know me. Violet might forgive you. I will never.*
>> *Your ex-daughter,*
>> *Lily Hilliard*

I hit Print and head out the door, feeling better than I have in a very long time.

CHAPTER FIFTY-NINE

After Everything Happened
Violet

There's a word for it, but I can't come up with it. When you buy a new car, suddenly you see nothing but that same car everywhere. It's as if they've multiplied into a mass in every parking lot, on every stretch of highway. It seems that whenever I go to the store, make a stop to get gas, or even drop something off at the cleaners, he's there. The detective that worked my mother's case is like that new car.

This time, I see Detective Hoffman in the drive-through at Dutch Bros. He's a tall man who has managed to fold his considerable lankiness into a Ford Mustang convertible. It's red. Not the "look how big my dick is" red, but worse. Obnoxious red. It's the kind of color that says, *Look at me. Now. Right now. Where are your eyes? Look at me!* I hate the color. I find a million little things to hate about him. His nose hairs. His cigarette-stained fingertips. His Pez-like manner of dispensing breath mints into his gaping mouth to camouflage his smoking habit. His shoes—scuffed. His eyes—extremely close together. The way spittle collects at the corners of his mouth.

Everything.

Mostly, however, it is because he won't go away. He just keeps on whack-a-mole-ing his way into my personal space.

I'm certain it isn't accidental. He's learned the schedule I keep when visiting my mother. It is possible that someone at the prison tipped him off in the beginning or he just knew that, considering everything that had happened, I would be a regular.

Two weeks ago, we talked, a mistake on my part. Something wrongly told me that if I engaged with him, he'd back off. He'd know that I didn't know anything about anything. How could I? I wasn't even there when it happened.

I was in the parking lot of the prison when he came up to me, crunching a mint and looking at me with what seemed like the eye of a cyclops. So close together.

"Saw your mom?"

I didn't smile at him, but I answered. "Who else, Detective?"

"Right," he told me, trying his best to look concerned. "How's she doing?"

He always asks and I always say the same thing.

"Not great, thanks to you and our messed-up legal system."

The detective didn't take the bait. He's not only nicotine stained, but he's also careful. He thinks I know more than I've admitted, more than I said in the interview room where we first met. He did the same thing that he did back then. He feigned concern. He pretended to make me feel as if we are somehow bonded in this sad story of my mother's crime. It's a game. And, so far, while my mother is clearly the loser, I'm doing just fine.

"Heard she's been in the infirmary," he said.

"Had her medications adjusted."

"Really," he said. "What's she on?"

I didn't tell him. And I didn't tell him to fuck off either. Instead, I pretended that I didn't hear him. I unlocked my car and swung the door open. Before I slid into the driver's seat, I gave him a cool stare.

"Detective, I'm beginning to think that you're stalking me. I don't know whether to be offended, frightened, or flattered. I am a married woman. If your frequent guest appearances in my life are by chance, that's fine. Creepy, but fine. If you are following me around for any reason, any at all, stop. If you want a complaint in your file, I can make that happen."

I shut the door and turned on the engine. I put the car in gear.

"I know that your mom didn't do it alone," he said, loudly enough to catch the attention of a couple who'd been visiting their daughter. "I know that you know more than you've ever let on."

He was right. Smoky. Creepy. But correct.

I pulled away, turning on the radio and letting some emo singer revel in the lost love that they can never forget. It nearly brought a smile to my face. Lost love? That was a real problem?

Going to prison was a problem.

Covering up facts in the quiet, solitary way cats cover their waste—that was not a problem. It was a way of life.

CHAPTER SIXTY

After Everything Happened
Rose

It had to happen. It was only a matter of *when*. Across the yard, I see Amy Woods. Her bright-yellow Crocs come at me like a flashing caution sign.

She sits down, and the bench boards move. She's in the camp that gains weight from our rib-sticking cooking. The other group picks at their plates to maintain figures that aren't going to be seen by anyone other than a tweaker at the next shower.

"Nice day," the former nurse says.

"Nice enough," I reply, looking straight ahead.

"How are you doing?"

"Fine. You?"

"The same."

It goes like that for a little while, a nothing conversation that is only broken by the sounds of gulls circling overhead, reminding me that the world stretches far beyond the curlicues of razor wire.

"I didn't kill your father," she finally says.

"I didn't kill the pervert," I throw back. "Guess we're both a couple of innocents."

"I'm far from that."

"Me too."

It's an odd conversation, to be sure. I don't want to be her friend, of course. That would be too strange, but I find myself thinking about what it was that brought us there, to that prison and to that bench. I know what I did. She knows what she did. We could be liars. We could be truth tellers. In prison, we can be whatever we want to be because no one knows the truth about anyone here.

"Your story got a lot of press," Amy says.

Our eyes meet the first time.

"Not as much as yours."

"You win locally—wall-to-wall coverage on TV and in the *Times*."

"You got *20/20*."

"A segment. Not a full show."

"Still."

We both laugh a little.

"You see your girls?" Amy asks.

"One," I answer. "The other not so much." I don't tell her that my youngest has never seen me. Not even one time. "What about you, Amy? You have family? Visitors?"

She doesn't answer for the longest time.

"No. No one will come here."

I shut my eyes. The sun feels good on my face, and it takes me, briefly, to another place. Hawaii. California. The coast of Italy. "I wondered if we would meet up," I say. "I thought they might separate us, you know, for our safety."

"I'm no threat, Rose."

I turn to face her. "I'm not either."

We're both speaking the truth, but it feels a bit forced, a stalemate.

"They think I'm here to pay the price for something I did, but in my mind, I'm here because I have nowhere else to go and I'm tired of being lonely. Frankly, I'm just tired. When you're still alive and have nothing to keep you going . . ."

"Like *The Walking Dead*," I say.

Amy gives me a smile.

Prison will be good for her teeth, I think. She's got one incisor that I name Brownie. The state will pay for dental work—one item for her win column.

"Without the gore," I add quickly. "My youngest loved that show."

"Blood and guts never bothered me. Probably should have been a doctor."

It should feel awkward beyond words, sitting here with her. Somehow it doesn't. Cars pull into a new office park on the other side of the prison fence. The traffic on Route 16 on the west side of the institution comes in waves like the ocean.

Amy's like me. We were both in prison long before we went to court.

The bell rings, a sound that makes us stand up in unison, and likely gives the prison the "campus" feel that outsiders seem to think is apropos when describing the place.

We get up and she looks me in the eye.

"I saw you there that night, Rose."

I let the air out of my lungs. "Where?"

"In the room. With your father."

I think hard. Anything I say is an admission of something evil. "Why didn't you say anything?" I finally ask.

She takes a step away. "I heard what you said to him."

"I see."

Amy knows. She's known all along.

She gives me a look that seems something like empathy.

"I'd have done the same thing," she says.

It's not that I don't think about it. I do. The night that I went back to the hospital. When I do, however, it isn't to wish it away.

Instead, I ask myself why I didn't do it sooner.

My father's eyes lit up when I approached his hospital bed.

"Rose," he said, his voice soft as a whisper, "I made a mess of the wedding. I'm sorry, honey."

"Sorry" was a word he'd used before. The truth was he probably didn't even comprehend what it really meant. He'd used that word the night he came into my room. It was the same night he'd sucked those black olives off my fingers at the dinner table. I thought it was silly he wanted me to do it again. After a while, he made me suck his penis. Then, penetration.

"It feels good," he kept saying. "Good girl. Daddy's girl."

When I cried, he put his black-olive-smelling hands over my mouth and told me to be quiet.

"Sorry," he said. "Daddy doesn't want to hurt you. Daddy wants us both to feel good."

I was frozen, scared. I hurt. A sliver of light came from the door. Then some movement and the door shut.

Mom had seen what happened. She had to have.

"I told you not to come."

"I didn't think you really meant it. I'm Violet's grandfather."

"Dad," I said, keeping my voice low too, "you raped her. Just like you did with me."

His features hardened, and he shut his eyes as though not seeing me undid the reality of what I'd said.

"You're a sick old man. You were a sick younger man. Mentally sick."

"That's not true," he said. "You know that. Stop it. Stop with the bullshit."

A tiny man. A weak man. A man who quietly gasped to take in oxygen.

"You made me think I had done something wrong. Do you know what that's like? When you went off to that rehab place, I thought it was my fault. That I made a mistake. You were the one who told me where to touch you."

He closed his eyes again.

"Damn you, Dad. You destroyed my life. My daughter's life. I blame Mom too. You two made me who I am."

I stop. A scene is the last thing I need. I came here to tell him off. To let him know that no one would ever see him again. Not me, Lily, or Violet. That he was as good as dead.

"You don't know what you're talking about. I think you should leave. Maybe get some help."

I wonder how many people feel the way I did just then. My father's face looked grotesque. A swirling sack of worms or snakes. Putrid. I wanted to kill that undulating mass of whatever it was. What I saw in the bed was no longer human but a monster.

I reached for the extra pillow.

It was easy and fast.

As I planted it on that ugly, squirming mass, I whispered into his ear.

"I hate myself more than I hate you. I hate myself, Dad, because I thought you'd gotten better. That you'd changed. I hate myself because I didn't do any better for my girls than Mom did for me."

I could feel him struggle under the pillow, under the sheets. I climbed up on top of him and pressed down as hard as I could. I prayed that I'd be able to kill him before anyone walked in.

Twitch.

Wriggle.

Gasp.

Die.

I felt woozy. Scared. Unsteady. Without even thinking, I found myself picking up the oxygen mask and breathing in as much as I could.

Better.

He was still.

He would never hurt anyone else.

No one saw me as I made my way to the elevators. I had done something that on the surface was unforgivable, and lately I've wondered if I could forgive myself. Not for killing my father. But for allowing history to repeat itself. The lying. The looking the other way. Believing in the fantasy that avoidance is some kind of fix for the things that we have a hard time talking about.

I should have known better.

Truth is, I did know better.

ABOUT THE AUTHOR

Amazon Charts and #1 *New York Times* best-selling author Gregg Olsen has written more than thirty books, including *If You Tell*, *The Hive*, *Lying Next to Me*, and *The Last Thing She Ever Did*; four novels in the Detective Megan Carpenter series; and *The Sound of Rain* and *The Weight of Silence* in the Nicole Foster series.

Known for his ability to create vivid and fascinating narratives, he has appeared on multiple television and radio shows and news networks, such as *Good Morning America*, *Dateline*, *Entertainment Tonight*, CNN, and MSNBC. In addition, Olsen has been featured in *Redbook*, *People*, and *Salon*, as well as in the *Seattle Times*, *Los Angeles Times*, and *New York Post*.

Both his fiction and nonfiction works have received critical acclaim and numerous awards, including prominence on the *USA Today* and *Wall Street Journal* bestseller lists. Washington State officially selected his young adult novel *Envy* for the National Book Festival, and *The Deep Dark* was named Idaho Book of the Year.

A Seattle native who lives with his wife in rural Washington State, Olsen is already at work on his next thriller. Visit him at www.greggolsen.com.